Ring of Lies

VICTORIA HOWARD

Cover design by Mae Phillips at
BabyfreshDesigns.com

Formatting by Jason G. Anderson at
Polgarus Studio

For more information about Victoria Howard's books
please visit:

www.victoriahoward.co.uk

ACKNOWLEDGEMENTS

To my wonderful friends and fellow writers, Dorothy Roughley, Daphne Rose, and Brenda Hill, for their encouragement and support on the long road to publication. I could not have written this novel without you and I'm honoured to call you my friends.

I'd also like to thank Jonathan Smith, of Loch Lomond Seaplanes, for answering my endless questions. Mistakes are mine, not his.

My thanks also go to the residents of Boca Grande, whose island home was the inspiration for this novel. Thank you for allowing me to share your piece of paradise.

The final thanks go to Stephen, who not only supports me in all I do, and makes me laugh, but for supplying me with endless cups of tea as the end drew near.

For Wendy and Paul

CHAPTER ONE

Grace Elliott followed her husband's coffin down the cobbled path from the church to the graveyard and tried not to stumble on rain-slicked stones. She shivered and grasped the collar of her suit jacket, holding it tightly against her neck as the winter rain seeped through her clothing and chilled her to the bone.

She felt hollow inside. And guilty.

Daniel's accident was her fault. If only they hadn't argued before he left for the conference, he might still be alive.

The small twelfth Century church stood on a hill on the edge of the village, its yellow Cotswold stone weathered with age. Moss-covered headstones dotted the graveyard, the inscriptions faded and barely readable. High in the branches of a gnarled yew tree, a rook cawed. Even the angels on top of the monuments seemed to frown on her.

Grace straightened her shoulders and kept her eyes firmly fixed on the single wreath of yellow chrysanthemums, solidago, and eucalyptus on top of the casket.

Apart from her heavily pregnant best friend, Olivia, only half a dozen mourners clustered around the open grave. Daniel had many friends and business associates. Where were they? She flitted between anger and sadness. He'd thought he was so loved; yet he was reduced to this—nearly forgotten on the day of his rest. She looked at the small group. Daniel's business partner, Shaun, and his wife—what was her name? Grace struggled to remember: Mary? Margaret? No, Margot, that was it. And there was Liz, Daniel's secretary, standing self-consciously to one side, constantly dabbing at her eyes with a crumpled handkerchief.

She didn't know the short, smartly dressed, middle-aged man with the pale, square jaw. But she recognized two of Daniel's friends from the local golf club, who had forsaken their daily round to attend.

But the person whose support she needed most of all was absent.

Despite numerous phone calls to Catherine's mobile phone and messages left on her answering machine, her sister remained silent. It wasn't unusual for Catherine to do her own thing. She had always had a selfish streak, going her own way, letting the family down, and today was no different. Yet it was, because Catherine was leaving Grace alone at a time when she needed her only sister the most.

Head bowed, Grace took her place next to the minister beside the open grave, her sense of loss beyond tears.

The minister's voice intoned over the heads of the mourners. 'We have entrusted our brother, Daniel, to God's mercy and we now commit his body to the ground. Earth to earth, ashes to ashes, dust to dust.'

She struggled to hold back her tears and concentrate on the words as grief and guilt squeezed her heart. Perhaps she should have organized a wake for Daniel's business colleagues and friends, but with his parents dead and her sister nowhere to be found, she couldn't face listening to their condolences and platitudes on her own.

At the minister's prompting, she stepped forward and picked up a handful of earth, allowing it to slip through her fingers, dusting the casket. The service over, the mourners crowded round her. Shaun was the first to step forward and take her hand.

'I just wanted to say how sorry Margot and I are. It's a very difficult time for you, Grace, and if there is anything we can do, please don't hesitate to let us know. Daniel was a good friend as well as my business partner.'

'Thank you, Shaun. Daniel... Daniel would have been pleased that you remembered him. I really appreciated your kindness in clearing his desk and returning his personal items to me when I know you're so busy.'

'It was no trouble, Grace. No trouble at all.' Shaun leant forward and kissed her cheek. 'Keep in touch.'

One by one, the other mourners paid their respects then silently drifted away. Only Olivia remained by her side.

'Poor, poor dear,' she said, draping an arm around Grace's shoulders. 'Here you are, and where is that sister of yours? Doesn't she care?'

'You know she does, Olivia. I'm sure she'd be here if she knew, but I've been unable to contact her. She has a career and—'

'—and a sister, whom she is leaving to twist in the proverbial wind on the darkest day of her life. I swear, Grace, I don't know how you're holding together.'

Grace shivered. 'I'm not.' She collapsed on Olivia's shoulder and shuddered with sobs. Olivia cradled her as a child—as the child she'd soon have, Grace thought. Another loss, she realized. She'd never have a child now that Daniel was gone.

'Oh, Grace. I know you loved him so.'

'I did. I do. What do I do now, Olivia? How do I continue without him?'

'I'm here for you, dear, as is Tom. Somehow we'll get through this together.'

Grace sniffed and blew her nose. 'I... I'd like a few moments by myself. Do you mind?'

Olivia narrowed her eyes. 'Are you sure?'

'Yes. I need to say goodbye. I have to. I won't be long.'

'Take as much time as you need. I'll wait in the car.'

Not trusting herself to speak, Grace merely nodded. She clasped her slender hands together and bent her head to hide the pain in her eyes. She felt empty. A flash of wild grief ripped through her, threatening to shatter her resolve not to cry anymore.

She remained at the graveside, ignoring the rain as it dripped from the brim of her borrowed hat onto the back of her neck, her eyes fixed on the rain-speckled brass plate on the coffin.

Daniel Elliott. 1971-2009

Tears blinded her eyes. Daniel was too young to die. At thirty-eight, he'd been the youngest partner in a firm of international accountants. And he'd been her rock—her one constant in ten brief years. How would she cope without him?

With her emotions barely under control, she made her way over the slippery cobblestones towards the car park. A man stepped out from beneath the moss-covered lych-gate and made her jump. She recognized him as the smartly dressed stranger from the graveside.

He doffed his hat. 'Mrs. Elliott?'

'Yes?'

'My condolences on the loss of your husband.'

'Thank you. I appreciate you coming today. If you don't mind, I'd like to be on my own.' Grace turned, but he grabbed her arm with the strength of a boxer. She winced. He relaxed his grasp slightly, but held her fast.

'What I have to say won't take a moment.'

Grace felt her temper rise. 'I don't even know you. I've just buried my husband. Have a heart!'

He grinned. 'A heart? An interesting choice of words. Hearts aren't standard issue in my business, Mrs. Elliott. Information is.'

Her head snapped up. 'Information? What sort of information?'

'The kind you are about to provide.'

Grace gave an involuntary shudder. The impenetrable blackness of his eyes and the way his tongue darted at the end of his sentences made her think of snakes. She glanced over her shoulder. Olivia beckoned from the car, no doubt anxious to get back to help her husband Tom, the local vet, with afternoon surgery.

'I have to go now. My friend is waiting.'

'I appreciate that this is not the most suitable time to discuss matters, but I assure you this will only take a few minutes. Your late husband looked after my business interests.'

'In that case I suggest you talk to Shaun, Daniel's partner. He's dealing with all Daniel's clients.'

'Perhaps I'm not making myself clear, Mrs. Elliott. This has nothing to do with your husband's business.' His tongue darted again. 'Daniel and I had a private arrangement. He had access to some very, shall we say, sensitive information. I just want to ensure that it doesn't fall into the wrong hands.'

Frightened, Grace tried to pull away, but his fingers tightened. 'Whoever you are, let me go.'

'In a moment, Mrs. Elliott.'

'You're hurting me!'

The stranger's lips twisted into a cynical smile. 'That's good, since it's my intention.'

'I'll scream. Someone will come.'

'We're quite alone out here. If I wanted to, I assure you I could drop you where you stand.'

Grace ceased to breathe. She knew he was right. 'What do you want from me? Who are you?'

'Your husband kept files that are of great importance to me.'

'All client files are stored at the office.'

The stranger shook his head. 'Not paper files. Electronic files—computer disks.'

'Whether the information you require is on paper or on a computer, I can assure you, I don't have anything belonging to you.'

He smirked, never blinking, and then released her arm. 'You're telling the truth.'

'Of course I am.'

'It's a good thing you are. I know when women are lying. You wouldn't want to lie to me, Mrs. Elliott. Not ever. It wouldn't bode well for you. Now I'll let you go. You'll be late for your appointment with your husband's solicitor.'

'How do you know that?' Her fingers tightened around the strap of her purse, until her nails dug into her palm.

'It's my business to know things. By the way, have you spoken to your sister lately?'

Grace's head jerked up. 'That's none of your business.'

The man merely smiled. 'No. Of course it's not. I won't keep you any longer, Mrs. Elliott. I'll be in touch again soon.' He turned and limped away into the mist.

Sweat gathered along Grace's spine as fear replaced grief. Her heart hammered beneath her ribs.

'Wait! Please! Is Catherine in trouble? If you know anything at all about her, please tell me.'

He didn't turn around. 'Goodbye, Mrs. Elliott.'

She stared at his retreating back. Who was he? Someone violent enough to instill fear, that much was certain. What did Catherine's whereabouts have to do with the stranger's computer disks, she wondered. And how did this man know about her appointment with the solicitor? Was it a lucky guess?

She took a deep, unsteady breath, and hurried out of the churchyard toward the waiting car.

'Who was that?' Olivia asked, as Grace slipped into the passenger seat.

'One of Daniel's clients.' Grace rubbed her arm absently. 'I told him to speak to Shaun.' She twisted in her seat to look back at the wooden lych-gate, but the stranger had vanished.

'Well, not to worry, my dear,' Olivia replied. She selected first gear and released the handbrake. 'Are you sure you don't want me to come with you to the solicitor's office?'

'Thanks for the offer, but no. I think this is something I should do on my own.'

Olivia sighed. 'Then I'll drop you off in town. But you need to know I don't approve.'

'I'll be fine. Besides, didn't you say one of the veterinary nurses is off with the flu?'

'Rufus, Tom's assistant, has come down with it too. Otherwise Tom would have come to the funeral. It's very difficult to find a locum vet at short notice. And you know how agitated Tom gets if he has to cope with reception duties as well as his patients. But if you wanted me to stay, I daresay he could manage on his own for another hour or two. Can I change your mind?'

'You and Tom have been marvellous. I don't know what I would have done without your support. And thank you for the hat. I just hope the rain hasn't ruined it.' She took it off and laid it on the rear seat.

'Darling, think nothing of it. That's what friends are for.'

Grace turned and smiled at the woman next to her. Olivia's dark hair was cut into a sleek dark, chin length bob, and despite the sadness of the occasion, her blue eyes brimmed with happiness. Pregnancy suited her.

'I have to get used to being on my own. Besides, you've the baby to think of. You should be sat at home with your feet up, not running around after me.'

'Well, I must admit, I'm starting to feel tired, and my ankles swell if I stand for too long. But if you would like me to stay until that wayward sister of yours contacts you, I can.'

Grace shook her head. 'No, really, I'll be fine.'

'Ah, here we are.' Olivia pulled the car into a vacant parking space outside the chemist. 'I'll call you this evening to make sure you're all right.'

Grace climbed out of the passenger seat. It was market day, and the small Cotswold town was crowded with Christmas shoppers. Grace felt anxious as she walked along the bustling High Street toward the solicitor's office. She hated dealing with people in authority: Daniel had insisted on handling everything himself.

As she passed the shoe shop, Grace caught sight of her reflection in the window. She looked gaunt, much older than her thirty-two years. The jacket of the hastily purchased black woollen suit hung off her shoulders, making her appear anorexic. Her normally pink cheeks were pale, and there were dark circles under her deep blue eyes. Even her chestnut-coloured hair lacked lustre. Perhaps she should have worn it loose instead of scraped back in a bun, which highlighted the hollows in her cheeks. She shrugged. It was too late to worry about her appearance now.

She took a deep breath, and pushed open the door of the solicitor's office. The staccato of her heels echoed on the polished marble floor. She hardly noticed the décor as the exquisitely groomed receptionist showed her into the conference room where an old, bespectacled gentleman sat behind an enormous desk. He creaked to his feet when she entered the room.

'Mrs. Elliott, please take a seat. I'm sorry to drag you here, especially today of all days, but it's best for all concerned if these matters are settled quickly. I hope you'll accept my condolences on your husband's untimely demise. It must have been a terrible shock for you.'

'Yes, it was. Your letter came as a surprise, too. I wasn't aware Daniel had made a will.' Grace's hands twisted in her lap. 'I didn't think it was necessary as we purchased the house in joint names and have a joint bank account.' To her dismay, her voice cracked.

'Mr. Elliott made his will quite recently. Of course, it simplifies matters from a legal point of view, but I am surprised he didn't discuss it with you first. He leaves the bulk of his estate to you, as you would expect. Applegate Cottage, as you pointed out, is held jointly between you and your husband so his share automatically passes to you. I am sure it will come as a relief to know there are ample funds from his life insurance to pay off the outstanding sum on the mortgage, so you needn't worry about that. There is only one other legacy, to a Miss. Catherine Peterson.'

'Catherine? Daniel included my sister in his will? Do you know why?'

'A will is a very personal thing, Mrs. Elliott, as I'm sure you appreciate. It is not my place to ask my clients the reason behind their decisions.'

'No, no, of course not.' Grace bent her head and studied her hands as she absently listened to the solicitor. Anger and confusion surged through her. Why had Daniel felt it necessary to make a will? And why had he made Catherine a beneficiary?

'—Probate should take four to six weeks to obtain and everything should be finalized within six months. I've already spoken to your bank and arranged to transfer your husband's savings account into your name. You'll need to make an appointment to see the manager and sign some papers, but it's all very straightforward. With regard to the beach house in Florida, I'm afraid your attorney in America will have to handle the transfer into your name.'

Grace's head jerked up. 'Excuse me? A house in Florida? An attorney in America? I don't understand. We don't own any property overseas.'

The solicitor examined the papers in front of him. 'Actually, you do, Mrs. Elliott.' He took off his reading glasses and smiled at her benevolently. 'I can assure you there's no mistake. Your husband purchased the beach house on Gasparilla Island some months ago. I have a copy of the purchase contract here in the file. As I mentioned, Mr. Parous, your American attorney, will be able to handle the transfer into your name. Now, is there anything else you'd like to ask me?'

'Mr. Parous?'

'Yes, that's right.' He handed Grace a business card. 'I've already spoken to him and faxed him a copy of the will. He sounds like a very competent chap. I'm sure he'll deal with the legalities in a prompt and professional manner.'

Grace glanced at it. Zachary Parous, Esquire, Attorney at Law. Beneath the neatly typed name were a telephone number and an address in Miami. She sat dumbfounded. Why hadn't Daniel told her that he'd purchased a house in Florida?

Her mind refused to accept what she'd been told. She was about to ask how Daniel could afford a second home when the solicitor pushed a pile of papers across the desk.

'If you would just sign these, Mrs. Elliott, I can get started. Mrs. Elliott?'

'I'm sorry? My signature? Yes, of course.' She signed every sheet without reading it. Daniel always told her what she was signing. Daniel—

It was dark when Grace left the solicitor's office. Numbness had finally set in. She moved without thinking, without emotion as if she were one of the stick figures at a theme park—flagging down a taxi and giving the driver her address.

Flicking on the hall light in her home, the home she and Daniel had shared and loved, the pain returned in a torrent. She dropped her purse on the table, and went straight to the study. Daniel's study, the one room in the house she never entered, not even to dust.

Grace rested her hand on the doorknob, and half expected to hear his deep-timbered voice scolding her for disturbing him. She'd ignored his warning only once, the ensuing argument had left her reeling. Ever since then, she had respected his wishes. All of them.

But Daniel was no longer here to wish for anything.

She pushed open the door and stepped inside. The air smelled stale. She told herself that the lingering aroma of pipe tobacco was permanently embedded in the furniture, but her feelings told her otherwise—that he was here, alive somehow, yet invisible to her. She fumbled with the catch on the window and threw it open, impervious to the frigid air that flooded the room.

An old leather chair, which had once belonged to Daniel's father, stood next to the soot-stained limestone fireplace where ashes of a half-burned log lay in the grate. A large oak desk, its surface covered with a faint film of dust, filled the bay window. The date on the desk calendar showed the seventeenth of November, the day Daniel had left for the conference. She tore off the pages without bothering to read the proverb printed underneath, and threw them into the wastepaper basket.

Daniel's face, and that of her own, smiled back at her from a silver framed photograph on the corner of the desk. She picked it up and wiped the dust from the surface with her fingertips.

'What other secrets have you kept from me?'

Daniel's brown, unfathomable eyes seemed to stare everywhere but at her. With a heavy heart, she replaced the photograph on the desk. She collapsed into the chair and rested her aching head in her hands. Their marriage hadn't been perfect; they'd had their fair share of ups and downs like every other couple, but she'd never thought of Daniel as being secretive. Yet, the last few hours had proved that he was just that.

She leaned back and rubbed her temples. Nothing the solicitor had told her made any sense. They weren't rich.

Their joint bank account, which last time she'd looked, held less than two thousand pounds. When they'd purchased Applegate Cottage four years ago, they'd put down the minimum ten per cent deposit and borrowed the rest from the bank. So where had the money come from to purchase a house in America, she wondered And more importantly, why hadn't Daniel told her about it?

The desk held seven drawers—three in each pedestal and one in the centre. Her fingers hovered over the small brass handle of the centre drawer. Feeling like an intruder, she pulled it open. It was empty. One by one, she opened the remaining drawers. Apart from an assortment of envelopes, a few credit card receipts, a letter opener shaped like a dagger, and some spare batteries for the hand-held dictating machine Daniel occasionally used, she found nothing connected to the beach house.

Daniel's briefcase, which the police had found in his car, and the personal items from his office, sat in a box next to the door. She slipped out of the chair, picked it up, and placed it on the desk. Item by item, she removed the contents: a desk diary, a box of post-it-notes, a calculator, and a framed photograph of her and Catherine. The desk diary she placed to one side, replaced everything else, and then put the box on the floor.

She'd given Daniel the Raffaello briefcase for his thirtieth birthday. It had cost two weeks housekeeping money, but it had been worth it to see the smile on his face when he opened the box. She ran her fingers over the now scuffed and torn calfskin.

Grace flipped the locks to open the case, but nothing happened. She dug the fingertips of her right hand into the frame and tugged at the handle. The catch on one side gave, and she realized that the force of the impact had warped the frame. With great care, she eased the blade of the letter opener into the lock on the opposite side and twisted sharply. There was a loud click and the lock popped open. Inside lay Daniel's MacBook and a number of manila folders. One by one, she went through the internal compartments, but found nothing else of interest.

Part of the silk lining had come away from the frame. When Grace ran her fingers along the edge, she felt something underneath. She pulled back the fabric and found an envelope taped to the bottom of the case. She tore it free and turned it over in her hand.

Why go to so much trouble to hide something as innocuous as an envelope? She slipped her fingernail under the flap and opened it. A passport and a tiny piece of paper fluttered on to the blotter. A series of numbers, written in Daniel's unmistakable scrawl, covered the surface. Perplexed, she counted the digits. Twenty-four. Daniel was fascinated by numbers and frequently designed puzzles as a way of relaxing. Were these something he was working on, or the combination to the safe at the office?

The latter seemed the most likely explanation, yet Daniel had an eidetic memory. There was never a need for him to write anything down.

Grace opened the passport at the photograph on the back page. Daniel's face stared up at her. Only the name in the passport wasn't his, but that of Lionel Lattide.

A flicker of apprehension coursed through her. She tried to catch her breath, but couldn't get any air. The more she struggled to control her breathing, the more terrified she became. Beads of perspiration dotted her forehead. She willed herself to relax, just as the doctor had told her to, but it was impossible.

She staggered into the kitchen. Her medication lay on the shelf next to the fridge. Standing on tiptoe, she reached for the bottle, but her hands shook so much it slipped from her grasp, the contents spilling out along the shelf and on to the floor.

She could get through this, she told herself. It was only a panic attack—she wasn't about to die. It wasn't real. Crying with frustration, her fingers trailed along the floor until she finally pinched a wayward pill between her thumb and forefinger. She popped it into her mouth, and washed it down with a glass of water from the tap.

Leaning against the sink for support, she forced herself to breathe deeply, in, out, in, out. The pill started to do its work, and the room began to steady itself. As her heartbeat slowed, she tried to ignore the questioning voice in her mind, but couldn't. She pressed her hands over her eyes in an attempt to blot out her fears.

What have you been up to, Daniel, that you needed a second passport?

She took another sip of water. The passport lay on the drainer next to her hand. With trembling fingers, she opened it and turned to the visa section.

It was stamped.

She froze. Her mind and body benumbed.

She peered at the faint impression and could just make out the words 'Department of Homeland Security.' America! She turned to another page, and found that too, had been stamped. During the last six months alone, Daniel or whoever he was, had travelled to the United States on five occasions.

Why?

She wrenched the calendar off the wall, and compared it to the passport. Every entry visa coincided with a date when Daniel had been away on business.

Waves of panic and nausea overwhelmed her, and she sank to her knees and sobbed. The man to whom she had trusted her heart had lied to her. Not once, not twice, but least four times.

Pain yielded to anger.

Who was her husband?

It seemed that the only way to find out was to fly to Miami and meet with the attorney, Zachary Parous.

It sounded so easy when she said it quickly. But the thought of such a journey aroused old fears and anxieties. She wasn't a traveller and certainly not alone. What if she had a panic attack mid-Atlantic? Who would help her?

Then there was the small problem of getting from Miami to some place called Gasparilla Island and locating the mysterious beach house. How hard would it be to find? Would she be safe?

She'd heard such things about Florida, stories of gangs, drug lords, and even worse. She snatched up the phone before she could change her mind and booked a seat on the nine-thirty flight to Miami the following morning.

Then there was only one call left to make.

CHAPTER TWO

Emilia was wailing. Again. Jack West waited a moment for the baby's shrieking to stop. It didn't. Emilia hit a new high note. He hadn't bargained for this.

He rammed the paintbrush into the jar of white spirit. Exasperated at yet another interruption, he washed his hands, and then stormed into the family room. He lifted the red-faced, screaming baby from the Moses basket and placed her on his shoulder, gently rubbing her back. How Rosa, Emilia's mother, could sleep through the piercing cries, he had no idea. Then most new mothers didn't stay out partying with their friends till dawn.

Emilia's cries settled into snuffling sounds. He gently bounced the squirming infant down the hallway. Over the course of the last two weeks, Emilia had changed from a placid, six-week old angel into an 'enfant terrible,' crying at every opportunity and for no apparent reason. During that time, they'd tried everything to placate her, including pushing her in the stroller and playing soft music. But nothing had worked. Finally, Rosa had given in to his pleas and taken the child to the Miami Children's Hospital be checked by the paediatrician, who said the most likely cause of the incessant crying was colic. Jack wasn't convinced. He thought it had something to do with Rosa's lack of interest in the child.

Emilia burped and threw up all over his shoulder. 'Damn it,' Jack muttered. It was his own fault; he knew better. Next time he'd remember to throw a towel over his upper arm before he picked her up.

'Shush, little girl,' he murmured, and carried her into the bathroom. He kissed the tufts of black curly hair. 'Need to change that nasty diaper. You're not only a noisy little thing, you reek, sweetheart.'

At six feet two and one hundred and eighty-five pounds, his large hands weren't designed for fastening diapers and easing tiny limbs into pink romper suits.

In the family room, his cell phone rang. He ignored it, but when it rang for a fourth time, then a fifth, he realized he'd forgotten to switch it over to the answering service. He fastened the last popper, scooped up the baby and snatched up the receiver, wedging it between his neck and shoulder as he rocked Emilia.

'West.'

'Hello, Jack West? This is—'

'Grace Elliott,' he interrupted.

'How did you know?'

'I have a good memory.' Her voice was rich, and smooth like honey, every word a caress. He put the hollow feeling in his gut down to surprise, not the images of a chance meeting six months previously that filled his mind. 'Why are you calling, Grace?'

'Daniel's dead,' she blurted out. 'He died in a car accident two weeks ago.'

'I'm sorry for your loss. It must be a difficult time for you.'

'Thank you, Jack. And no, the last few weeks haven't been easy.'

'So why are you calling and why should your husband's death interest me?'

'It doesn't have anything to do with you, not directly. But do you remember the last thing you said to me?'

'Remind me.'

'You said that if I ever needed any help, I should contact you.'

He chuckled mirthlessly. 'You never fail to amaze me. Look, Grace, things have changed. I'm no longer attached to the embassy in London.'

'I know that. That's why I need your help. It's difficult to explain over the telephone. My flight gets into Miami International at two twenty-five tomorrow. Could you meet me? I'll explain everything then, I promise.'

'I don't know, Grace. I have commitments,' he said looking at the sleeping baby cradled in the crook of his arm.

'Please, Jack. I've no one else to turn to. I don't fully understand, but something odd has happened. And you're the only person I know in America who can help.'

The strain was evident in her voice. For a moment, he didn't answer. Instead he closed his eyes and remembered the day he'd first seen her — a beautiful woman with glossy, sable hair, sad blue eyes, and a shy smile. She'd slid past his defences then, just as she was doing now.

'Jack? Jack, are you still there?'

'Look, are you sure there's no one else who can help?'

'I'm sure.'

'All right, Grace, I'll meet you. But I can't promise you anything, you do understand that?'

'I understand, and thank you, Jack. I'll see you tomorrow.'

He laid Emilia in the Moses Basket. Her eyes fluttered open, and then closed as she stirred briefly. He brushed a finger over the cap of dark fluffy hair. Satisfied that she was indeed asleep, he tiptoed out of the room. As he passed the kitchen, he grabbed a clean T-shirt from the stack of laundry waiting to be ironed and changed his shirt.

While he slapped buttercup-yellow paint on the wall of what was once his study, and was now the nursery, he thought about Grace. Early June last summer, they'd been two people in a crowd of thousands attending the Wimbledon Tennis Championship. His two-month secondment with the Embassy in London over, he'd taken what was left of his accrued leave and purchased a seat for the duration of the tournament. As it happened, Grace had been allocated the seat next to his. When rain showers halted play, he'd offered her shelter under his umbrella, and they started chatting. Equally knowledgeable about the game, it turned out that they both played for their local clubs. Their relaxed banter soon developed into an easy I-like-you kind of rapport.

Whenever there was a break between matches or play was abandoned due to inclement weather, they found a quiet spot to share a bowl of strawberries and a bottle of wine. By the end of the first week, they were constant companions.

Then on the final day of the tournament, he'd suggested they have dinner together. At first Grace had said no, but changed her mind on condition they split the bill. Somewhere between the entrée and dessert, their relationship changed. The conversation became more personal. He'd told her about Rosa, his Cuban girlfriend, from whom he'd parted some month's earlier on less than friendly terms, and about his life in Florida. In turn she'd told him about her sister, and the village in Gloucestershire where she lived.

When it came time to say goodnight he saw her safely back to her hotel.

'Thank you for dinner.'

'My pleasure. Are you going to ask me in for a nightcap?'

Her smile faltered. 'I'm sorry, I can't.' She took a deep breath and looked up at him. 'I—oh, I don't know how to say this, so I'll just come out with it. Jack, I'm sorry. I'm married.'

His smile didn't falter, it collapsed. 'You're married?'

She nodded.

A combination of disappointment and bewilderment clouded his features. 'That's a hell of a thing to hear. Couldn't you have told me before this?'

'Oh, I tried, believe me, but it never seemed be the right moment. I... I like you, Jack.'

'Like me enough to lie to me.' He glanced at her left hand and wondered why he'd never noticed the thin platinum band on her finger. Something in her eyes told him the marriage wasn't all it should be. For the longest time he just stared at her, saying nothing.

Eventually, she held out her trembling right hand. 'It was wonderful meeting you, Jack.'

He took her hand, leant forward, and brushed his lips against her cheek. 'You too.'

'Have a safe journey home.'

'Grace—'

'I'm sorry. Goodbye, Jack.' She turned and walked quickly toward the bank of elevators before he could say anymore.

That was the last time they'd had any contact. He'd often wondered what might have happened if she had invited him back to her room for a drink.

Rosa padded into the room. 'You've been painting the same piece of wall for the last five minutes.'

Startled, he jumped at the sound of her voice. The can of paint in his hand tipped, threatening to spill its contents over the polished wood floor.

'Damn it, Rosa, do you have to creep up on me like that?'

She yawned, and then brushed her long black hair from her eyes. 'You were someplace else, what were you thinking about?'

'I was thinking that I'd finish this a whole lot quicker if I wasn't interrupted every five minutes.'

'You haven't been interrupted by me, so there's no need to be a grouch. Did I hear the phone?'

He looked at her with something akin to disgust. 'Christ, Rosa. You wake up when the phone rings, but not when your daughter cries. What sort of a mother are you?'

Hands on hips, Rosa glared at him. 'Don't start, Jack. You've no idea what it's like to give birth. I just can't stand her needing me all the time.'

He sighed. Rosa hadn't told him about the pregnancy until it was too late to do anything about it, not that he believed in abortion. It was just that fatherhood had never featured high on his list of priorities. But whether the pregnancy was due his carelessness or her forgetfulness in taking the birth control pill, he'd accepted the responsibility and moved her into his condo. What he couldn't tolerate was her total lack of interest in the child, and the home he was providing for them.

'Besides, I'm not feeling well. I've a terrible headache.'

'Yeah? That's not surprising is it? You should be looking after our daughter rather than spending the evening drinking with your friends.'

'You don't understand, Jack. I can't cope with her on my own. Not when she cries all the time.'

'It's what babies do. You've got enough brothers and sisters with kids to know that. I can't be around all the time, Rosa. I'll have to go back to work at some point.'

'But not yet. Please, Jack, stay at home a little longer. At least until we get her settled into a routine.'

'Another week, that's the best I can do. The condo is a mess. There are dishes stacked in the sink, laundry waiting to be done. It's about time you started pulling your weight. I can't be expected to look after the baby, as well as cook, clean, and fix up the nursery. You're going to have to learn to manage on your own.'

As if on cue, Emilia started bawling.

Rosa put her hands over her ears. 'For God's sake, what's the matter with her?'

'She's hungry.'

Rosa rested a hand on his arm and offered him a smile. 'Can't you feed her, Jack? She always settles after you've fed her.'

Jack put down the brush, and removed her hand from his arm. 'No. I'm busy. You might try breastfeeding her for a change. It's the motherly thing to do.'

'No way! I've seen what breastfeeding does to a woman.' She wrapped her arms around her generous chest. 'I don't want my tits ending up down by my knees.'

'In that case, there's a bottle of formula in the fridge. You can nuke it in the microwave. Now go on, go and feed our daughter. And don't forget to burp her before you put her back down.' He pushed her in the direction of the lounge. She hissed something in Spanish, but did as she was told.

****

The following afternoon, with his ears still ringing from his and Rosa's latest futile argument, Jack pulled the black Ford Explorer into a vacant parking space at Miami International Airport. He glanced at his watch. Two o'clock. He locked the SUV and walked the short distance to the main terminal building. With half an hour to kill before Grace Elliott's flight landed, he headed to the nearest coffee shop. He chose a stool at the counter nearest to the exit and ordered a double espresso.

Airports fascinated him, not because he wondered where everyone was going to, but rather what they were hiding. He rubbed the dark beard on his cheeks. He didn't like the man he'd become — cynical, bitter, and when occasion demanded, tough and mean. He had the Bureau of thank for that, or rather fourteen years working as an undercover agent.

Jack drained the last of his espresso and headed for the international arrivals hall. The officer on the customs desk recognized him and waved him through. If anything, the hall was more crowded than the concourse. He glanced at the overhead display. Three flights had landed in quick succession: a British Airways flight from London, an American Airlines flight from Bogota, and an Air Taca flight from San Salvador.

Angry voices filled the air as people jostled for trolleys and stood shoulder-to-shoulder in front of the carousels waiting for their luggage. To his left, a small, wizened man was arguing with the custom official in a mixture of Spanish and halting English over the inspection of his luggage. Jack grinned. It reminded him of his arguments with Rosa. Whenever she thought she was in danger of losing the point, she reverted to her native tongue.

Out of habit, he watched the arriving passengers for telltale signs of nervousness and anything that seemed out of place. A sniffer dog and its handler worked the luggage from the Columbian flight. The dog gave no reaction, but Jack knew from experience that agents from the DEA, the Drugs Enforcement Agency, would be closely monitoring the passengers, selecting those who acted suspiciously, for a more thorough examination of their luggage.

He turned his attention to the carousel for the London flight and recognized Grace straightaway. She stood to one side waiting for her luggage. Dressed all in black, she was thinner than he remembered and her complexion more translucent. She looked more ethereal than ever, if that was possible.

More than one man glanced in her direction, openly appraising her. Jack grinned. He wasn't the only man to find her attractive. He started to turn away, but one individual in particular caught his attention. A short, stocky man, dressed in a well-cut suit, continued to stare at Grace from the opposite side of the carousel. Without seeming to, Jack memorized the face. He wasn't sure if Grace had noticed, but something unnerved her. She constantly put a hand to her throat. He shrugged and put her nervous behaviour down to a combination of jetlag and unfamiliarity with her surroundings. It took him several minutes to cut through the crowd and reach her side.

'Grace? It's good to see you again. I just wish it could have been under happier circumstances.'

She offered him a tremulous smile. 'Me too. Thanks for coming, Jack. How have you been?'

'I'm fine, all things considered. You look tired. How are you holding up?'

Her blue eyes clouded with tears, she lowered her gaze. 'Oh, you know. Some days are better than others.'

'Did you get any sleep on the flight over?'

'Not much. The passenger behind me had a young baby, and it cried for most of the journey.'

Against his will, he smiled. Despite what she said, she looked great. All the 'if only' feelings he fought to contain threatened to spill out. He looked away.

The conveyor belt whirred into life. Grace stepped forward to reclaim her suitcase.

'Here, let me get that for you.' He dragged it off the carousel, then took her elbow and urged her toward the exit. 'I'm parked in the multi-story. Do you want to wait while I get the car? Or do you feel up to a short walk?'

'A walk would be good.'

Without speaking, they made their way through the terminal to the exit. As they neared the door, Jack caught a glimpse of the man who'd been staring at Grace. For a millisecond their gazes locked. Something about the man's demeanour and his overt interest in Grace brought Jack's senses to full alert. He lengthened his stride and hustled her towards the parking garage, where they took the elevator to the second level.

Jack couldn't stand the silence anymore. 'So where am I taking you?'

'I made a reservation at the Island Palm Hotel. Do you know it?'

'It's about half an hour from here on Collins Avenue in South Beach.' He stowed the luggage in the trunk, then helped her into the passenger seat, before climbing behind the wheel. The engine growled to life with the first turn of the key. He cranked the air conditioning up to full, then steered the Explorer out of the parking lot into the steady stream of traffic heading for the city.

Grace sat in silence; her arms folded across her chest, and stared out the window.

'Jet lag is the pits. Trust me. After a hot shower, and something to eat, you'll feel a whole lot better.'

'I'll take your word for it. Right now my nerves feel as if I've drunk a year's supply of coffee.'

Jack turned onto the Dolphin Expressway and followed the traffic towards the MacArthur Causeway. 'All right, Grace. Time to tell me why you're here.' He stole a glance at her.

She shook her head. 'Not yet.'

'Then when?'

'Soon,' she whispered. Her eyes closed, she sat rigid, her fingers plucking at the fabric of her shirt.

He knew what it was like to feel strung out, and if her tight-lipped expression was anything to go by, she was near breaking point. But what had brought her to this?

He reached for her hand to offer a little comfort, and then thought the better of it. Nothing had changed between them.

Everything had.

Instead, he pulled his sunglasses out of his shirt pocket and concentrated on getting her safely to her hotel.

The traffic on Collins Avenue consisted of the usual snarl-up of tourist buses and private cars. Jack drummed his fingers on the dashboard while an elderly matron tried to reverse into a parking space that was obviously too small for the Lincoln she was driving. After three attempts, she gave up and drove off, much to his relief and the queue of vehicles behind him.

The Island Palm Hotel, one of the more upmarket hotels in South Beach, was situated just north of the Art Deco District. He swung the Explorer into the hotel's forecourt and parked in front of the entrance.

'Grace? Wake up. We're here.' He climbed out from behind the wheel and retrieved her luggage. By the time he walked round to the passenger side, she'd clambered out of the vehicle. Together they mounted the marble steps to the hotel.

The lobby, a mixture of South Beach Chic and Southern Charm, was quiet and blessedly cool. The concierge was on the phone, talking rapidly in Spanish, as they approached the desk. Jack understood enough of the language to know that he was berating whoever was on the other end of the line for taking a break rather than delivering fresh towels to room four-oh-six.

After a little haggling, he got Grace's reservation upgraded to a one-bedroom suite on the ninth floor overlooking the ocean. He picked up her suitcase, and ushered her toward the elevator. Once inside the suite, he placed her suitcase in the bedroom on the stand provided, and handed her the room key.

'I'll give you an hour to get settled and freshened up. I'll wait for you in the lobby. Then you can tell me why it was so important to travel six thousand miles to ask for my help.'

CHAPTER THREE

The door closed softly. Grace shot the bolt. She draped her jacket over the back of a chair, and dropped her oversized black leather purse and the room key onto the coffee table. Elegantly decorated in muted shades of cream and chocolate, the large airy sitting room felt welcoming after her long journey. She kicked off her shoes, stretched, and then winced. Hours of sitting cramped in one position had made her back, neck, and shoulders ache.

She removed a bottle of mineral water from the mini bar, emptied the contents into a glass, and added ice. The cold liquid tasted like nectar and was a welcome change from the bitter, semi-warm airline coffee she'd drunk for the last ten hours.

After the cold of England, the room felt overheated. She crossed to the balcony and threw open the door. Warm, humid air billowed through the curtain. Nine floors below, the half-naked bodies of sunbathers stretched out on loungers around the pool. Through the palm trees, she could just make out the white sand beach and turquoise waters of the Atlantic Ocean beyond.

Grace let the curtain fall and walked into the bedroom. The digital clock on the nightstand showed three-thirty.

She picked up the telephone and dialled Olivia's number. While she waited for her to answer, she tried to work out the time difference, but her weary, jet lagged mind refused to make the calculation.

'Olivia? It's Grace.'

'Hello, my dear.'

'I'm calling from Miami, so I won't stay on the line for long.'

'Miami? Good gracious! What on earth are you doing there?'

'It's a long story, but it seems that Daniel owned property here. I'll know more once I've spoken to his attorney.'

'Well, I always said he was secretive. But Miami? Why couldn't he have purchased a house in France like everyone else?'

'I've no idea. Hopefully, I'll find out why tomorrow.'

'All right, but be careful. I've heard Miami can be a dangerous place.'

'Don't worry, Olivia. I have a friend helping me. I just wanted to let you know where I was. I'll be in touch again in a couple of days. Give my love to Tom.'

Grace replaced the receiver. The king-size bed looked soft and inviting, but even if she had time to undress and slide between the cool cotton sheets, she knew she wouldn't sleep. Instead, she opened her suitcase, took out her bag of toiletries along with some fresh underwear, and walked into the bathroom.

A quick look in the mirror told her she looked worse than she imagined. Her clothes were so crushed and travel-weary they looked as though they'd never seen an iron since the day she'd purchased them. Fatigue settled in dark pockets under her eyes. Her hair was a mess; tiny curling tendrils escaped her once-neat braid and now framed her pale, pinched face. She pressed her hands over her eyes and tried to wipe away the sadness. She felt empty and drained, and so tired that her nerves throbbed.

You've come this far. You can't fall apart now. A few more days, and then you'll know the truth.

She undressed like an automaton. Shook her hair free from its braid, and then stepped into the fancy marble and chrome shower cubicle. Turning the faucet full on, she let the hot water stream over her body and face, but it did nothing to relieve the tension in her neck and shoulders.

Seeing Jack again had re-kindled old emotions. Six months ago she'd been within minutes of falling into bed with him. Only her strong sense of righteousness had stopped her — that, and the platinum band on the third finger of her left hand. Tall, dark, lean, self-assured, he was everything she remembered, everything she wanted but couldn't have.

Desire washed over her, followed by a wave of shame. Other memories filled her mind; his ready smile, the way his eyes crinkled at the corners when he laughed. But most of all she remembered his gentle, sensual touch.

Grace knew she ought to walk away, find someone else to help her uncover the truth. Yet she knew he was the only man she could trust.

The only man who could protect her.

She'd told herself she could handle being close to him again. But she wasn't fooling anyone, especially herself.

She lathered herself with the complimentary orange and ginger scented shower gel, and then slathered shampoo and conditioner through her knotted hair. After rinsing off, she turned the faucet to cold and stood under the fine spray until her skin puckered and she began to shiver.

Most of the clothes she'd packed were more suited to a harsh British winter rather than the milder sub-tropical climate of Miami. But after much rummaging, she finally she settled for a pair of smoke-coloured linen trousers and an apricot silk shirt. She towelled her hair dry, shook her head, and finger-combed it into soft waves.

The woman in the mirror looked more together than the one who'd stepped off the plane a couple of hours ago, but her face remained chalk-white. A few strokes of blusher and a little mascara was all she could manage by the way of make-up. The next time she looked, her cheeks at least had some colour.

Conscious that Jack was probably pacing up and down she grabbed her purse and made her way to the lobby. She found him seated in a quiet corner reading a newspaper. He stood as she approached.

'Feeling better?' he asked.

Grace offered him a small, shy smile. 'More awake, certainly.'

'In that case, let's grab a bite to eat and something to drink.' He took her arm and steered her towards the exit.

Grace fell into step beside him. Once outside, the heat and humidity took her by surprise. She fanned her face with her hand.

'Is it always this hot in winter?'

Jack grinned. 'This isn't hot. You should be here in summer. Give it a day or two and you'll acclimatize.'

Collins Avenue, flanked by Art Deco buildings with a mixture of up-market hotels and trendy shops, was bustling with tourists. Grace struggled to keep up with Jack's long strides as he wove his way in and out of the crowds.

Without any preamble of any kind, he said, 'You've let your hair grow.'

'What?'

'Your hair, it's longer than last time we met.'

Grace looked away from his intense green eyes. 'I felt like a change.'

'It suits you.'

She swallowed hard. 'Thank you.'

'Still play tennis?'

'Occasionally. Look, Jack, this isn't a—'

He gave her a sideways glance. 'A good idea? Probably not, but I'm only making small talk, Grace. I'm not asking you to fall into bed with me. God knows I gave up on that idea months ago.'

An unwelcome blush crept into her cheeks. 'I just assumed that you'd treat this like a business meeting, that's all.'

They walked on in silence. After two blocks, they turned left and made their way to Ocean Drive. Like those of Collins Avenue, the buildings were a mixture of pastel coloured mansions, ultra-chic hotels, bars and clubs.

Jack ignored the enticing aromas wafting from the stylish restaurants and upscale eateries. Instead, he chose a table at one of the crowded sidewalk cafés. Once seated, he ordered two shrimp salads, a glass of Pinot Grigio for Grace and a small beer for himself, then turned to face her.

'Okay, Grace. What's so important that you need my help?'

She took a deep breath and organized her thoughts. 'Two weeks ago Daniel was killed in a road traffic accident. On the day he died he was supposed to be in Birmingham attending a conference, yet the police found his car on a country lane not far from Heathrow Airport.'

'There could be any number of explanations for that. He might have changed his mind at the last minute and decided to fly.'

'Jack, you and I both know it takes longer to drive to Heathrow than it does to drive to Birmingham from my home.'

The kitchen staff had been uncommonly quick. Jack waited until their server was out of earshot before continuing. 'Maybe he'd arranged to pick someone up and take them to the conference.'

'That doesn't make sense either. Besides, the police told me he was alone in the car. But that's not the only strange thing about his death. As I was leaving the church after the funeral service a man approached me.' She shivered at the recollection. 'I'd not met him before and had no idea who he was. He asked about some electronic files Daniel was keeping for him. When I said I knew nothing about them, he threatened me, and grabbed my arm. Not only that, he knew all about my appointment with the solicitor. He even mentioned my sister, Catherine.'

'Electronic files? You mean the computer disks they're stored on? What did Daniel do for a living?'

Grace stared at Jack, trying to see past the cold eyes and expressionless face. 'He is… was an accountant.' She speared a shrimp and took a bite.

'That explains it then,' Jack said with a smile. 'The guy must have been a client.'

'He said not. And even if he were, it doesn't explain how he knew about my appointment or Catherine.'

'I don't know, Grace. It could just have been a lucky guess.'

'I don't think so. When I got home I went through Daniel's briefcase. I found these.' She opened her purse and handed him the passport and the slip of paper.

He flicked it open. 'Lionel Lattide. Do you know this guy?'

Grace held his gaze. 'Oh, yes, I know him. He's Daniel Elliott, my late husband. At least that's who I thought he was.'

Jack let out a low whistle, but said nothing.

'That's not all.' She took a sip from her glass.' Six months ago, Daniel or Lionel, or whoever he is, purchased a beach house on Gasparilla Island. I knew nothing about the purchase until I heard that he'd bequeathed it to me in his will. We're not rich, so I have no idea where he found the money to purchase another property, especially one overseas. So you see, Jack. I had no choice but to come to Miami.'

'You've got my attention, Grace. Do you know which real estate agent sold him the house?'

'Actually, it looks like it was handled by an attorney. Our family solicitor gave me his business card. I have it here.'

He took the proffered card. 'Zachary Parous. Can't say that I've heard of him or his firm, but that doesn't mean a thing. How about we pay him a visit?'

She tipped her head to one side and smiled. 'I was hoping you'd say that.'

Jack pulled out his cell phone, punched in the number off the card, and hit send. He handed Grace the phone.

While she listened to it ring, he said, 'Try and set up an appointment for tomorrow. If they say no-can-do, insist.'

The phone answered on the third ring. 'Parous and Associates. How may I direct your call?'

'I'd like to speak to Mr Parous, please. My name is Grace Elliott. I'm calling in connection with my late husband's estate.' Grace covered the phone with her hand. 'They're connecting me.' She angled the phone so that Jack could listen to the conversation.

'Hi, Mrs Elliott. Your solicitor told me to expect your call. I'm kind of surprised to hear from you so soon, though. What time is it in England?'

'Actually, Mr Parous, I'm calling from here in Miami.'

The attorney paused for three beats. 'You're here? Right now?'

'I arrived this afternoon. I was rather hoping we'd be able to meet—tomorrow morning, perhaps?'

'That's pretty short notice, Mrs Elliott. Or Grace. May I call you Grace?'

'Yes, of course, but—'

'How about next week? I've got space on my calendar on Thursday at ten-thirty. I can fit you in then. In the meantime, you can relax and enjoy our fair city. Take a couple of tours, maybe a day cruise. Those are great. My assistant can get you hooked up with a couple of tour operators.'

She looked at Jack. He shook his head and covered the mouthpiece with his thumb.

'Sound tearful. If he still says no, tell him you'll be there tomorrow at two, and then hang up.'

'This is a difficult time for me, Mr Parous, as I'm sure you appreciate. I had rather hoped to have everything settled and be on my way home by then.'

'I need to draw up some documents before we can meet, Grace. I'm not sure I can be ready any sooner. That's stretching it.'

'I'm sure your assistant will appreciate the overtime, Mr Parous. I'll see you tomorrow at two.'

Jack nodded, took the phone, and hung up. He took a pull on his beer.

'Parous should be able to tell us how Elliott paid for the house. He'd also know whether or not Elliott had a bank account here or whether the funds were transferred from a British bank.'

Without thinking, Grace rested her hand on his. It felt warm and strong, just like she remembered. When she realized what she'd done, she pulled back. He didn't react either to the touch or the retreat.

'Thanks, Jack. I feel better knowing that you'll be coming with me. It's hard enough understanding English legalese without having to get my head round the American legal system too.' She speared another shrimp with her fork, dipped it into the chilli-lime dressing, and took a bite.

He shrugged and looked away. 'No thanks necessary. I'd do the same for any friend.'

Silently she watched him. There were more lines around his eyes than she remembered, and his once black hair was now threaded with silver. But apart from that, he looked no different than when she'd last seen him.

'I've never heard of Gasparilla Island. Is it part of the Florida Keys?'

'No, it's a Barrier island on the Gulf Coast about two hundred miles from here. Why? Are you thinking of going there?'

'I don't know. I haven't thought that far ahead. I guess it depends on what the attorney says tomorrow.'

'I'll ask around, see if I can find out whether Zachary Parous has any unsavoury connections.'

Grace frowned. 'Unsavoury connections? I don't understand.'

'Miami is full of people with underworld connections. Racketeering, money laundering, drug peddling, murder; you name it this city has it all.'

'Surely an attorney would be above all that?'

'You'd think. But not everyone is as honest as a newborn babe. People get sucked in one small dirty deal at a time. A favour for a friend, and then another, and another, until they're in so deep there's no way out.'

'What are the police doing about it?'

He smirked. 'Not a lot. They don't have the manpower. For every criminal they take out of circulation, there's another waiting on the sidelines to take his place. And a lot of the force is crooked too. It's no wonder Miami has one of the highest crime rates in the country.'

Grace didn't like what she was hearing. She toyed with her salad, trying not to think about the reasons behind Daniel's trips to Miami.

'You've gone quiet. You okay?'

'I'm worried, that's all.'

'Don't let your imagination get the better of you, at least not yet. You said Elliott was an accountant. What was his speciality?'

She frowned. 'Daniel never really discussed his work with me, but I do know he monitored the foreign exchange rates. There are numerous books in his study on overseas tax laws. I could ask his business partner, Shaun, for more details if you want.'

'No need.' Jack leaned forward, his dark eyes intense. 'Had there been any change in his habits? Did he stay later at the office than usual, that sort of thing.'

She glanced at him sharply. He was asking a lot of questions. But he was also listening. Talking to him helped, but made her feel uneasy. She took a breath and answered his question.

'After our marriage he stopped trying, as if it were too much effort to ensure I was happy. He became very critical, unfriendly, cold almost.'

'In what way?'

'He stopped buying me flowers and taking me out for dinner. We never had a holiday. He was very particular. The house had to be spotlessly clean, yet he didn't want anyone apart from Catherine to visit.'

'What about the friend you mentioned?'

'Olivia? We met in town or at her house.'

'That's indicative of abusive behaviour. First you isolate your victim, undermine their confidence, and make them feel worthless. Did he ever—'

'Hit me?' She hesitated, wondering how much to reveal. 'No. But verbally, Daniel could be very cruel.'

Jack swore under his breath, but said nothing. Instead, his hand closed over hers, his thumb brushing the soft skin on the inside of her wrist.

'It was just after we were married. I entered his study without knocking. I'd never seen anyone get so angry. After that, I did as he requested and never went in there, even when he was at work.'

'What about more recently? Any changes in his routine or behaviour?'

She paused to take a sip of water. 'He seemed nervous, more tight-lipped. When I asked if there was anything troubling him, he didn't answer. I assumed it was pressure of work.'

Grace sat back in her chair. There was a slight tremor in her hand as she reached for her coffee.

'Did you ever consider divorce?'

She looked at the platinum band on the third finger of her left hand. 'I made a commitment. Why should I break my vows?'

'Not even after you found out about his uncontrollable temper?'

'I told you, that was my fault.'

'Bullshit! Let's put the question of whose fault it was to one side for the moment. The dates in the passport—'

Grace cast her eyes downward. '—correspond with dates Daniel was supposedly attending work-related seminars or conferences.'

'And you had no idea he was actually out of the country?'

She shook her head. 'Why would I? He was never away for more than five days. He phoned each evening and we'd chat for a few minutes.' That now familiar feeling of uneasiness crawled over her skin. 'Do you think Daniel was involved in something illegal?'

'I can't tell you at this point, but I can tell you property, especially a beach house, is very expensive. Unless your late husband won the lottery or inherited a whole stack of money, then he must have been involved in some pretty heavy stuff.'

Grace stared at Jack. She wanted to scream at him. Tell him he was wrong. Daniel was a good man. A kind, thoughtful man. He would never jeopardize his career by being involved in a criminal activity. But the truth was there in Jack's eyes. Her world spun, her breath came in great wheezing gasps.

'Oh, shit!' Jack yanked her chair back from the table and pushed her head between her knees. 'Don't you dare faint on me,' he said roughly. 'Breathe! In. Out. In. That's it, slow and easy.'

Grace struggled to sit up, but the weight of his hand on her back held her in place. 'Not... fainting... pills... in... my...' she hissed.

Jack released her, grabbed her purse, and riffled through the contents. Finally, his hand closed on a small brown bottle.

'These?'

She merely nodded her head. He quickly read the instructions on the label, shook one into her hand, and held out a glass of water. He waited while her breathing gradually settled into a more normal rhythm and the colour returned to her cheeks.

'Damn it, Grace, you scared the hell out of me. Feeling better?' His gaze roved over her face.

'I'll be fine. It was just a minor panic attack. Give me a minute.' She squeezed her eyes shut and concentrated on her breathing. When she opened them again, Jack was watching her intently.

'When did they start?'

'Seven months ago. My doctor says they're caused by stress and are probably only temporary.'

'I have to ask. Were you and Elliott having marital problems?'

Grace felt the colour flood her cheeks. 'We had our differences, but we got through them.'

He held up his hands. 'I'm sorry. I'm just trying to figure out why Elliott would lie about his business trips. Could he have been involved with someone else?'

'You mean having an affair? No, definitely not.' But as soon as the words escaped her lips, Grace realized she wasn't certain. Most days Daniel would come home from work, eat his dinner, and then lock himself in the study for the rest of the evening. His interest in their sex life amounted to a two-minute fumble once a month.

'How can you be so sure? You've just admitted he lied to you.'

'Because—' She was about to say I trusted him, but she knew that was no longer true.

'The first thing I learnt about my job is always expect the unexpected. That way when your world turns from sugar to shit you're prepared for the worst.'

Grace stared at him, trying to see past the cold eyes. 'When did you become a cynic, Jack?'

'Maybe I've always been one.'

'I don't believe that.'

'There's too much history between us, Grace. You should hire a private detective and let him investigate this for you.'

Her hands clenched. 'I can't. I couldn't trust a stranger. Besides, I need to do this for me.'

'Last June when—when—'

'Yes?'

'Oh, nothing. It doesn't matter.' He gave a fake shrug and threw some bills on the table, then stood and pushed his hands in his pockets. 'Come on. It's time I took you back to your hotel.'

Grace picked up her purse and followed him out of the café. It was only when they reached the steps of her hotel that he spoke again.

'You've got your room key?'

She nodded. 'Would you like to come in for a coffee?'

Jack's dark eyebrows rose. 'What?'

'I'm sorry. I just meant coffee. I didn't mean—' She saw the flash of impatience on his face, and suddenly felt embarrassed.

'Yeah, that's right. I almost forgot. You don't always mean what you say. I'll see you tomorrow at one-thirty. He spun round and stormed towards his car.

Grace stood on the marble steps and watched him drive away. Twin spots of scarlet stained her cheeks.

CHAPTER FOUR

Jack climbed into the Explorer and gunned the engine. He glanced in the review mirror. Grace stood on the hotel steps watching him.

Damn it! I don't need this!

He sped out of the car park onto Collins Avenue and nearly collided with a red Mustang. The driver sounded his horn and yelled obscenities. Jack ignored him. He couldn't face going back to the condo and whatever awaited him there, instead he drove north.

Agreeing to help Grace had been a bad idea. A real bad idea. Hearing the pain in her soft voice made him want to pull her into his arms and hold her until the sorrow went away. But that would be stupid. He'd watched her struggle for composure and knew that one kind word from him would make her collapse like a marionette with cut strings.

He should have walked away, left her to sort out her own problems, but he hadn't. Couldn't.

He'd been attracted to her from the moment of their first meeting. That hadn't changed, and he wondered if it ever would. Whether it was her eager smile and easy-going manner, her radiant vitality or the gleam in her eyes that had caught his attention, he couldn't say for sure. But his instinctive response to her had been so powerful that he hadn't been able to get her out of his mind since.

His instincts told him that he had too much to lose. His life was with Rosa and his beautiful baby daughter, not chasing after half forgotten dreams and desires.

Rosa. He'd never intended her to be a permanent fixture in his life. He certainly didn't love her, not in the way a man should love his partner. And certainly not enough to marry her.

But Emilia, she was different. Nothing could have prepared him for the surge of love and joy he'd felt when the nurse placed her in his arms. She was so beautiful—so perfect—with her cap of wispy black hair and big blue eyes. He'd watched her take her first breaths and knew that he'd lay down his life to keep her safe.

She was only a few weeks old and already bore a strong resemblance to his elder sister, Charlotte, who by all accounts, had broken every teenage boy's heart by the time she was fourteen. He had no doubt that Emilia would do the same.

He turned left and headed west onto Interstate 95. He kicked down the accelerator and watched the needle climb, when it settled on sixty, he set the cruise control. The traffic on the three-lane highway was heavy with commuters returning home from work. Out of habit, he glanced in his mirrors. A silver Mercedes convertible sped past him. The driver was in for a shock. Jack had already spotted the cop car coming down the ramp and adjusted his speed. Sure enough, within seconds the cop had switched on his siren and was giving chase.

Jack wove the Explorer through the traffic and took the off ramp. At the next intersection he turned right, then right again into the parking lot of a non-descript building. From the outside it looked like a warehouse, in reality it housed the FBI shooting range.

He showed his ID and signed in, then made his way through to the changing rooms. He swapped his jeans and

T-shirt for a pair of coveralls, collected a pair of ear defenders, four clips of bullets, and a SIG Sauer 228 from the range manager then took up position in one of the booths. He adopted a shooting stance, and fired at a silhouette suspended from a wire twenty metres away. When he checked the target, his aim was off. He replaced the clip and was about to fire again, when the door opened and Mike Zupanik walked in.

Bald and a few pounds overweight, Mike was head of the Miami field office. He'd exchanged his normal work outfit of a three-piece suit for black coveralls. With twenty years service under his belt he was counting the days to his retirement when he planned to buy an RV and travel the country with his wife, Chrissie.

Jack watched the older man take aim and fire, hitting the target dead centre every time. When Mike paused to reload, Jack walked over to talk to him.

'Hi, Mike. Nice shooting.'

'Thanks, Jack. I'm surprised to see you here. I thought you'd be busy with your new baby daughter.'

'I decided I'd get some practice in before my leave's up.'

The SAC smiled. 'More like you wanted to get away from all that crying. I remember what it's like. Chrissie went months without a decent night's sleep when our two were babies. The endless round of feeding, changing diapers, your life stops being your own for a while. Another week and you'll be begging me to come back to work.'

Jack nodded. 'Mind if I ask you a question, Mike?'

'Sure, go ahead.'

'You've got kids.'

'And two grandkids, don't forget. David's seven and Angie's nine.'

Jack dragged a hand through his hair. 'I wondered, after they were born did… did Chrissie lose interest in them?'

Mike snorted. 'Hell, no. Hey, what kind of a question is that? You got problems at home?'

'Rosa — she doesn't pay much attention to Emilia. Doesn't want to feed her, hold her or do anything for her. It's not natural.'

'You spoken to her doctor?'

'Not yet.'

'I'm no expert, but I know what Chrissie went through giving birth, and I'm telling you, I'd rather face a bullet than that kind of pain. May be that has something to do with it.'

'Rosa had all the pain relief drugs known to medical science.'

'Then I dunno. Maybe it's that post-partum depression you keep hearing about. It happens sometimes.'

'Maybe. Thanks for the advice, Mike. I'll make sure Rosa gets it checked out.' He patted the other agent on the shoulder and turned to walk away.

'Aren't you going to practice some more?'

'No, I've left Rosa with Emilia for long enough. Better head back.'

'Wait up. I know you well enough to know there's something else bothering you.'

Jack frowned. 'You're right. You ever heard of an attorney by the name of Parous, Zachary Parous?'

'Never heard of the guy. What's up with him?'

Jack shrugged. 'I'm not sure. A friend has an appointment with him tomorrow, and I said I'd ask around, that's all.'

'Make sure that's all it is, Jack,' Mike said curtly.

'Don't worry. I have no intention of getting involved in anything you don't sanction.'

'Glad to hear it. Any chance you could cut short your leave and come back to work? The office is short-staffed since Hayes and Santos transferred to Chicago.'

'Sorry, Mike. But with things the way they are—'

'That's okay, I understand. Just thought I'd ask all the same.'

Jack returned his gun and ear defenders to the range manager, then left. Rather than take the freeway back to his condo in Coral Gables, he drove downtown.

The central business district was a mixture of high-rise luxury condominiums and modern office blocks, and home to the tallest building in the State, the Four Seasons Hotel. According to the card Grace had shown him, the offices of Zachary Parous and Associates was located on South Biscayne Boulevard.

He pulled into the kerb, and rolled down the driver's window. A blast of sultry air filled the vehicle. He read the building directory etched into the wall at street level. Apart from the offices of Parous and Associates, the steel and glass skyscraper housed a bank, a collection of brokerage firms, international financial advisors and a public relations company, as well as a number of luxury apartments.

One thing was certain; Parous was no two-bit lawyer to afford offices in such prime real estate. Jack's gut tightened. Whatever Elliott had been involved in, it was bad news.

He put the car into gear and drove home.

Rosa was waiting for him when he opened the door of the condo. The first thing he noticed was the stain on her shirt. The second was that her generous full lips were compressed into a tight, thin line. He bent to kiss her cheek, but she deftly turned her head to one side.

'You're late. You said you'd be home by five.'

'My meeting took longer than expected. And then I bumped into Mike from the office.'

Rosa's husky voice took on a sharp edge. 'What meeting? Damn it, Jack. You're supposed to me helping me with the baby, not working!'

'Her name is Emilia. She's not just 'the baby,' Rosa.'

She clicked her tongue. 'Okay, Mr Metrosexual, Emilia. Are you happy? That little monster's been screaming since you left. Driving me nuts. And who were you meeting, anyway? Out with some other girl?'

He flinched. How the hell did she know these things?

'I met an old friend. She wanted my advice.'

'What kind of old friend? You bastard! You're cheating on me!'

'Shush! Calm down or you'll wake Emilia. Grace really is an old friend, nothing for you to get worked up about.'

Rosa folded her arms across her chest. 'You're lying.'

'I don't lie, Rosa, you know that. Now, instead of standing here arguing over nothing, why don't you tell me how Emilia is?'

She shook her head; her thick black hair tumbled loose from its clip. 'I don't know what to do with her. I fed her and she threw up all over my shirt. It's silk. It's ruined. The stain will never come out.'

'Who feeds a baby in a silk shirt?'

'I do, you asshole!'

'Okay, you do. I officially give up.' He groaned and walked down the hallway to the family room. He'd hoped that looking after the baby for a few hours would have enabled Rosa to bond with the child. He was obviously mistaken. Emilia lay on her back in the Moses basket; her unfocused eyes stared at the mobile hanging from the frame. Then she saw him and cooed, favouring him with a gummy grin. He tickled her tummy and she gurgled. He turned back to Rosa.

'She looks all right now. Probably ate too quickly.'

'But what about my shirt?'

He closed his eyes and fought his anger. 'Screw the shirt, Rosa. Is that all you can think of? If your clothes are more important than our child why did you go ahead with the pregnancy?'

She started shrieking in Spanish, and slapped him hard across the face.

'Stop it.' He placed a hand on her arm. 'You know I can't understand you when you speak so quickly.'

'I said I only had the baby so that you'd marry me.'

'And that's not going to happen — ever.'

The blunt words made her flinch. She stared at him with something akin to disgust in her chocolate brown eyes.

'You're a cold bastard, Jack. I hate you! Jorge and Ramon told me about you.'

Jack looked at Rosa and wondered what he'd ever seen in her. 'What do your brothers have to do with this?'

'Jorge said that if I got pregnant you'd never marry me. He warned me. He was right.'

'Warned you? Wait a minute—' Then he realized that he'd been played. 'Green cards. That was it, wasn't it?'

Rosa said nothing, but hatred burned in her eyes.

'That's what you really wanted, wasn't it? You wanted me to sponsor the whole damned brood for green cards? Well, I never promised marriage. I said I would take care of you and Emilia.'

'But—'

'Look, Rosa. I've seen what working in law enforcement can do to a family. My mother watched my father walk out the door each day never knowing if he was coming back. It tore her apart. When I was six she had a breakdown and spent the rest of her life in a mental institution. I promised I'd never risk that happening to someone I care about.'

Silence stretched.

Rosa gave a broken laugh. 'But what will I tell my family?'

'I don't give a shit what you tell them. Marriage was never part of the deal for us.'

'So what is the deal for us?'

Jack rubbed the back of his neck. 'I don't know, okay? I just don't know. Now, I going to get changed, have a beer, and then I'm going to finish painting the nursery.'

He stormed into the master bedroom. The door closed behind him with a thud. Emilia began shrieking again and he instantly regretted what he'd done. He hadn't intended to fight with Rosa, but he only had to open his mouth and she found something to complain about. He supposed it had something to do with her hormones and Latin temper, but he sure could do without having an argument every time he walked through the door.

He stripped off his shirt and threw it in the laundry basket along with his jeans. He wasn't in the mood for painting and had planned to spend the evening doing some research on his laptop, but that was out of the question now. If he went anywhere near the family room Rosa would glare at him and pout her lips like a spoilt child. No, it was better to let her work the angst out of her system on her own.

He pulled on a pair of shorts, and an old T-shirt, and then walked into the kitchen. He dumped the laundry in the machine then turned his attention to the sink full of unwashed dishes. He stacked the dishwasher, and mixed sufficient baby formula for the following day. He placed the bottles in the fridge, and took out a Budweiser. He took a long swallow from the bottle, and carried it into the nursery, along with the brushes and paint. Across the hall Rosa had the TV on, no doubt watching some mindless reality show as usual.

He opened the tin of gloss, dipped the brush in and started painting the mouldings on the cupboard. If he'd known how things were going to turn out he would never had moved Rosa and Emilia into the condo. Instead he'd have done what many other men did, and simply paid child support.

He'd talk again to Rosa in the morning. Maybe she'd be less pissed off by then. Or more. Who knew? It didn't really matter if she ever understood why he needed to go with Grace to see the attorney.

CHAPTER FIVE

Located on the twenty-first floor of the city's most enviable high-rise, the offices of Parous and Associates were furnished with an eclectic mix of glass topped chrome desks, leather chairs, and modern art. Jack and Grace followed the executive assistant down a long hallway lined with offices. Each bore the nameplate of a junior attorney and his para-legal assistant. At the end of the hallway they were shown into a conference room overlooking the bay.

Behind the large oval-shaped desk hung the most garish, unframed oil painting Grace had ever seen. She looked at it from every angle, and tried to make sense of the random splashes of reds, blues and blacks, but only succeeded in making her eyes cross and her head ache.

Jack sat next to her as they waited for the attorney to appear. The familiar spice of his cologne filled her senses. She closed her eyes and tried to blot out the memory of a sunny June afternoon, and the easy laughter they'd once shared. He'd smiled more back then; now all he seemed to do was frown. Even his voice, once softer, more seductive, had a hard edge and she wondered what had brought about this change in his demeanour. When she opened her eyes again, he was watching her.

She tugged at the skirt of her newly purchased azure blue silk suit in an attempt to show Jack less of her long legs. 'Stop staring at me, Jack.'

'I'm not staring, I'm regarding. There's a difference. I can see this isn't easy for you. You okay?'

'I'm coping, that's all that matters. I wonder what's keeping Mr Parous.'

'He's probably snorting coke in the executive bathroom or meeting his dealer.'

'Attorneys don't do drugs or hang out with drug dealers,' Grace said. 'That would be unprofessional and illegal.'

'Bullshit! Don't you read the papers or listen to the TV? Who do you think defends the drug barons when they come up in court? I'll tell you. It's a thousand-dollar-an-hour attorneys like Parous. How do you think they afford offices like this? And don't tell me it's from legitimate earnings, because I won't believe a word of it. Corruption is rife in Miami; bankers, attorneys, cops, even high court judges — they're all on the take.'

She wanted to disagree, but the morning paper had carried the news that a district attorney in another state had been charged with corruption.

'Are you corrupt, too, Jack?'

'Hell, no. I'm just another patsy being taken for a ride!'

Grace opened her mouth to say something but was silenced by his dark, angry expression.

He rubbed his beard. 'Forget I said that. I didn't get much sleep last night and it's been a rough morning. When Parous shows up introduce me as a distant relative or a friend of the family. Whatever he tells you about Elliott's affairs, act like you already know.'

'I'm not sure I can.'

'Look, Grace, if you want learn the truth about your late husband you have to trust my instincts. If I tell you to do something, you do it, no questions asked. Now, you do all the talking. I won't interrupt unless I think he's hiding something or lying, okay?'

Grace nodded. Her fingers played with the strap of her purse, the only outward sign of her nervousness. The longer the attorney kept them waiting, the more she wished she'd stayed in England.

Suddenly, the door to the conference room opened. Zachary Parous stepped inside, a manila folder tucked under his arm. He appeared younger than Jack. Tall, athletic-looking, with wide-shoulders and a deep tan, he had blond hair and blue eyes. He looked as if he'd stepped straight out of the pages of a fashion magazine. His suit, like the furniture in his office, hadn't come from the local K-Mart store. Everything about his appearance shrieked money—from the handmade leather shoes to the heavy gold cufflinks and designer watch on his wrist.

'Grace, it's good to meet you. I can't believe you actually came here and at such a tragic time.' He took her hand in his own soft, well-manicured one, and held on to her fingers longer than considered necessary. His gaze settled on Jack. 'And you are?'

Grace withdrew her hand. 'This is Jack West, an old family friend. He's helping me while I'm here in Florida.'

The attorney eyed Jack suspiciously for a moment, and then took his seat behind the massive desk.

'Daniel always spoke fondly of you, Grace. And I can see why he chose to leave you at home rather than have you travel with him. With such a charming smile, you'd be prey for every beach lothario within a hundred miles.'

Grace lowered her head, and glanced at Jack from under her lashes. His expression was one of derision, but he said nothing.

'Thank you for the compliment, Mr Parous. As you know, I'm only here for a few days and I'd like to settle Daniel's affairs before I return to England. So, if we could get on?'

'Daniel was quite a character, always telling jokes, and a hell of a golfer, too.' The attorney looked out of the window at the Miami waterfront. Then he looked at Grace without meeting her eyes. 'Do you play golf, Grace?'

'I wasn't aware that you knew my husband in anything other than a professional capacity, Mr Parous.'

'Daniel and I played whenever he was in town, and had dinner together afterwards. He often talked of you two moving here permanently one day.'

Grace drew in a breath and tried hard to keep her expression neutral. But the shock of Daniel's duplicity was hard to hide.

'The purchase of the beach house was the first step in his plans for our future. Unfortunately, he died before he could tell me exactly what they were. My priority now is to ensure that the house is—'

'Sand Dollars, you mean?'

'Sand Dollars?'

'That's the name of the house.'

'Oh, yes. I forgot. Sorry.'

'You can hardly be blamed. You've been through a lot. By all accounts it's a stunning property, although I've only seen pictures. Seems likely you're a very rich widow.'

Jack's temper finally snapped. 'Look, Parous, Mrs Elliott is here to sign the transfer papers. She didn't come to listen to you ramble on for an hour in order to justify your exorbitant fee.' He turned to Grace. 'Give him the documents.'

Grace glared at Jack. 'I apologize for Jack's rudeness, Mr Parous.' She pushed an envelope across the desk. 'Inside you'll find proof of my identity — certified copies of my birth and marriage certificates.'

The attorney ignored Jack. He quickly scanned the documents. 'These all seem to be in order.' He opened the folder in front of him and spread the contents out on the desk. 'My assistant has prepared the necessary papers. If you'll just sign where indicated, I'll arrange to get them filed with the court.'

Grace leaned forward and angled the document so that Jack could read it too. She took her time, although the legalese was beyond her comprehension. Under the cover of the desk Jack squeezed her knee lightly. She glowered at him. He ran his fingers down the page to where the address of the property had been entered. Grace gave a slight nod, then lifted the pen, and added her signature.

The attorney stood and took her hands again, squeezing her them too tightly for her comfort.

'It was really good meeting you, Grace. Sorry to cut this short, but I have some important calls to make.'

Grace managed a stunning smile before pulling her hands free. 'Just one more thing; I wonder if you could tell me the name of the bank my husband used here in Miami. I want to set up a checking account so that any maintenance staff I employ to look after the house in my absence can be paid.'

'It's the First Apopka Bank on the corner of First and Third. If you wait in reception I'll ask my assistant to call ahead and see if the Manger is available.'

'No, that's okay,' Jack said. He stood and touched Grace's elbow lightly, urging her toward the door. 'We'll take our chance and see if he's free.' He cast a glance over Grace's drawn face as they strode down the hall to the elevators. 'Feel up to visiting the Bank, or have you had enough for one day.'

'I'll cope. The sooner I learn the truth, the sooner I can return to England and get on with my life.' The warmth of his hand seeped through the fine silk fabric of her jacket. She felt her pulse leap, and a shiver run down her spine. The attraction she'd felt for him six months ago was still as strong. She let out a long breath and stepped away from his body.

The elevator doors opened. Jack pushed her inside. 'The house belongs to you now, but what if Daniel bought it with dirty money? What will you do then?'

Suddenly angry, her head snapped round. 'You mean illegally? I don't know. I hadn't thought about it.'

'Maybe you should.'

'Why are you so sure that Daniel was involved in some form of criminal activity?'

'Instinct. Gut feeling. Call it what you like, but something tells me your late husband's business dealings were less than honest. How long were you married?'

Scowling, she shifted the strap of her purse on her shoulder. 'Ten years. Why?'

'And in all that time Elliott never talked about his work?'

Tension vibrated through Grace. It took all of her willpower to remain calm. 'I've told you. Daniel never discussed his work or clients with me.'

'So you keep saying. But can you prove it?'

'I… no.'

'You may have to.'

Ever since the solicitor had revealed the contents of Daniel's will the fear had been building. She fought the panic bubbling within her chest, but even so her breath hitched.

'You're scaring me, Jack.'

'Good.'

'I had nothing to do with it, remember?'

'I believe you, but others in authority might not. In fact, they probably won't. Let's hope Daniel didn't use money he scammed from his clients.' The elevator doors glided open. He let go of her arm. 'Come on, the bank is this way.'

Downtown Miami bristled with life. Office workers mingled with tourists, newspaper and street vendors. Buses battled with taxis, cars, and delivery trucks in a city where every building appeared to touch the sky.

Grace felt overwhelmed; she'd never been comfortable in big cities. To her they were places she visited to shop for that special occasion dress or a trip to the theatre, but she could never live in one. She matched her stride to Jack's, and kept close to his side, as he zigzagged his way in and out of the pedestrian circus. The hot, moist air felt oppressive, and overhead storm clouds gathered. She wondered whether they were about drop their contents on Miami or on her.

The First Apopka Bank was situated in an older, brick building, and at only five storeys high, it was dwarfed by the skyscrapers on either side. Distinctly Spanish in design, the ornately carved façade reminded her of buildings she'd seen in Seville on the only occasion she'd accompanied Daniel on a business trip.

She tilted her head. 'What happened here? Did the city run out of steel and glass?'

Jack grinned. 'Give it another few years, and some crazy architect will tear it down and put up another glass monstrosity.'

He held open the swing door and allowed her to pass. But rather than take a place in the line of people waiting to be served by the tellers, he steered her toward an advisor sat at desk on the left hand side of the banking hall.

Grace paused to catch her breath, the feeling that Jack was about to be proved right, that Daniel had been embezzling his clients, was stronger than ever. She swallowed hard, lifted her chin, and stepped up to the desk.

The dark-haired young woman in a smart grey business suit and crisp white blouse, turned away from her computer screen to study them.

'Hi, there. My name's Tracy. Please take a seat and I'll be with you in a moment.' She tapped away at her computer keyboard for another minute until satisfied with the entries she'd made.

'So what can we do for you, Mr and Mrs?'

'Jack isn't my husband, he's just a friend.' Grace answered quickly. 'I'm Grace Elliott. My late husband held an account with your bank.'

'I'm so sorry to hear about your loss,' Tracy said, with the appropriate sadness. As quickly as she manufactured the condolence, she snapped back into business mode. 'How can we help you today?'

'I wish to transfer his account into my name. I have the necessary documentation — a copy of his will, my birth and marriage certificates, along with a copy of the death certificate — to prove that I'm entitled to contents of the account.'

'And to any safety deposit box Mr Elliott had,' Jack added.

Tracy swivelled her chair and fixed her gaze on him, then turned back to Grace.

'You'll need to speak to someone more senior. I'm not authorised to deal with such matters. I'll see if someone's available.' She picked up the phone and punched in a few numbers. The brief conversation was held in hushed tones.

Almost immediately, a short balding man with spectacles approached the desk.

'Mrs Elliott, it's good to see you again,' he said, and shook her hand warmly. 'Come into my office.' He turned on his heel and strode towards a door at the rear of the bank.

See you again? Grace's knees buckled. She stumbled, and would have fallen had not Jack's arm circled her waist, and pulled her to her feet. She bit down hard on her lip, lest the scream that was bubbling inside her should escape.

'What's going on, Jack?' she whispered. 'I've never met this man before.' She took a deep breath punctuated with several even gasps, and clung to reality, praying she wouldn't betray her shock.

'I think I know what it means. Stick close to me, I'll explain later.'

Grace stared at him, speechless. Just thinking about all the lies and deceit made her feel physically sick.

'Can you hold it together for a bit longer?' Jack asked.

Her voice wobbled. 'I think so.'

He let her go. His thumb skimmed her cheek as his fingers brushed the hair back from her face.

'Remember what I said earlier about going along with whatever you're told?'

Grace forced a smile and gave a tense nod of her head.

The bank official held the door to his office open, and motioned them inside. As she entered, Grace squinted at the name badge on his lapel. She settled into the chair nearest to the large oak desk, and rested her hands in her lap.

'Forgive me, Mr Cody, if I seem forgetful. It's been a difficult time.'

'I understand. You have my condolences on your loss. Your husband's account shows a healthy balance. My assistant will prepare a duplicate set of statements for you. Do you plan on keeping funds here in the United States or would you prefer to transfer the balance to your bank in England?'

'I'm not sure. My plans are fairly fluid at present.'

'In that case, why don't we set you up with a checking account and bankcard? I see you have a house on Gasparilla Island. Will you be staying there?'

'Oh… yes. Of course.'

'That's fine, then. We'll show that as your residence here. That way you'll have access to your money while you're stateside. Then, at a later date, if you decide that you want to transfer the money into some other account, it'll be easy.'

'That sounds reasonable. Did Daniel have an ATM card, only I didn't find one among his effects?'

'We issue all our customers with an ATM card.'

'What about a safety deposit box?'

'If Mr Elliott owned one, it wasn't with this bank. We don't have that facility here. Now, if you'll just sign these forms, Mrs Elliott, I'll take care of everything for you.'

'I'm staying at the Island Palm Hotel here in Miami... just for a few days. If you could direct any correspondence there, I'd be grateful. Of course, I'll be in the house in a week or two, I'm sure. Just not today.'

'I see.'

'I mean, I've only just arrived and—' Jack nudged her knee with his. She got the message. 'I'm sure you understand, Mr Cody.'

'Of course. Thanks for dropping by today. You'll be hearing from us.'

Grace shook hands with the banker, and then she and Jack left. They'd only walked the length of one block when he pulled her toward the window of a jewellery store.

'If you're expecting me to buy you a Rolex in return for all your help, forget it,' she said, scanning the price tags on the skilfully displayed watches. 'They are way out of my price range.'

'Just pretend to be interested.'

'Why?'

'Because the plate glass makes a good mirror and I want to check out the guy who's following us.'

'We're being followed?' More surprised than frightened, she started to turn.

His hands clamped around her upper arms. 'Don't turn around. Point something out to me, as if you want me to buy it for you.'

Grace tilted her head and pointed to a ladies watch with a mother of pearl face. 'You're sure someone's watching us?'

'I'm sure. A man wearing dark glasses, black jeans, and blue shirt followed us from the attorney's office to the bank. He got into the teller line. When we left, he was standing next to the newspaper stand outside. He's not too careful about blending in. A pro would have changed his appearance, different jacket, a hat, glasses—or switched places with a partner.'

'It could be just a coincidence.'

'I doubt it, but there's only one way to find out.' He glanced at her feet. 'Those shoes make your legs look great, but can you run in them?'

Grace shot him a withering glance. The navy blue Italian leather shoes with four-inch heels were new. 'Run? In these, in this heat, are you serious?'

'Yep.' Jack looked in the window. Their tail had crossed the road and was standing at the edge of the sidewalk talking into his mobile phone.

'These cost me all of two hundred dollars.'

'Then take them off.'

'You're mad.'

'Very probably, but sometimes it's the only way to stay alive. Listen carefully. Act as if we're having an argument, then walk away as quickly as you can. Do you think you can find your way to the parking lot?'

'I think so.'

'Okay.' Jack slipped the keys to the Explorer into the palm of her hand. 'I want you to go there and lock yourself in the car. If I'm not there in ten minutes, drive until you see a cop and tell him you were followed. I'll catch up with you as soon as I can.'

'But—' She stared wordlessly at him, her heart pounding.

'No buts. Now do what I told you to do.'

Grace turned to face him and froze. His eyebrows rose. He lifted his palms upward. Feeling terrified and foolish, she gesticulated wildly, then pulled off her shoes, and ran down the street. Jack stomped inside the store, and pretended to examine the merchandise. Through the shop window he watched their shadow take off after her.

He waved the approaching sales assistant away, with a 'another time, maybe' and exited the store. By the time he reached the intersection, he'd caught up with their stalker.

The lights changed to red and pedestrians queued impatiently at the curb, waiting to cross. Jack grasped the man by the arm and spun him round.

'Carlos, how you doing?'

'Hey, let go of me!'

The little guy tried to wriggle free, but Jack's grip tightened. He bowed his head and said, 'How about you and I have a chat about who sent you, and why you're following me and the lady?' Jack pulled him out of the crowd and led him toward an alleyway.

'You're crazy, man. I'm not following anyone.'

'You've been clinging to me and the lady like shit to a shovel ever since we left the bank.'

'You're mistaken. I've never seen you before in my life.'

'Don't lie to me. Who sent you?'

Suddenly, the man twisted and kneed Jack in the groin, following it up with a punch to his jaw.

Jack tasted blood and fell to his knees, the air whooshing out of his lungs. Before he could move his attacker was hoofing it back down the alleyway and on to the crowded street. He cursed his stupidity; he should have backed the guy up against the wall before questioning him. He staggered to his feet; his breath came in great heaving gasps. At least he'd remained conscious, but his jaw was going to ache for the next couple of days and he was going to have one hell of a bruise. He wiped the blood from his lips, brushed the dust off his jeans, and stumbled out of the alleyway.

When he reached the Explorer, he found Grace sat in the driver's seat, her knuckles white where they clutched the steering wheel.

'Oh my God! Your face!' she cried. She stretched out her hand to touch him, but thought the better of it, and hastily withdrew.

'It's nothing that a stiff drink, and a long soak in the tub, won't cure. Move over. I'll drive.'

She shifted across the seat. 'Why would anyone want to follow us?'

'Not us, you. The bastard made off before I got chance to ask. But I think he and your mystery man from the graveyard are maybe connected.'

'That's impossible. I only decided to come to Miami after the funeral.'

'Yeah? Then either you were followed here or Zachary Parous has some real nasty associates who are keen to get their hands on either the money in that bank account, or you.'

CHAPTER SIX

Jack watched Grace for the space of a long breath; saw the fear in her eyes, and without stopping to think about the consequence of his actions, pulled her into his arms.

'Don't panic. As long as you're with me you'll come to no harm,' he whispered against her hair. He tried not to notice the warmth of her body against his, and exotic scent of her perfume filling his senses. While he rocked her in his arms, he told himself he was just offering comfort as he would to any other woman who'd just lost her husband. He even tried to believe it. But while he could fool his brain, he couldn't fool his body. He tilted her face to his.

'Say something, Grace.'

She blinked and focused her gaze. 'None of this makes any sense.'

'The way I figure it, Elliott or Lattide or whatever else your late husband called himself, got involved in a scam. A bad one. Now his boss or clients want their money back. And the only way to get it is through you.'

The stricken look on her face made him wish Elliott was alive so that he could beat the crap out of him for putting his beautiful wife in such danger. As it was, he was glad the son-of-a-bitch was dead.

Grace shuddered. He reached out and caught her slender hand in his.

'I don't believe—' Her voice broke.

'Honey, I hate to say this, but your late husband was a bastard. Not only did he keep secrets from you, he was having an affair. If he hadn't died in that car accident, then sooner or later his criminal friends would have caught up with him, and chances are the outcome would have been the same. I know that's cruel, but it's true. And you have to accept it.'

Grace shot him a cold look, and pushed free of his grasp.

'You don't know that! You've no idea what Daniel was like. He would never do anything to place his family in danger.'

Jack bit back a searing curse. When he spoke his voice was deceptively calm. 'No? Then why did that guy back there follow us and try to kick my head in?'

'I don't know. I wish I did. But I wish you wouldn't talk about Daniel as if he's on the 'most wanted list.' He was my husband. I would have known if he was involved in anything… in anything illegal.'

'For Christ's sake, open your eyes! You've already told me he never discussed his work with you. It's pretty clear that the jackass who followed us was going to tail you as far as your hotel, and then call his buddies. They wouldn't be quite so polite when asking questions.'

Grace covered her face with her hands. 'Stop it! Stop it! You're scaring me! I'm sorry I ever called you. You're horrible!'

He covered her hands with his own, and drew them into his lap. 'Yeah, I'm horrible, but I'm also right. You should be scared, Grace. Shit happens, and when it does, we can't bury our heads in the turnip patch and ignore it. And this, love, is serious shit.'

Grace turned and looked out of the window. She stopped chewing her bottom lip and stole a look at him. When she spoke her voice was barely a whisper.

'So what happens now?'

He started the engine and drove out of the parking lot.

'We go back to your hotel. You pack your bags and we find you someplace else to stay. Then we go over those bank statements with a magnifying glass. Hopefully, we'll find some clue as to where the money for the house on Gasparilla Island came from.'

'And if we don't?'

'Then we go visit your new home.' He pushed hard on the accelerator and cut across two lanes of traffic. The driver of the car following took exception to the manoeuvre and sounded his horn.

Grace grabbed the door handle. 'Are you nuts? You nearly got us killed.'

His fingers clenched around the wheel. 'Not hardly. I plan to lose anyone else who might be following us.'

'And are we… being followed?'

'Not yet.'

'Thank God for small mercies. But I don't see why I need to move to another hotel.'

Jack steered the Explorer into the parking lot at the Island Palm. 'Parous knows where you're staying. So do the people at the bank. And I'm betting whoever sent our tail knows where you're staying, too.'

There was no sign of the concierge as they passed the front desk on their way to the elevators. Jack thought it odd, but said nothing. All the same, he unbuttoned his jacket thankful he was carrying his weapon. He touched Grace's left elbow lightly, urging and yet protective. The ride to the ninth floor took seconds.

Jack held out his hand. 'Give me your room key.'

She shot him a hard glance.

'Okay, I'm sorry. Give me your room key… please,' he sighed.

Grace dug in her purse and pulled out the electronic card. Jack swiped it through the lock and pushed open the door. He listened for the sound of movement, but the only noise came from the air conditioning unit. Satisfied that everything appeared as it should, he stepped aside to allow her to enter.

'Go and start packing. I'll ring down to the front desk and ask them to make up your bill.'

'Which hotel are you taking me to?' Grace asked, kicking off her shoes and walking barefoot into the bedroom.

'I'm not sure yet. Depends which of the hotels in Coral Gables has a vacancy.'

Grace popped her head back round the bedroom door. 'Just so long as it's not some soulless motel down by the railway tracks, where your shoes stick to the carpet and breakfast consists of lukewarm coffee from a machine.'

'No soulless motel, I promise,' Jack smiled. 'How do you feel about a bed and breakfast, instead?'

'So long as it has a comfortable bed, and serves decent food, that's all that matters if it means I'll be safe.' She started tossing clothes out of the wardrobe onto the bed.

Jack rang the front desk, and then made one other call. He replaced the handset, and joined her in the bedroom. He leant against the door and watched her fold her clothes. She placed them in the suitcase with such care, as if they were fragile and might break if she didn't do it perfectly. He wondered if that's how she approached life—as if it too would break if she weren't careful. Or maybe it had already broken, and he was called in to sweep up the shards.

If only she knew how destroyed his life was.

He considered telling her about Rosa, and the hell their life had become. He thought about telling her about Emilia, the bright and shining star he never expected to see in any firmament. Then he saw the sadness in her eyes, and his resolve to tell her about any of it collapsed in a heap.

'Grace,' he said softly, and took a step towards her. 'Under different circumstances, I'd ask you stay at the condo with me. As it is, I can't. And I can't be with you twenty-four/seven, so having you switch hotels is the next best thing until I can get you a bodyguard.'

Grace's smile flickered, and then vanished. 'A bodyguard? Isn't that taking things a bit too far?'

'Possibly. But I can't take any chances with your life, Grace. You mean—'

Grace dropped the pair of trousers she was folding, and wheeled round to face him, an almost hopeful glint in her blue eyes.

'Yes?'

Unable to stop himself, Jack crossed the room and swept her into his arms. 'Damn it, Grace, you know how I felt about you — then. It hasn't changed. But the timing is wrong for us, and always will be. You're grieving and my life... well, my life's complicated.' He closed his eyes, savouring the feel of her body against his, then let her go, swearing that he'd never allow himself to get this close to her again.

'Jack—'

He rubbed his beard, and then ran his hand round the back of his neck. 'Accept it, Grace. I have. There's no point in fretting over what might have been. Now, if you're about done, let's go. I want to get you settled before I leave you alone for the night.'

Stunned, Grace snapped the locks on her suitcase, and picked up her purse. A quick glance around the room told her she'd not left anything behind. Jack dragged her case off the bed and strode out of the suite.

In the lobby, Grace paid her bill, and arranged for any mail to be held, then followed him out to his car.

'Did you leave a forwarding address?' Jack asked.

'I could hardly do that, seeing as I don't know where you're taking me,' she replied curtly.

'Sorry, I was thinking about something else.' Like how Rosa is going to react when he told her he wasn't going to be around to help with Emilia tomorrow.

While he waited for a tourist bus to clear the exit of the parking lot, he studied Grace's face. Tight-lipped and sombre, her expression was easy to read. Was she angry because he'd suggested that her husband was a crook or because he'd admitted that he wanted her? Or both?

The drive to Coral Gables didn't take long, and by the time Jack pulled up in front of the Cutler Inn he'd had enough of the silence and tension in the car.

'You'll be safe here,' he said. 'It's run by Frank Davis, and his wife, Maisie. We're old friends. I'd trust both of them with my life.'

Grace didn't even look at him. 'Why should I trust them with mine?'

'Because Frank's an ex-cop. One of the best. And he's real keen on security, and short of taking an axe to the doors, there's no way for anyone to gain entry to the guest rooms. That's why.' He clambered out of the Explorer, pulled Grace's luggage off the back seat, and herded her toward the front door.

The two-storey Florida mansion house had been lovingly restored. Painted white, with double galleries supported by pillars, it overlooked the Coral Gables Waterway.

Jack shouldered open the massive carved oak door and stepped aside to let Grace pass. He dropped her suitcase on the floor.

'I'll go find Frank.'

While she waited, Grace wandered around the room. Decorated in soft cream, with oak floors, rattan furniture and colourful cushions, the reception room was a picture of elegance and old Southern Charm. Overhead, a huge brass fan stirred the air. She was busy examining an old, framed photograph of the property when Jack returned with a man wearing a green, blue and yellow Hawaiian shirt and khaki shorts.

'Hi, I'm Frank,' he said, and held his out hand.

'Grace Elliott.' She took it and felt the inherent strength in his fingers. Frank Davis might be in his sixties, but he was stronger and looked fitter than men half his age. Nor had age dulled the sparkle in his blue-grey eyes. Deeply tanned, his white hair was cut crew-cut short.

'Jack tells me you've had some trouble. Don't worry; you'll be safe here. I've given you the room next to Maisie and me. Ordinarily we don't serve dinner, but for you, I'm making an exception.'

Grace forced herself to smile. 'That's very kind of you Mr Davis.'

'Naw, call me Frank. Everyone else does. And it's no trouble at all.' He picked up her suitcase. 'I'll show you to your room. After you freshen up, we'll eat. Maisie is a great cook. You staying for dinner, Jack?'

'Thanks, Frank, but I'd better get back. Things do to.'

Grace and Jack followed him upstairs to a room at the front of the house. The bedroom, complete with private bathroom, was large and airy and tastefully decorated in muted shades of green. A king-sized bed, covered by a rose coloured throw, with a bedside cabinet on either side, filled the centre of one wall. The furniture, like that of the reception room, was made of oak.

'This is wonderful. It's very kind of you to take me on such short notice,' Grace said.

'It's always a pleasure to help Jack. Okay, I'll leave you to settle in and see you downstairs when you're ready.'

Jack closed the door. 'Frank is a good man, Grace. He sleeps with a .38 next to the bed, so you only have to holler and he'll come running.' He nodded towards the phone. 'I've asked him to ensure you have an outside line at all times. If you hear anything that makes you nervous, you call me no matter what the time is, and I'll be here right away. Otherwise, I'll see you in the morning, and we'll go over the bank statements then. In the meantime, try and get some rest.' He bent to kiss her cheek then decided it wasn't such a good idea after all, so settled for giving her shoulder a re-assuring squeeze, then left.

Grace crossed to the window and leaned her head against the glass. Outside, coloured lights twinkled in the branches of the trees, reminding her that Christmas was but a few short weeks away.

Her first Christmas without Daniel.

Life would never be the same again. She felt hurt, empty, lost. Unlike Catherine, her sister, she'd never been one for the social scene, and the idea of forging new friendships was abhorrent. But, then so was the prospect of spending the rest of her life on her own.

Too weary to unpack, she flopped down on the bed, and buried her head in the pillows. Tears she'd fought so hard to contain spilled down her cheeks.

Coming to Miami had been a mistake. If she'd been thinking straight she'd have stayed in England and instructed the family solicitor to sell the house. But her strict upbringing had instilled such a strong sense of right and wrong in her that she had no option but to uncover the truth.

And then there was Jack.

One minute he was full of concern and hinting that he cared for her, the next he was pushing her away. Her skin tingled whenever he touched her, and she couldn't deny the gravitational pull he exerted on her, but allowing her feelings to exceed the bounds of friendship would be dangerous.

And lying there wallowing in self-pity didn't help her situation. She knuckled her tears away, conscious that her hosts were waiting to serve dinner. A quick shower and a change of clothes at least made her feel more human but did nothing to calm her swirling emotions.

When she emerged from her bedroom twenty minutes later, she found Frank and his wife waiting for her in the lounge.

A small, plump, brown-haired woman came forward and wrapped her arms around Grace. 'I'm Maisie, and you must be Grace, Jack's friend. It's a pleasure to meet you.'

Unprepared for the show of affection, Grace withdrew. 'It's good to meet you too, and I'm sorry if my sudden appearance has inconvenienced you.'

'Don't be silly. Now, I hope you don't mind, but Frank and I usually eat in the kitchen when the Inn has guests.'

'Please don't go to any trouble just for me.'

'Come on through. Dinner's nothing fancy, just red snapper and fresh greens. Frank! Are you going to sit reading that newspaper all night?'

He folded it up and tossed it aside. 'I'm coming, ma. I wouldn't want to ignore our lovely guest!'

The kitchen was warm and homely. The aroma of freshly baked biscuits filled the air and Grace realized that she was hungry. At the end of dinner Maisie produced what Grace determined was the largest key lime pie she'd ever seen.

'It's our speciality,' said Maisie.

Frank beamed at his wife. 'This is citrus country. Maisie makes the best key lime pie in the state, so you can imagine how many wayfaring strangers flock to us to get a little taste.'

Grace took a bite. 'It's absolute heaven. I'm a fair baker, but I've never tasted anything like this. You must give me the recipe.'

Maisie beamed. 'You're awfully sweet, dear. Just enjoy it.'

'Thanks. Have you known Jack long?'

'Since he was a baby,' Frank replied. 'His daddy, Hank, and I worked in the same precinct. Jack was six when his mom took ill. She died three years later. Hank found it hard to cope with two boisterous youngsters, so Maisie and I kind of stepped in. Jack and Lottie, that's what we've always called his sister Charlotte, came here after school. Maisie would feed them, see that they did their homework, and if Hank was working the late shift they stayed over. Jack was fifteen, when Hank passed on. Charlotte was away at university by then, and rather than bring her home to look after her baby brother, Maisie and I took him in until he was old enough to go to college.'

'He's been like a son to us,' Maisie smiled. 'Never forgets my birthday, and spends Thanksgiving with us whenever he can. We don't often see Charlotte. She's married now and living in Buffalo. Three kids too! She's a heck of a mom. What about you, Grace? Are your folks still alive?'

'They died in a boating accident while on holiday in Thailand some years ago. I have a sister, Catherine. She was sixteen at the time of their death. I gave up university to look after and support her. A year later, I married my husband, Daniel. Jack's probably told you he died a few weeks ago.'

'How tragic for you, child,' Maisie said. 'Are you and your sister close?'

'We were, but lately she's been busy with her career. She's a marketing executive for a pharmaceutical company. Her work is very involved, and she spends a lot of time on the road visiting hospitals and attending conferences.'

'It's sad when siblings grow apart,' said Frank. 'Your sister should be supporting you at a time like this. Do you have any children?'

Grace felt a twinge of disappointment. 'No. I'll have to hope that Catherine settles down one day and gives me lots of nieces and nephews.'

Frank placed the coffee tray on the table and poured Grace a cup. 'Has Jack shown you the pictures of his daughter, Emilia? She's a real cutie.'

Grace's heart stopped. 'No, he hasn't as a matter of fact.'

'Oh, she's going to be a heartbreaker, that one. Six weeks old and already she's got him wrapped round her little finger. He'll be riding shotgun by the time she's old enough to date.'

Grace's hand shook, spilling hot coffee into her lap and all over the white lace tablecloth. She jumped to her feet, her face a vivid scarlet. 'Oh, I'm so sorry. I… I'm not usually so clumsy.'

A war of emotions raged within her. Jack had a daughter, a six-week-old baby daughter.

She tried to do the math, and was even more shocked to realize that Rosa was already pregnant when she and Jack met at Wimbledon. No wonder he didn't invite her to stay at the condo — he was married and his wife and daughter were living there.

Frank grabbed the roll of paper towel and started mopping up the brown liquid. 'No harm done. I'm ham-fisted myself at times.' As he passed her chair on the way to the trashcan, Maisie glared at him, a silent, 'How could you' message in her eyes.

'What'd I do?' he whispered. Her only response was to thump him hard on the arm.

Grace swallowed the despair in her throat. 'Jack and I have been so busy trying to straighten out my late husband's affairs that we haven't had chance to catch up.' She turned to Maisie. 'Thank you for a delicious dinner, but if you don't mind, I think I'll go to my room. I… I didn't get much sleep last night.'

She all but ran up the stairs. Once inside her room, she flung herself on the bed and sobbed.

CHAPTER SEVEN

If Frank and Maisie noticed the dark rings under Grace's eyes when she came down to breakfast the following morning, they said nothing.

While Maisie flipped pancakes with ease that came from years of practise, Grace sat down at the table. She helped herself to a cup of coffee, added a splash of cream and stirred the cup. After a night spent tossing and turning she felt drained, hollow, lifeless.

'If you stir that cup any longer you'll take the pattern right off the china.'

Grace jumped at the sound of Jack's voice. 'What?'

'You were someplace else. Maisie asked you three times if you want syrup or fruit with your pancakes.'

Grace pushed the cup away. 'I'm sorry, Maisie, I seem to have lost my appetite this morning.' She swivelled in her chair to look at Jack who leaned against the doorframe. 'I didn't hear you come in.'

'I'm not surprised. That was some day-dream you were having.' His smile was as intimate as a kiss.

Grace rose from the table. Anger replaced pain, slicing through to her soul. 'I'll go fetch the bank statements,' she said tersely.

Jack caught her hand. 'Hey, what's up?'

Grace frowned. 'I didn't sleep well.'

'That's as maybe. But something else is bugging you. I can see it in your eyes.'

The screen door creaked. Frank came in from the garden. He took one look at Grace and Jack squaring off and tactfully withdrew.

'There's fresh coffee in the pot, help yourselves,' Maisie announced. 'I'm going to help Frank in the garden.'

Jack didn't move. He just waited for Grace to answer, his expression one of barely suppressed tolerance.

'Are you hell bent on making my headache worse, or just being obtuse?'

'Neither one, but I'd sure like to know who, or what, made you so cranky this morning.'

Grace regarded him impassively then strode out of the room.

Jack watched her walk away. The pale peach linen dress she wore couldn't conceal her curves. She'd left her hair loose, and it glistened against her creamy skin like polished amber. He caught the citrus and jasmine notes of her perfume, swallowed hard, and tried to forget how good she felt in his arms. He had no business thinking about her in anything other than a platonic way, but she was like a drug, and right now he couldn't get enough of her.

While he waited for Grace to return with the bank statements, he poured a cup of coffee. Maybe a shot of caffeine would stop him thinking about what might have been, and concentrate his mind on more important matters, like finding out what Elliott had been involved in.

When Grace re-entered the kitchen a few moments later, he was sat at the table reading the newspaper. She pulled out a chair, sat down next to him, and opened the envelope from the bank.

'Did you look at these last night?' Jack asked, putting down the paper and taking the sheaf of papers from her hand.

'Only briefly. The first statement is for March — four months before the date of the first entry in the passport. So that suggests someone other than Daniel opened the account.'

'I'm guessing Parous. It'd be easy enough for him to do that on behalf of a client.' He examined the first statement, and then compared it to the next three in the pile. 'There's a pattern here. Each weekly deposit is small enough not to attract attention of the banking authorities who track transfers of more than ten thousand dollars.'

'The same amount is transferred a week later. Where does it go, back to the client?'

'Probably into an offshore account or a limited liability company that no one individual technically owns. That way the authorities, such as the Inland Revenue Service have hard time unravelling the paper trail.'

'How do you know that?'

His eyes narrowed. 'Years of experience. When did Daniel buy the beach house?'

'June.'

Jack flipped through the statements until he found the appropriate one. 'Look,' he slid the sheet of paper toward her. 'Five withdrawals—I'll bet a year's salary that they are equivalent to the down payment on Sand Dollars.'

Grace blanched. 'Half a million dollars?' She quickly did the math. 'Why, that's nearly two hundred and fifty thousand pounds. Where did Daniel get that amount of money?'

'Guess.'

'Honestly, I have no idea.'

'Well, start thinking. This ain't no board game, honey. You don't collect two hundred pounds every time you pass go. He got the cash from somewhere very real, Grace.'

'Do you think Daniel embezzled the money from his clients?'

'No, the deposits are regular and the sums involved are too great. My bet is on a money laundering scam.'

'Money laundering? She stared at him, baffled.

'The criminal takes his profits from drug trafficking or other activities and moves it from one offshore account to another or from one offshore company to another. They may even do this several times every day. By the time the money arrives back in the country, no one knows that it was anything but legitimate. It's been washed clean, so to speak.'

'Can't the authorities do something to stop this?'

Jack shot her a twisted smile. 'Banks follow pretty strict codes, so it's not easy following the paper trail. It's like trying to net a single fish in a shoal of thousands. Offshore banks and secrecy havens make it easy for drug traffickers to build complex international networks. Asia, the Caribbean, Central America and Europe all have major offshore centres.'

Stunned and sickened, Grace gazed at Jack in despair. 'You're kidding me.'

'Nope.'

'And you think Daniel was involved in a scheme like this?'

'There's absolutely no doubt in my mind. I'm also sure that when we dig deeper, we'll find this isn't the only account your late husband had. Go grab your purse. There's someone I want you to meet.'

Grace shook her head. 'Where are you dragging me to this time?'

'I'm taking you to meet my boss.'

Her hands clenched. So did her whole body. 'Wait a minute. I thought you worked for the embassy?'

Jack's green eyes narrowed. 'I was on secondment.'

'What are you? Some sort of cop?'

'Not exactly. Now, are you ready, or do I haul you out of here in steel bracelets?'

'You wouldn't dare.'

The glint in his eyes said he would. 'Mike doesn't like to be kept waiting.'

Grace blinked and re-focused her gaze. 'You're unconscionable!'

'That's putting it nicely. Anyway, let's hope that Mike believes your explanation.'

Grace said nothing on the drive downtown; she looked out the windshield, unblinking, filled with icy rage. By the time Jack pulled his SUV into the parking lot the silence had become unbearable.

Despite the anger seething in his blood, his voice remained smooth, and calm. 'You asked for my help, Grace, and that's exactly what I'm giving you. As much as I'd like to keep this just between us, I can't. It's against Bureau policy.'

'What Bureau?'

'There's only one.'

'As in FBI?'

Jack nodded. 'Before I met him, Mike worked with a number of international organisations, including your Serious Organized Crime Agency. He cracked quite a few money laundering rings in his time.'

'Which is why you want him to meet me.'

'Which is why I want you to meet him.'

They walked toward an unremarkable single-storey grey concrete building. The Bureau's Miami field office looked the same as every other building on the block. There was no sign. It didn't need one. At the door, Jack showed his ID to the guard on the desk, signed in, and handed Grace a visitors' badge.

'This way.' He took Grace's hand and ushered her down a long corridor and into a sterile white office. Three darkly suited men and an equally darkly suited woman sat in front of a bank of computers. They murmured a brief 'hello' in acknowledgement of Jack's presence then went back to what they were doing.

At the far end of the office was another room. Jack knocked on the door and then stood aside to allow Grace to enter.

'Grace, meet Special Agent in Charge, Mike Zupanik. Mike's head of the Bureau's field office here in Miami.'

Mike shook her hand then rested his hip against the corner of this desk. 'Mrs Elliott, why don't you take a seat? Jack's already filled me in on why you're here.'

Grace sat down, her gaze fixed on the older man's face.

'I don't know what he's told you Mr Zupanik, but I assure you I've done nothing wrong. Jack seems to believe that my late husband, Daniel, was involved in some sort of criminal activity. All I know is that he left me a property on Gasparilla Island. I refuse to accept he's done anything illegal until evidence proves to the contrary.'

Mike ran a hand over his baldhead. 'Now, Mrs Elliott, no one is accusing you or your late husband of anything. However, we do need to clear up a few things. Let's start with this one. Where did your husband get the money to buy the beach house? You have to admit that was a pretty big wad of cash.'

Grace bit her lip, but said nothing. Jack tossed the bank statements on the table. 'Mike, take a look at these. There's over two million dollars in that account. And what's more, the account manager, a guy called Cody, implied he'd met Grace before.'

Mike raised an eyebrow. 'They say accountants stay close to the money, but that's a lot of cash for a bean counter. Excuse me, Grace. That's American slang. So here's another question. Can you explain how that amount of money came to be in your husband's account?'

'No.'

'You were his wife. Why not?'

Grace coloured under Zupanik's steady gaze. 'When Daniel died our bank account held less than two thousand pounds and there was roughly twice that sum in our savings account. Our home is mortgaged, and my car is six years old. Daniel's was leased through the business. As far as I'm aware, Daniel's partnership in the accountancy firm was our only source of income.'

'I understand your husband never discussed his work with you. Is that correct?'

'Daniel believed in client confidentiality. He preferred to stay late at the office rather than bring work home.'

'Was your husband's business in trouble?'

'I have no idea. You'd have to speak to Shaun, his partner.'

'What about debts? Did he have a gambling habit?'

'Not that I'm aware of.'

Mike frowned. 'Could someone have been threatening him?'

Grace lifted her chin, meeting his icy gaze. 'Why are you asking me all these questions, Mr Zupanik?'

'I'm trying to establish whether or not your husband had reason to kill himself.'

'Daniel was as well balanced as you or I, and had no reason to take his own life.'

Jack leaned against the window ledge and let out a long sigh. 'I told you, Mike. Grace knows nothing.'

'Everybody knows something,' Mike said, his steely eyes bored into Jack.

'Not this time.'

Mike gave an impatient shrug and turned to Grace once more. 'Tell me about the guy who approached you in the graveyard.'

'We only spoke for a few minutes.'

'But surely you can recall what he looked like?'

'He was short. I remember, because I didn't have to look up to him. And smartly dressed.'

'You mean he wore a suit?'

'Yes, I could see the collar of the jacket under his overcoat. His clothes were well cut, as if they'd been made-to-measure rather than purchased from a chain store.'

'Okay, but what about his build? Was he average for his height, thin or heavily built?'

'I don't remember.'

'Try!'

Grace's hands twisted in her lap and she began to shake as the image focused in her memory. 'S-stocky, like a boxer.'

'Now, this is important, Grace. Can you recall what colour his eyes and hair were?'

'He wore a hat, so I couldn't see his hair.'

'Anything else? Any distinguishing features? A scar on his face perhaps?'

'It was raining and we sheltered under the lych-gate. I couldn't see his face that well in the gloom. His eyes… I'm not certain, but I think they were brown.'

'What about his voice, Grace? Was he English or did he speak with an accent?'

'I… I'm not sure.'

'Come on, you must remember. The man threatened you.'

'Stop bullying me. I've told you all I know!' She cradled her head in her trembling hands.

Jack reached out and patted her shoulder. 'Take it easy, Grace. Mike's only trying to help.'

'A limp. He walked with a limp. He was strong, very strong.' Absentmindedly she rubbed her forearm. 'And he had this odd habit of licking his lips at the end of every sentence.'

'It's not much to go on,' said Mike. 'I'll get one of the guys to run it through the computer. Do you have a photograph of your husband?'

Grace took her wallet out of her purse, and removed a snapshot. 'It was taken a couple of years ago.'

Mike picked up the bank statements and flicked through them. 'Grace, I'm going to hold on to these, along with the photograph.' When she started to object, he held up his hand. 'Jack will give you a receipt and we'll get you some photocopies. I'm going to assign one of our forensic accountants to take a closer a look at the listed transactions, see if we can track the deposits and find out where the money originated.'

'What about Cody, are you going to pull him in for questioning?' Jack asked.

Mike flicked an imaginary speck of lint off his shoulder. 'I don't see much point at present. We'll keep him and the bank under surveillance. See if anyone tries to access the account. Jack, hate to do this, but your vacation just ended. I want you to pay a visit to the house on Gasparilla Island.'

'You're not going without me,' Grace said, surprised at her own bravery.

'No, not without you. Jack, you take Mrs Elliott with you. See if you can find out what her husband did to while away the lonely hours when he was there. Now Grace, if you don't mind, I'd like to have a word with Jack in private.'

Starchily, Grace stood and strode out of the room. When the door closed behind her, Mike turned to Jack.

'She seems innocent. What do you think?'

'She is. Daniel Elliott dominated his wife. He paid all the bills, and gave her a monthly housekeeping allowance to cover food and clothes. He didn't tell her anything about what money he had or how he spent it. If she asked too many questions he verbally abused her and undermined her confidence.'

'And she stayed with him?'

'Grace had a strict upbringing and she married young. Her father was a minister, so divorce was never an option for her. I wouldn't say she's entirely naïve, but whatever Elliott told her, she believed.'

'She sounds totally gullible to me.'

'I like to think there's some fight in her.'

'Now, Jack,' Mike counselled. 'You aren't developing some feelings for the pretty widow, are you?'

Jack kept his face impassive and hoped he sounded convincing. He knew what happened to agents who had a relationship with their informants — they were either fired or despatched to some backwater to end their career in obscurity.

'Me? Oh, hell, no. You know me.'

'I do. That's why I'm asking you.'

'The answer is no, Mike. Really.'

'Okay,' Zupanik sighed. 'So this lady's husband was a control freak who kept secrets. Accountants can access a lot of financial information. But he wasn't siphoning money from his clients' accounts or the British Tax authorities would have picked up on that, most likely.'

'Most likely.'

'Which means, Jack, the money had to be coming from other sources. You know what I'm getting at.'

'That's my thinking, too. Elliott had a second passport in the name of Lionel Lattide.' Jack handed it to his boss, along with the piece of paper Grace had found in Elliott's briefcase. 'He used it whenever he flew between here and London.'

'Lionel Lattide? Hmm. I'll organize a background check on both names, and a search to see if he had any other bank accounts. I'll also get the guys to show his photo round the hotels, see if anyone recognizes him. I don't like it, Jack. My gut tells me this case has all the makings of a chimpanzee's tea party.'

Jack raised an eyebrow. 'Another one of your quotable quotes, eh? What's this one mean, Mike?'

'It means anything can go wrong, so be careful.'

'Don't worry, Mike, I will.' Jack headed for the door.

'Before you go — things any better at home?'

Jack frowned. 'No, and Rosa's not going be happy when she learns I'm taking on another case. It means she'll have to actually take care of Emilia.'

Mike didn't respond immediately. When he did, his face was creased with lines of worry. 'If your personal life is going to interfere I can always assign someone else to look after the widow.'

'It won't. Grace barely trusts me. You assign another agent and she'll fly back to London faster than you can order a pizza.'

'Okay, Jack. But any problems, you let me know. I'll ask Chrissie to drop by your apartment in a day or so to see how Rosa's coping. Now get going before Grace starts getting agitated.'

CHAPTER EIGHT

For most of the two-hour drive to Gasparilla Island Grace stared out of the window. Apart from the other vehicles on the highway, there wasn't a house or building in sight, just mile after mile of tarmac, tall sawgrass and marsh.

'This place looks godforsaken.'

'It's not surprising, the road is known as Alligator alley,' said Jack. 'It runs right through the Everglades. If you look carefully, you might see one on the bank of a marsh, but the most I've ever seen in a bunch of egrets.'

'I don't like it.'

'I don't either. I wouldn't recommend taking a walk in there, that's for sure.'

Unseasonably hot, Grace wiped her damp palms on a tissue. Even with the air conditioning on, the air inside the car was oppressive.

'Have you been to the island before?'

'No, but I've heard of it. Jed Bush, onetime Governor of our state, has a place there. It's also famous for the Tarpon fishing tournament held each year. The town is named Boca Grande.'

'What Grande?'

'Boca. It means 'mouth'. Grande means 'big.' It's Spanish for 'big mouth' and comes from the waterway at the southern end of the island.'

'Oh,' said Grace, and continued staring out of the window. The deep orange sun slowly sank toward the horizon as Jack brought the Explorer to a halt at the tollbooth. He paid the four-dollar fee, and then drove across the swing bridge.

'Sand Dollars — I wonder why Daniel chose that name.'

'I think it's rather apt.'

'How do you mean?'

'A Sand Dollar is a type of burrowing sea urchin. The name comes from the shape and colour of the skeleton, which resembles a silver dollar. They are very popular with shell collectors, but pretty hard to find, especially whole.'

Grace frowned. 'I still don't understand why he chose that name.'

'I think Elliott was sending a message to anyone who tries to trace the money. The truth of where the money came from is buried deep, like a Sand Dollar.'

'I see. Will you be able to find the house?' Grace asked.

'I memorized the zip code when we were in Parous' office and entered it into the Sat-Nav,' Jack replied as they crossed another bridge. 'That will take us right up to the front door. The island's only a few miles long.'

Grace stared at the large colonial styled houses silhouetted against the setting sun. No two properties appeared the same, although most had wide verandas, and windows bordered with plantation shutters. Occasionally, she caught a glimpse of a lush hedge of pink bougainvillea, and a tropical garden filled with palms and hibiscus.

'It's not the sort of place where I'd expect someone involved in illegal activities to live. If I were a criminal, I'd choose the anonymity of a big city rather than somewhere as quiet and beautiful as this.'

'It's December. The time of year when the snowbirds come to Florida.'

'Daniel wasn't into bird watching; he didn't even like sport unless it was—'

Jack's rich laughter filled the car. 'Snowbirds are what we call affluent east coast retirees who come here to get away from the worst of the winter weather.'

'Oh, I see. You mean old age pensioners or seniors as you call them. This is more like millionaire's paradise than skid row.'

'Even criminals can be snowbirds. Tell me more about Daniel. Did he have many friends?'

'There's his business partner, Shaun and the guys at the golf club. Most of the people he knew were business associates or clients. He spent his evenings in the study, although what he did in there, I have no idea.'

'What about his old college buddies? Did he ever attend any class reunions?'

'He lost touch with them years ago.'

'Which means he met whoever is behind this scam through his accounting firm.'

Grace turned to face him. 'Are you suggesting Shaun or one of the junior associates is involved too?'

'It's possible. Whoever it is, has business interests on both sides of the Atlantic. Importing, exporting, that sort of thing.'

'That could include anyone of the firm's clients.'

Jack grunted and turned off Gasparilla Road and onto Fourth Street. 'We're going to need a list of them.'

'I'll ask Liz, as I doubt Shaun would comply because he'd be breaching client confidentiality.'

'Okay, I'll give you a number she can fax it to. If we need more information we can always subpoena Shaun. Let's hope Sand Dollars reveals what your late husband was up to. In the meantime, are you hungry? I spotted a restaurant back there. What do you say we go grab something to eat?'

'Good idea. There won't be any food in the house.'

'It'd be interesting if there was,' Jack murmured.

She gave him a sidelong glance. 'What did you say?'

Jack kept his eyes on the road. 'Nothing.'

The town of Boca Grande could be summed up in two words – small and quaint. Grace counted two real estate offices, a post office and a couple of clothing stores, as well as a restaurant housed in what appeared to be an old railroad station. Down one of the side streets she spotted the sign for the island bakery. Directly outside stood a pink gas pump. Nearly everyone they passed on the road drove a golf cart rather than an expensive, gas-guzzling car.

'I feel as if I've stepped back in time,' Grace said, as she climbed out of the SUV. 'It's like that TV show they're always repeating on British Television – The Prisoner. I half expect a big white balloon to come rolling down the street.'

Jack grinned, took her arm, and steered her toward the restaurant. 'I saw the re-runs of that show on the Sci-Fi channel. The guy was a spy and continually tried to escape. Charlotte, my sister, had a crush on the star, whatever his name was. He was in Secret Agent and a couple of movies, too. Her bedroom walls were plastered with his pictures. I used to tease her until she got so mad, she'd throw shoes at me. Did I ever tell you high heels make painful weapons?'

'No, you didn't. Is that a joke?'

'A very bad one, I guess.'

Grace sighed. 'Do you want to eat inside or out?'

'Inside. Now that the sun's set, the temperature's dropped by a few degrees. It can get mighty chilly all of a sudden on islands like this.'

They passed a party of noisy teenagers sat under one of the many umbrellas shading the tables in front, and found a table in the corner of the dining room. The menu wasn't extensive but if the number of diners crowded into the small room was anything to go by, the food was excellent.

'I didn't know you had a sister,' Grace said after the waitress had taken their order.

'There's a lot you don't know about me. Charlotte's older by eight years.'

'And I'm five years older than Catherine. She was still at school when our parents died. I gave up university and took a job to support her.'

'Is that where you met Daniel, at university?'

Grace shook her head. Bronze-gold curls glistened in the glow from the overhead light. 'No, I'd left by then and was working as a secretary for a firm of accountants when Daniel joined the company as an associate. We dated for three months before he proposed. We we're married two months later. A year after that, Daniel and Shaun set up their own practice.'

'Did you go work for them? You'd have been a natural, managing the office.'

Grace shook her head. 'I offered, but Daniel insisted I give up work as soon as we were married.'

'That's a shame. I can see you keeping things going.'

Grace winced. 'He said I wasn't cut out for it. I don't have the level of business acumen Daniel needs... Daniel needed.'

Jack just let it slide. 'Are Daniel's parents alive? Did he have any siblings?'

'His parents died before we met, and he was an only child.'

'What about Catherine? She'd have been what, fifteen when you and Daniel married?'

'Sixteen. She'd just finished taking her GCSE's and wanted to study for her 'A' levels so that she could go on to university. I didn't have it in my heart to deny her the chance of further education. Daniel agreed to help with the fees if she studied hard and got the necessary grades.'

'I hope she appreciates all you've done for her.'

Grace's smile faded. She looked away. Catherine was demanding. Rarely said 'thank you' no matter how small the favour, and more often than not, placed her needs above those of others.

'I can't exactly say. Catherine is—'

'Selfish?'

'What makes you say that?'

'Well, it's obvious. She'd be with you now, if she wasn't.'

'Catherine has a high profile career. She's rarely in the office and spends most of her time on the road.'

'Did she and Daniel get along?' Jack asked, as their server approached the table with their order.

Grace regarded him with a speculative gaze. 'Why the sudden interest in my sister?'

'I'm just trying to get a picture of Daniel's life and that of the people around him, that's all.'

'Daniel and Catherine got along fine. He said she was the sister he'd always wanted, but never had. Once she started university she rarely came home during term time. When she graduated, she and a friend rented a flat in Clapham. Eight months ago she bought a place of her own.'

'Unless things are different, property in London is pretty expensive. How did she afford to buy an apartment?'

'I—I don't know. I'm assuming she has a mortgage like everyone else. Anyway, we've never discussed her income. It's considered the height of rudeness and ignorance to ask someone what they earn in Britain.'

'Okay, no need to go on the defensive. Eat your pasta before it gets cold.'

Grace pushed a forkful of linguine round her plate. She no longer felt hungry. Jack's questions about Catherine made her realize that her sister still hadn't returned her calls. She glanced at her watch, it was too late to call now, but she'd try again in the morning, assuming there was a phone in the house.

'You're not eating,' Jack said, breaking into her thoughts.

'Sorry, I was just thinking about my friend, Olivia. She's due to have her baby in few weeks' time.' Grace stared pointedly at Jack, with the hope that he'd tell her about his daughter, but his expression remained unchanged. She looked down at her plate but felt his eyes watching her. She scooped up a forkful of pasta and made a show of enjoying it, even though it was cold.

As they lingered over coffee a tall, thin man with jet-black hair, tied back in a ponytail, approached their table.

'Hey, Mrs Lattide. I didn't know you and Lionel were back on the island.'

Caught off guard, Grace sat there dazed and shaken. She put down her cup and looked at the stranger. Dressed Bermuda shorts and a brightly multi-coloured T-shirt, he looked no different than any of the other dinners. It was only when Jack nudged her foot with his own that she managed to mutter, 'I-I've only just arrived. Forgive me. I'm not very good with names.'

'That's okay; we only met once. I'm Pete Jacobs. I run the island seaplane charter. I flew Lionel down to the Keys a couple times when he was last over.'

'Then you won't know that Da… Lionel is dead?'

'Wow. I'm really sorry to hear that, Mrs Lattide. What a shocker. I had no idea. How'd it happen?'

'He died in a car accident.'

'That's tragic. He was such a fun guy, you know. Always laughing and joking. He was one of my best customers. I'll miss him. Well, if there's anything I can do for you, you let me know, you hear?'

'Thank you, I will.'

Nervously, Pete backed away and sped out the door. Grace slumped over the table, her face contorted with worry. She didn't want to believe what she'd just heard, didn't want to think she'd spent ten years living a lie. But she couldn't deny the facts any longer.

'All along I've thought this is some sort of nightmare and that I'll wake up and find everything has returned to normal. That Daniel is still alive. But now, I don't even know who I married. Lionel Lattide or Daniel Elliott?' She smiled sadly at Jack. 'I feel dirty, used. Who was Daniel? I don't have any idea. Isn't that terrible?'

Jack reached across the table and took her hand in his. His grasp was warm and comforting. His fingers slipped around hers with assurance. He squeezed her hand as if it was the most natural thing in the world.

'This isn't the place for such a profound discussion. You sound like you're having a hard time breathing. Do you need your medication?'

'I'm—' Her voice broke, so she shook her head.

'Then let's get out of here.' He downed the last of his coffee, and threw some cash on the table.

Grace staggered to her feet. Jack slipped his arm around her waist and escorted her to door. She leaned into him. He felt solid, reassuring, yet she knew she ought to pull away. She felt her pulse quicken, her instinctive response to him so powerful that she stumbled again.

Jack's grip on her waist tightened. A sigh escaped her lips. If only she hadn't had such strong principles and he wasn't married, things could be so different. As it was… she pushed the thought from her mind.

The streetlights cast amber coloured halos into the early evening dusk as they returned to his car. Jack helped Grace into the passenger seat, then walked round to the driver's side, and climbed in behind the wheel. Five minutes later, he drove through the gates of Sand Dollars and down the dark, tree-lined circular drive.

When no lights came on and no dogs barked, he opened the driver's door and strode up to the house. The porch light came on, triggered by a motion sensor, but the solid oak door remained firmly closed.

Grace stepped out of the vehicle to the distant sound of waves crashing upon the shore and the tang of salt filled air. She gazed up at the house, reluctant to enter. One and a half storeys high, surrounded by trees and a lush tropical garden filled with hibiscus and palms, it stood in semi-darkness, the large bay windows shuttered, and bare. A screened porch ran down the side of the house towards the sand dunes behind.

'Don't stand their gawking, try acting as if you own the place.'

'I do own it. That's why I'm staring,' Grace replied.

'How do you feel about a little breaking and entering?' Jack asked as he climbed the steps to the front door.

'Isn't that illegal, even for the FBI?'

'Technically, yes. But an agent can use reasonable force to gain entry if he suspects a crime has been committed.'

'That might not be necessary.' Grace dug in her handbag and pulled out a set of keys. 'These were Daniel's,' she said, and handed them to Jack. 'The small brass key belongs to the house in Gloucester. The black electronic fob to what remains of his BMW. The rest — well, I have no idea what they are for.'

He bent and examined the lock, selected one of the keys, inserted it, and turned. The door opened with a soft click.

'Let's hope there's no alarm and that it's not connected to the Sherriff's office. Stay here.'

'Why should I? It's my house.'

'Because it's safer.'

'I'll be just as safe standing behind you.'

Jack knew it was pointless arguing. 'Then make sure you don't get in the way of my right arm.'

Grace gave him a long look. 'Why?'

'Because it's my gun arm, and I don't want to accidently shoot you,' he said, and removed the weapon from the holster at the back of his jeans then stepped inside.

Grace's voice wedged in her throat. She ran her damp hands down her dress, and followed Jack. The aroma of tobacco filled the hallway — the same blend that Daniel smoked. Cold sweat trickled down her spine, making her shiver. She ignored it along with the heavy rhythmic beat of her heart, and closed the door.

Jack cocked his head to one side and listened, but there was only silence.

'See if you can find the light switch.'

Grace's fingers trembled as she ran them down the wall. She found the switch, and flicked it on, bathing the hallway in a soft yellow light. Overhead, a fan hummed into life and gently stirred the air.

'Someone has been here recently,' Jack said, putting his gun on safety and returning it to the holster.

'How can you tell?'

'There's no dust on the furniture,' he said, running his fingers along the hall table to prove his point. 'Wait here while I have a look around.'

Grace drummed her fingers against the table, and gazed at the large piece of modern art hung on the wall. It reminded her of the painting she'd seen in the attorney's office only this time the colours were a garish mix of yellow, black, and green. Fed up of waiting for Jack, she opened the nearest door and stepped inside.

Large and airy, the lounge was a sharp contrast to the one in Applegate cottage. Two over-stuffed sea-green leather sofas stood either side of the marble fireplace, with an elegant glass topped table between. A thick cream coloured carpet covered the floor. The walls were painted in the same shade of cream and dotted with paintings. No modern art this time, but powerful seascapes in varying shades of green.

'This is so different to the house Daniel and I shared,' she said when Jack entered the room a few moments later. She felt a stab of jealousy and anger. 'I've lost count of the times I suggested we buy new furniture and decorate, but he always came up with some excuse. Now I know why.'

Jack walked over to the glass fronted oak cabinet that stood in the corner of the room. He took out a crystal tumbler, and held it up to the light. A rainbow of colours shimmered in the glass. He replaced it in the cabinet.

'Come on let's see what the rest of the house is like.'

At the rear they found a large spacious kitchen/family room with a screened porch and views out over the garden to the ocean. A centre island, topped with a marble counter, divided the cooking and eating areas. Jack opened the refrigerator. It contained a quart jug of orange juice, a pack of butter and some cheese. He removed the jug and cautiously sniffed the contents.

'The juice is still fresh.' He replaced it on the shelf and closed the door. 'Check the cupboards. I bet they're full of tinned goods.'

Grace opened the nearest cupboard. As he'd predicted, it was neatly stacked with tins. She slammed the door shut. Betrayal clawed at her chest as her heart refused to believe what her mind was telling her. Struggling for control, she stormed out of the kitchen.

Like a drunk seeking his next drink, she sought out the bedrooms. On the landing she hesitated until curiosity and the desire for truth got the better of her. She pushed open the nearest door and stepped inside.

It was his room — she was sure.

Spasms of panic ran through her body, for here too, the scent of Daniel's favourite tobacco lingered in the air. Decorated in blue and cream, the room overlooked the ocean. An elaborate, carved oak king-size bed, with matching nightstands stood against one wall. Unable to stop herself, she ran her fingers across the navy blue chenille bedspread. Anger born of grief made her throw back the covers and toss the pillows onto the floor.

Darkness spun around her, as the room tilted alarmingly. Bile filled her throat. She swallowed hard and pushed it back down, as she lurched toward the French doors and threw them open. She stepped out onto the veranda, and gulped in a lung full of fresh clean air. Moonlight cast a silvery glow on the sea, but all she could think about was Daniel's treachery.

'I thought you loved me, Daniel,' she said with a hoarse cry. 'How could you lie to me like this, and how could I not know?'

Only the gentle breeze blowing off the ocean answered.

Grace wrapped her arms around her chest, and leaned heavily against the handrail. Shudders racked her body. She willed them to stop. Her breath came in chest-heaving gasps. Her heartbeat throbbed in her ears, and she felt so lightheaded that for one heart-stopping moment she thought she would topple over the balustrade onto the tiled patio below. She stepped back, her face a glowering mask of rage. She stumbled inside, determined to uncover what other secrets the room held.

The dressing area contained a large walk-in wardrobe. Her hand shook as she slid back the door. One section was filled with a selection of men's designer suits, shirts, and jackets. The other held a rail full of women's clothes. She bit her lip until it throbbed like her pulse. One by one she studied the contents. A sapphire blue cocktail dress caught her attention. Something about the design seemed vaguely familiar.

Grace lifted it out and examined it more closely. The notes of some heady oriental fragrance lingered on the fabric. She wadded it into a ball and threw it onto the floor, then removed a trouser suit. It too ended up on the floor, as did the rest of contents of the wardrobe.

The dresser contained underwear. She took out a peach teddy and held it up. Delicate lace and silk shimmered in the light. She pulled at the lace until it ripped in two then tossed the shreds on the floor along with everything else.

Her breath hissed out between her teeth. She teetered, then ran and kept running until she was out of the house and heading toward the ocean.

It was true. It was all true.

Daniel hadn't loved her.

All the devotion she'd felt — everything she'd done had been for him. And he'd kept someone else, here in this house. And who knew where else?

Pain shredded her eyes, her mind, and her heart. She was seized and crushed by gasping, tearing agony. There was no more reason to live. No more reason to breathe. Instead of breathing, there was screaming, endless screaming.

CHAPTER NINE

Across the hall from the family room, was a small study. Floor to ceiling bookcases filled one wall. A large, 'L' shaped desk faced the window which offered views over the garden to the ocean beyond.

Jack closed the drapes and turned on the small desk lamp. The glow from the blub shed a tiny golden circle of light on the polished wood surface.

The desk drawers were locked, but that didn't surprise him. None of the keys on the ring Grace had given him earlier fit. He pulled a small folding knife out of his jeans pocket and inserted it between the lock and the frame, and twisted. There was a sharp click and the topmost drawer slid open. He was examining the contents when Grace screamed.

His stomach turned over, then clenched. Adrenaline flooded his veins, sharpening his senses, as a second ear-splitting scream filled the house.

He reached for his gun. The clip was full, plus he had a spare in his back pocket. He slipped off the safety, and stepped into the hallway just in time to see Grace drag open the front door and dart outside, shrieking the whole way.

'What the hell?' He cursed again, and took off after her. He jumped the porch steps, landing hard. The driveway was empty; the Ford Explorer where they'd left it. He spun round toward the back of the house in time to see Grace's slim figure running through the garden. He prayed that whatever had spooked her didn't have two legs and a gun, and wasn't about to come charging out of the house after them.

He listened.

A branch snapped.

Leaves rustled.

Then all he could hear was the steady thump of his heart and the murmur of waves washing the shore.

A motion sensor clicked on, then off. The brief blaze of light enabled him to track Grace's progress through the garden. Uneasiness crawled over his skin. He took a deep breath and forced himself to remain calm. He tightened his grip on his gun and stepped onto the wooden deck, silently praying that none of the boards were loose or weak. A second sensor lit up, the sudden blinding light almost destroying his night vision. He squinted, trying to cut out some of the glare, all the while assessing the danger. He wanted to call out to her, tell her to stop, but training over-ruled instinct.

Somewhere in the trees to his right an owl hooted, its call strangely high-pitched and unnatural. Sweat popped on his spine, adding to the chill carried on the breeze. He took a chance and broke into a run. The pool lights came on; the water shimmered with an eerie turquoise radiance.

A low wooden fence covered by a flowering shrub separated the end of the garden from the beach. Thorny branches clawed at his jacket, tearing the fabric. Knowing better, he yanked it free, shredding a large hole in the process. He crept along the path, his gun arm constantly sweeping from side to side. A large Banyan tree stood by the open wooden gate, its thick woody trunk casting sinister shadows in the moonlight. He hesitated, then stepped through, and followed the path through the Sea Oats and Sea Grape, past the tall hexagonal structure of the rear range light, to the beach.

Grace stood in the ocean oblivious to the water lapping around her. Her sodden dress clung to her slender legs and thighs. Her head tilted towards the moon, a strange high-pitched moan escaped her lips. Her fists pounded against her thighs, and her body convulsed as she continued keening like some wounded animal that had gone to the sea to die.

Jack groaned, holstered his weapon and waded in after her. The waves rippled around his calves, the cold water sending an involuntary shudder through his body. He placed a restraining hand on her shoulder then did the one thing he knew he shouldn't. He reached for her, and cradled her in his arms.

'Talk to me, Grace. Tell me what's wrong.'

Her arms beat against his chest as she pushed him away.

'Leave me be, Jack. I don't need your help. I don't need anyone's help. My life is ruined, that's all.'

'I'm not leaving you out here on your own, not like this. What were you thinking running out of the house like that?'

The moonlight glinted off the tears that streamed down her face. 'You… have no… idea what… I'm thinking,' she gasped.

He pulled her roughly, almost violently against his chest. 'I think I can guess.'

'Daniel's clothes… her clothes. Her clothes.'

'Shush.' He rubbed her back with the same rhythmic strokes he used to sooth Emilia when she was crying. Only Grace wasn't a baby and his response to her was anything but platonic. He wanted to lean into her, hold her until there was nothing left in his mind but her.

Grace lifted her tear-stained face to his.

'I should have stayed at home instead of doing what is morally right. I can't stay in this house knowing… knowing Daniel and his mistress slept here.'

The haunted look in her eyes made him wish he could bear some of her pain. But he couldn't. So he settled for offering her what little comfort he could. He wiped away her tears with the ball of his thumb, and watched the play of emotions on her face.

'I know this is hard on you, Grace, but you don't have any choice, not if you want to know the truth.'

With a final wail her body sagged against his. He hesitated, then swept her into his arms and carried her out of the ocean onto the beach. Her arms wrapped around his neck, her head rested on his shoulder. His pulse kicked as her breasts brushed against his chest. Her scent filled his nostrils, mixed with the tang of salt and flowers from the garden, adding feelings of lust and tenderness to his adrenaline filled veins.

He told himself that he was just protecting an informant, that he'd do the same for any woman in a similar predicament. But he was lying. His feelings for Grace went way beyond duty.

Grace wept aloud. Jack rocked her back and forth until her sobs subsided. He tipped her face to his, and brushed his lips against her forehead. When he was sure she could stand without falling, he set her on her feet. He took off his jacket, wrapped it around her shoulders, and clasped her body tightly to his.

'I'm here for you,' he said, not knowing what else to say that wouldn't sound maddeningly inappropriate to her pain.

Her response was raw. 'I know. You're a good friend, Jack. I know that. I just can't make myself accept that Daniel was cheating on me, even after the banker and that guy in the restaurant said they'd met me before. Even now, now that I've seen her clothes, smelt her perfume I still can't believe it. I want to die, Jack. I want to die and make it all go away!'

'Stop it, Grace. That's crazy talk. I know it's hard to turn off your feelings, but Daniel's not worth your tears.'

'I'm not crying for him, Jack. I'm angry. Angry because I didn't see what was happening, what sort of person Daniel had become. Maybe the person he always was.' She wriggled free of his embrace and stepped back. The cool night air fanned her cheeks and calmed her mind. She turned to face him.

'I know the truth now, Jack. He never loved me. Not for a minute. How he must have laughed at my naivety.'

'You're not naïve, Grace. If you were, you would have accepted the contents of the will without question. As it is, Daniel didn't deserve to have you as his wife. End of story. Now come on, let's go back to the house before you catch pneumonia.' He wrapped his arm around her waist and guided her up the beach.

They reached the dunes when Jack heard the unmistakeable throb of a powerful outboard engine. Swiftly, he pulled Grace into the shadows cast by a Cabbage palm. It wasn't much protection, but it was all there was. A powerful searchlight swept the beach then settled on the windows of Sand Dollars.

'What—'

'Don't move,' he breathed, reaching for his gun once more. He pushed her further into the shadows.

'It looks as if word has got out that Daniel's widow is back on the island.' He slipped off the safety and braced his legs, ready to take aim.

'But less than half a dozen people know I'm here,' she hissed.

'Yeah. Which means one of them is in direct contact with Daniel's associates.' He felt her pulse quicken, and gooseflesh ripple over her skin where he held her wrist.

'All the more reason to move into a hotel,' she said softly, and filled her lungs with one deep breath, then another.

'Wrong. All the more reason to stay,' he whispered.

'But—'

Jack clamped a hand over her mouth. The engine died. Two more men appeared on deck. Heavily accented voices floated on the wind. One of them turned and shouted something in Spanish.

Jack held his breath, while the cruiser drifted with the current. He tightened his grip on his gun as the searchlight travelled the length of the house one more time before alighting on the dunes.

'Do you think they saw us?' Grace whispered.

'If I was them, I'd have seen us.'

'Then we're in danger,' she whimpered. 'We have to go—now!'

When the searchlight lit up the bushes on Jack's left, he swung Grace into his arms. His lips brushed against hers as he spoke. 'Don't fight me, Grace. This is just for show. I want the guys on the boat to think we're a couple of sex starved adolescents making out.'

Grace watched him with a kind of intensity that made his blood heat, and his hormones leap. He continued to stroke her back, telling himself he was only soothing her, keeping her calm. He didn't believe it. His fingertips brushed her cheek and felt her shiver in response. The need to kiss her, feel her lips on his, sent desire pulsing through his body. He closed his eyes for the space of a long breath and fought an inner battle. Only the imminent threat presented by the men on the boat prevented him from doing what he'd wanted to do six months ago.

As suddenly as it had stopped, the engine growled into life once more. The searchlight went out and the boat roared off into the darkness.

Jack waited a few minutes to be sure no one had come ashore then stepped out onto the path.

'Let's go.' He kept his arm firmly around Grace's waist and started running toward the house, but instead of going inside, he continued down the drive until he reached his car. He unlocked it, pushed her inside, and handed her the keys.

'Lock the doors. Wait here until I've checked the house. If anyone other than me comes drive to the nearest house, pound on the door, and tell whoever answers to call nine-one-one.'

'But I can't ask a total—'

'I mean it. Don't ask them. Tell them. Understand?'

Grace bobbed her head.

Jack heard the locks click, then turned and climbed the porch steps. The hallway was empty, just as he'd left it. He went through the rooms, one by one, checking the windows, and ensuring the doors were securely locked. Satisfied that no one was in the house, he went back for Grace.

By the time he got her inside she was shaking with cold and her skin had taken on a ghostly pallor.

'We need to get you warm,' he said, and herded her up the stairs and into the bathroom. He turned on the faucet. When the water ran hot, he said a silent pray of thanks to whoever had the foresight to install solar panels.

'Get out of those wet clothes and into the shower. I'll fix you a drink.'

Left alone, Grace stripped and stepped into the stream of hot water. While steam swirled around her body the realization that she'd have welcomed Jack's kiss sent a quiver of heat of a different kind surging through her veins.

She was grieving and vulnerable, yet the need to be touched and held by a man was so strong that she'd almost given into temptation. She rested her head against the tile. No longer bound by her marriage vows she was free to do as she chose, yet an affair with Jack would be perilous for both of them. She was free, but he wasn't. He had a wife and a daughter. And no matter how strong the attraction, she couldn't destroy his marriage and the lives of his wife and child.

Tears mingled with the flow of water from the shower. She washed them away along with her grief. Jack was right. Daniel didn't deserve her tears. And this would be the last time she cried for him. From now on she was going to live her life her way.

Gradually, her muscles relaxed and the tension of the day seeped away. She stepped out the shower and vigorously rubbed herself dry. A pale green, silk and lace bathrobe hung on the back of the door. She held the fabric to her face. No perfume lingered in the folds. She slipped it on, cinching the belt tightly around her waist.

She found Jack in the kitchen.

'Here, drink this,' he said, and handed her a steaming cup of coffee.

She took a sip. The alcohol burned her throat and made her cough.

'This is lethal, what's in it?'

'Brandy, it was all I could find.'

'Your jeans are wet through, Jack. Why don't you go and change?'

'I'm a whole lot tougher than you are, Grace. A little cold water won't do me any harm. Whoever was out there just now, will be back. Keep the drapes closed and stay away from the doors and windows.'

'Isn't it a bit late for precautions?'

'It's never too late. Besides, I don't want some drug crazed or trigger happy criminal letting off a shot every time a shadow crosses in front of a window.'

Grace swallowed her fear, determined that Jack shouldn't see how rattled she felt. 'How... how do you know that they weren't teenagers mucking about or fishermen out for a night's sport?'

'Since when did fish start crawling out of the ocean and waiting on the beach to be caught?'

Grace went still.

Jack finished his coffee and put the mug in the sink.

'Look, I'm not trying to frighten you any more than you already are. I'm just telling you how it is. The guys on the boat were interested in two things. Sand Dollars and who might be inside.'

'If it's so dangerous we should move into a hotel.'

'If we did, we'd never find out who is behind this scam or who killed your husband.'

Startled by his comments, Grace's mug clattered down on the counter.

'Daniel's death was an accident!'

'Says who?'

'The police and the coroner. He was driving too fast and lost control of his car.'

'Accidents are easy to fake, Grace. Shoot out a tyre, just before a bend and the driver will lose control. Or tamper with the steering, cut a brake cable — the result will be the same — you're dead.'

Grace wrapped her arms around herself in defence. She fought the impulse to run out of the door and keep on running.

'You're… you're making some rash assumptions.'

'You're a smart woman, Grace. Way too smart to say that. Do you really think Daniel's death was an accident after everything that's happened to you in the last few days?'

'I—' She chewed on her lower lip, her gaze fixed on him. 'I don't know.'

'Sure you do. And you know something else. The bad guys aren't going to stop until they get their money back. If that means killing you too, they won't hesitate, which is why I'm calling Mike and asking for back-up.'

Grace looked away. The harder she tried to ignore the truth the more it persisted. She'd asked for Jack's help. The fact that he was destroying her world tiny piece by tiny piece wasn't his fault. There was no anger in her voice, just acceptance.

'What do you need me to do?'

'I need you to put on an act.'

'What sort of act?'

'We take control. You're the one who has the money. So when they make contact, you tell them you're not going to hand it over without some guarantees for your safety.'

'And if I don't get them?'

'Then there's no deal. Instead, you pass on whatever information we've uncovered along with the cash to the Government, and we bury you in the witness protection scheme.'

'But won't they know I've talked to the FBI?'

'We've been careful. I see no reason why they should.'

Grace tried to measure the risk rationally. If she walked away chances are she'd end up like Daniel, her body broken and crushed beyond recognition. If she stayed her life would still be in danger, but with Jack to protect her, the odds were marginally in her favour.

'It's your call, Grace. I can have you on a plane and out of the state within the hour. Or you can stay, and we bring Daniel's killers to justice. The choice is yours.'

She offered him a bleak, tight light-lipped smile.

'I'll stay.'

'Good. Mike will have two other agents here by morning. In the meantime, you and I get to share a room.'

She grasped the collar of the bathrobe and held it tightly against her throat.

'Now just '

Jack's smile was almost apologetic.

'I said share a room, Grace, not a bed. The guest room has two. We'll sleep in there. That way I can keep you safe.'

He watched her face as she glanced at the bolts securing the kitchen door. It took her less than a minute to come to the same conclusion he had, that they wouldn't deter anyone hell bent on breaking in.

'So we stay here, then what?'

'I found a safe in the study. I want to take a closer look at it. Find out what, if anything, is inside. Any idea what the combination might be?'

'It could be anything. Daniel loved numbers and liked to design puzzles.'

'Okay, I'll try using birthdays — yours, Catherine's, and Daniel's. If that doesn't work I'll ask Mike to send out a Bureau safe cracker. In the meantime, I suggest we get some sleep. We'll go and talk to Pete Jacobs, the guy who runs the seaplane charter, in the morning, find out exactly where he took Daniel. And how often.'

CHAPTER TEN

Mike Zupanik's expression was grim. He'd spent the last three hours bent over his desk going through old files and crime reports searching for any reference to Daniel Elliott, Lionel Lattide and Zachary Parous. So far all he had was a stiff neck and a killer headache.

According to the passport, Lionel Lattide had passed through immigration five times in the last six months. Apart from the first occasion when he'd stayed for two weeks, his other visits had been relatively short — five days, roughly once every four to six weeks. And the pattern was always the same. He flew direct from London to Miami, spent a day, two at most, in the city then left town, presumably to stay at the house on Gasparilla Island. He met with Parous, his attorney, played a round of golf, ate in the same restaurant each evening and appeared to be a model visitor.

Yet something about Lattide bothered him.

Mike extracted a yellow legal pad from his desk and started doodling, a habit he'd developed very early on in his career. The random squiggles helped him relax, clear his mind of all but essential thoughts.

Something linked Parous and Elliott/Lattide. Parous handled the purchase of Sand Dollars, but was that sufficient reason for the two men to continue to meet? There had to be some other reason. A mutual client perhaps? He could subpoena the attorney's files and records and compare them with the list of Elliott's clients. But with so little to go on, a judge would laugh him out of the courtroom.

He needed one tangible clue, one tiny piece of information that would tie the two men together. He continued to doodle. When drawing stick figures brought no fresh ideas he turned to a fresh page on the pad.

Daniel Elliott/Lionel Lattide

Mike stared at the two names. He played with the letters, arranging them and re-arranging them. Could it be a simple code, the kind his grandchildren played with? Then it struck him. Both names contained the same letters, just arranged differently. Lionel Lattide was an anagram of Daniel Elliott. But which was the alias and which the real name?

What's more, Grace Elliott had told Jack that her husband was an accountant and that he liked puzzles. Daniel Elliott's passport showed his date of birth as January tenth 1970, but what if he was actually born on October first?

'Diego, get yourself in here.'

A short, dark man in his mid-thirties stuck his head round the corner of the SAC's office.

'You wanted me, boss?'

Clean shaven, and sporting the requisite short, slicked down hair, Alejandro Diego was highly intelligent, quick-witted and diligent, and one of the Bureau's rising stars. Born in Dulzura on the Mexican border to mixed race parents, he'd joined the US Navy on his eighteenth birthday and spent the next five years in various hot spots around the world. A short stint with the DEA followed, before he signed up with the Bureau. An expert on the

Cuban drug trade, he'd settled quickly into the Miami office.

'Take a seat. This Elliott/Lattide,' Mike tapped the passport in front of him. 'I've got a feeling he had more than two passports or was on his way to getting others.'

'You mean the 'five flag' scenario? At least two passports, a safe location for any assets, an offshore tax haven, and still be a bone-fide resident of a country even though he may not spend much time there.'

'Yeah, that about covers it,' Mike said. 'He's supposedly a British citizen, yet he had an American passport and owned property here. Check with the IRS to see if he's got a Social Security Number. Then I want you to start checking with our associates in all known tax havens — South America, Aruba, Cayman Islands, Switzerland — the usual places. See if any of them issued him with a passport recently and whether he opened any bank accounts.'

'It won't be easy. Some of those countries have strict banking laws.'

Mike shot him a dark glance. 'If the banks won't give you the information, put the skills you learned at Quantico to good use and hack into their systems. He had to get that money from somewhere. Jack seems to think Elliott/Lattide was involved in money laundering, but I wonder if it was a Ponzi scheme, one that pays high returns to investors from money put in by subsequent investors.'

'In that case, why would anyone threaten the widow?'

'Those schemes inevitably collapse; it's only a matter of time. One or more of the investors could have hired some heavy to threaten Grace, only to find out she doesn't know anything about her husband's business dealings.'

Diego shook his head. 'Sorry, boss, I'm with Jack on this. I think Daniel Elliott was the banker for a money laundering scam. As an accountant, he knew his way around the system, which countries operated tax havens, and so on. He used some of that money to buy this house on Gasparilla Island. His boss found out and had him killed.'

'Let's be completely sure his death wasn't anything other than an accident. Get a hold of the accident and autopsy reports from the British Police. I also want a full background check on Zachary Parous — where he grew up, which law school he went to, what sort of clients he represents, where he buys his suits. I want to know everything about him and I want the information on my desk in the next twenty-four hours.'

Diego rose to leave.

'Oh, and have Mancuso get hold of the phone records for Sand Dollars, and check them against those for Parous and Associates. Let's see if any numbers show up on both sets of records. And one more thing — check the flight manifests. I want to know who sat next to Elliott each time he travelled to Miami.'

'You've got it, Boss,' Diego said, and charged out of the room to start his assignment.

Mike pushed back from his desk and went to the coffee machine. He'd already drunk too much of the thick black brew and wondered if his ulcer could handle anymore. As it happened, the pot was empty. He grunted, and selected a bottle of water instead. Jack should have called by now. He opened the bottle and took a lukewarm mouthful.

After twenty odd years with the Bureau, he was too old to be pulling back-to-back shifts. Good thing Chrissie is so understanding, otherwise our marriage would have crashed and burned a long time ago.

He yawned, took another long swallow of water, then capped the bottle, looked once at the recycling bin, and smirked. Then he tossed the bottle in the trashcan. The pile of reports on his desk wasn't going to get any smaller if he just sat looking at them. With a sigh, he adjusted his reading glasses, and slid the first folder across his desk.

An hour later, his research confirmed what he already knew. Lionel Lattide wasn't associated with any known criminals, which left two possibilities. Either there was a new mob in town or Lattide was acting on behalf of an international group.

The mastermind behind any successful scam was a devious one, and if there were a loophole to be exploited, that person would find it. Banks had a strict code of practice, and employees weren't immune from prosecution if they failed to report suspicious activity. Mike stared at the bank statements Grace had left with him until his eyes glazed over. He wasn't an accountant, but even he could see a pattern in the deposits and transfers. So why hadn't the employee overseeing the account at First Apopka Bank alerted the bank's compliance department?

There was only one answer. Someone had paid the bank employee to ignore the rules.

Over the years he'd built up contacts in every law enforcement agency in both hemispheres. He started emailing his contacts in the hope that one of them might know if someone was working a new money laundering scam crossing international borders.

Mike ran his hand over his baldhead and massaged his throbbing temples. He couldn't do any more until Diego and Mancuso finished their research and someone replied to his email. He stood, picked his jacket off the coat rack in the corner of his office, and turned out the lights.

He got as far as inserting the key in the lock, when a ringing telephone punctuated the silence. Training overrode the desire to ignore it. He kicked open the door and snatched up the receiver.

'Zupanik.'

'Hi, Mike, sorry it's so late,' Jack said. 'I was waiting for Grace to go to bed before calling you.'

'I was about to go home and find out if Chrissie had kept my dinner warm or fed it to the dog.'

'Tell her it's my fault you're late. We had some unexpected guests.'

Mike hitched a hip on the edge of his desk. 'You and Grace okay?'

'Grace was spooked for a while, but otherwise we're fine.'

'I figured we'd have three or four days before word got out that the widow was in town,' Mike said.

'Me too. They blasted a pretty powerful search light on the house. I couldn't make out a name on the boat it was too dark. But the perps were definitely speaking Cuban Spanish.'

'Found anything else interesting?'

'I haven't had chance to look around, too busy preventing Grace from trying to drown herself.'

'You are shitting me,' Mike's eyes narrowed, at times like this he wished he still smoked.

'Absolutely not.'

'The woman sounds like a nut. Where is she now?'

'In the bathroom, getting ready for bed. She's pretty sane considering everything she's been through. But finding out her husband was unfaithful, didn't help. She's okay now. We bumped into a guy called Pete Jacobs while we were out eating dinner. He recognized Grace, called her 'Mrs Lattide.' He runs a seaplane charter company. Can you have him checked out?'

'Sure,' Mike said, and scribbled the name on his legal pad. 'This woman impersonating Grace — do you have any idea who she might be?'

'No. Hair and eye colour are easy to change. Coloured contacts, a cheap bottle of hair dye, or inexpensive wig and she could transform her appearance in minutes. But height and build, that's a different matter. Whoever this is, she either had major plastic surgery or came straight out of the box looking like Grace.'

'I've got Mancuso checking the flight manifests. If Lattide was travelling with a companion, we'll know soon enough. Anything else, or can I call it a night?'

'This place is too big for me to cover alone. I need some back-up. Whoever you send will have to camp on the beach, so you'll need to speak to the parks department, there are strict no-camping rules on the island. Any chance you could persuade the coastguard to patrol the area behind the house? I don't want someone sneaking ashore in the dark.'

'Anderson and Kennedy will be with you by morning. Can you handle things until then?'

'Yeah, I'll manage.'

'Okay, Jack. I'll get the sheriff to do a drive-by now and again. As soon as anything breaks I'll let you know. In the meantime, be safe.'

Mike broke the connection. Other than himself and Jack, and now this Jacobs character, only Zachary Parous and Cody, the banker, knew Grace was going to Gasparilla Island. Either one of them could be responsible. Or neither.

He sighed. Jack West was one of his best agents. Occasionally headstrong, his impetuosity had got him into a few scrapes, and he had more than a few enemies within the upper echelons of the Bureau. His instincts and investigative skills were excellent, but Mike had a feeling that there was more to Jack's relationship with Grace than he was letting on. He just hoped it wasn't affecting his judgement.

CHAPTER ELEVEN

Jack knocked at the office marked 'Seaplane Charters' expecting it to be staffed by Pete Jacobs. Instead, a plump woman barely five feet tall opened the door. Her dark brown skin and chocolate coloured eyes were framed by a mass of jet-black curly hair. She looked up at Jack.

'Won't you come in? I don't normally lock the door, but I was in the back office making coffee.'

'That's okay. Is Pete around, we'd like to talk to him, if he can spare the time?'

'He's down at the marina refuelling the plane ready to fly a group of Canadian tourists over the island later this afternoon. If you take a seat, Mr—'

'West. Jack West, and this is Grace Lattide.'

'I'm Mercedes, although folks usually call me Mercy. I run the office; take bookings, keep the accounts, that sort of thing. So you want to book a special charter?'

'Yeah, that's right,' Jack lied. 'I promised Grace a trip down to the Keys.'

'That's nice. It's lovely down there at this time of year.'

'You worked here long, Mercy?'

'Mr Jacobs hired me a couple of weeks ago after his last assistant left. I guess island life wasn't her thing. That sounds like the plane now. If you'll wait here, I'll go and see if Pete's available.'

While they waited for Jacobs, Grace strolled around the room. It was small, barely sixteen feet square, three chairs stood against one wall, on which hung a series of aerial photographs. One in particular caught her attention.

'Isn't that Sand Dollars?' she said, and tapped the frame.

Jack scrutinized the foot square photograph. 'Could be. I wonder when it was taken.'

'I took that eight months ago when the previous owner decided to sell,' Jacobs said, as he entered. He wiped his hand on an oily rag and crossed the room to stand next to Grace. 'Photography is a hobby of mine. When I'm not flying charters, I work for the island's realty companies. I gave your husband a copy a couple of months back.'

'That was kind of you.'

'No bother at all. Come through to my office.'

Grace and Jack followed Jacobs down a narrow corridor to an even smaller room at the rear of the building. A huge plate glass window looked out across the bayou toward Charlotte Harbor.

'Take a seat. Can I get you some coffee?' Jacobs asked.

Grace shook her head. 'Not for me, thank you.'

'I'll pass, too,' Jack said. 'Yesterday, you mentioned that you flew Mr Lattide down to the Keys on a regular basis.'

'That's right.'

'Was there anything different about the last trip?'

Jacobs shifted in his chair. 'What's this all about?'

Grace chose her words carefully. 'I was at home when my husband died, Mr Jacobs. I'm just trying to get a clearer picture of his movements during the days preceding his death.'

'I'm sorry. I don't like giving out information about my clients.'

Grace smiled softening the lines of tension around her mouth. 'Lionel was my husband. Under the circumstances, I think you could make an exception, don't you?'

'Point well taken. I flew Lionel down to one of the small private islands off Marathon Key, as usual. It's little more than a sand bar in the middle of the Gulf. I don't even think it's on the charts, and as far as I know, it doesn't have a name.'

'If it's not on the charts, how did you find it?' Jack asked.

Jacobs scooped a handful of peanuts out of the bowl on his desk, popped them in his mouth and chewed for a minute before answering.

'Lionel gave me the GPS co-ordinates. There's only one house. It's built on stilts and surrounded by palm trees. It's hard to see from the air. On the seaward side, there's dock that leads out into deeper water, and a helipad.'

Jack kept his gaze firmly fixed on Jacobs. A nervous tick played at the corner of his face.

'What happened after you landed, did you taxi up to the dock?'

'Depends on the tides. Most times a boat came out for him.'

'Did you hang around?' Jack asked.

'Sometimes. It depended on whether Lionel was staying over. Whenever he did that, I came back here, waited for him to call, then flew down and brought him back.'

'Do you know who owns the island?'

'No, but I can fly you down there if you like.' Jacobs looked hopeful.

'That won't be necessary,' Jack said. 'But I would like the GPS coordinates.'

Jacobs walked over to the filing cabinet that stood in the corner, and took out a folder. He scribbled something down on a pad and handed it to Jack, who slipped the piece of paper into the pocket of his jeans.

'Thanks. Did you see or meet anyone while you were there?'

'Like I said, I dropped Lionel off, and either hung around until the launch brought him back or returned to Boca Grande. Look, are you sure you're not a cop?'

'Jack is a friend, Mr Jacobs, a close friend. He's acting on my behalf. If you have a problem answering his questions I can always put this on a more formal footing and involve the police,' Grace bluffed.

'I'm sorry, Mrs Lattide. I keep forgetting how difficult this must be for you,' Jacobs said. He turned to Jack. 'I only saw the guy handling the boat, but I didn't get a good look at him.'

'Will you be around for the next day or so in case we need to ask you anything else?'

'I'm flying a party over to Sanibel, and then taking a honeymoon couple down to Key West, but other than that, yeah, I'll be around.'

'Thank you for your time, Mr Jacobs,' Grace said.

'Lionel was a nice guy and a good customer. Always paid cash and turned up on time. You don't usually get that kind of business in my line of work. I'm gonna miss him.'

Jack caught hold of Grace's elbow and led her towards the door. 'Just one more question — did anyone accompany Lattide on these trips to the island — a woman perhaps?'

Jacobs looked away. 'Lionel always travelled by himself. Why do you ask?'

'No reason. Thanks for your help,' Jack said. He ushered Grace out the door. They crossed the street and got into the Explorer.

'Did you believe him, Jack?' Grace asked, snapping the seat belt into place.

Jack hesitated, wondering whether she was up to hearing the truth.

'He knows the name of the island and who owns it.'

'Then why didn't he tell you?'

'Because he's protecting someone or he's been paid not to talk.'

Grace swivelled in her seat to face him. 'What happens now?'

'I'm going to keep pushing until I get some answers. In the meantime, we grab something to eat, and then go back to the house. I want to examine the desk and see if I can open the safe.'

The island deli and bakery occupied a corner lot just off Main Street, and was full of sun worshipers shopping for goodies for their picnic baskets. Jack and Grace stepped inside to the aroma of freshly baked bread and coffee. An elderly couple wearing matching T-shirts and shorts stood at the cheese counter debating whether to purchase some Brie or Gorgonzola. Grace smiled at a small redheaded boy who tugged at his mother's hand, pleading for an ice cream, and took her place in the queue at the deli counter.

While she waited for their order to be filled, Jack wandered around the store. A middle-aged man, wearing beige chinos, a pale blue shirt, and a Stetson, entered the shop. For someone with a limp, he moved confidently, and seemed intent on watching Grace.

Intrigued, Jack edged closer without ever looking directly at him. When he saw the man replace the tin of tuna he'd been holding on the shelf and head for the sandwich counter, his interest sharpened. As Jack drew level with him, the man muscled his way into the line behind Grace. He leaned into her at the same time his right hand pulled something out of his pocket.

Jack cut into the line, elbowed the man out of the way, and stepped on his foot at the same time, ignoring the shouted curse that came from his lips.

'I'll carry that,' he said, and snatched the brown paper sack from Grace's hand. He hauled her through the checkout and out the door. He kept looking over his shoulder as they hurried toward his SUV.

'What's the matter, Jack? Are we being followed again?' Grace asked.

'No.'

'Then why did you drag me out of the bakery?'

'Because I didn't like the way the dude with the Stetson and the limp cut into the line and crowded you.'

Grace looked back at the entrance to the bakery over the rim of her sunglasses. 'Limp? The guy in the graveyard had a limp.'

'I know which is why I don't want you out in the open one minute longer.'

Grace put a hand to her throat. She had to fight to catch her breath. Her heart was beating too fast, making her skin damp and her head spin.

'You don't think—'

'I'm not thinking, but there are way too many coincidences for my liking. Now hurry up.'

She swallowed hard and almost ran to keep pace with Jack's long strides. She'd no sooner climbed into the passenger seat than Jack started the engine.

'Aren't you going to wait until he comes out of the store so that I can get a look at his face?'

Jack slammed the Explorer into gear, and roared down Fourth Street with a squeal of rubber.

'I guess that answers my question,' Grace panted. 'You know, it might not have been the same man.'

He looked sideways at her. 'Do you want to go back and take that chance?'

She drew in a deep breath, but remained silent. Her fingers clutched the door handle, tightening until they were white and bloodless.

'I didn't think so,' Jack said. 'I slipped up. I shouldn't have let you out of my sight for a moment. I could have got you killed.'

'That's being over dramatic.'

Jack lifted his foot, and dropped his speed to comply with the island's limit. 'First thing they teach us at Quantico is that you stay alive by being overly cautious.'

Stunned by Jack's bluntness, she snapped her mouth shut and stared out of the window.

A road-weary motor coach, its roof bristling with antennae and satellite dishes, huddled underneath a large Banyan tree fifty feet from the entrance to Sand Dollars. The headlights flashed twice as they approached.

'Someone you know?' Grace asked.

'Yeah, Anderson and Kennedy, the two agents Mike assigned for back-up. I'll introduce you later so you don't get scared if you bump into them. They'll be taking the night shift — watching the house while we get some sleep.'

'When Catherine and I were young, our parents owned what we Brits call a caravan. It was very basic, just a tin can on wheels. Catherine hated it, especially when it rained. Everything would be damp, bedding, clothes, shoes, everything. And when it was hot, it was even more unbearable, so I don't envy your colleagues in this heat.'

Jack smiled. 'Tin can—I'll remember that next time I have to use it. It's newer than it looks, and is equipped with an array of high-tech gadgets and a decent A-C.'

'A-C?'

'Air conditioning. Never fails to amaze me how we say we speak the same language… but we don't speak the same language. Do we?'

His eyes met Grace's and a thrill of something more than fear twisted her heart. She wondered if Jack felt it too. He glanced at her again. His look said nothing. She stared straight ahead at the motor coach.

Jack slowed the SUV to a crawl and wound down the driver's window as he drew level with the vehicle. To anyone who might be interested it appeared as though he was telling the guy behind the wheel to move away from his property.

'You're clean, Jack. No one, not even the mail man, has gone near the house since we got here.'

'Thanks, Kennedy. We'll be in for the rest of the day. Get some shut-eye.'

The Explorer picked up speed and turned into the driveway. Jack pulled on the brake and swivelled in his seat to face Grace.

'You need protection and I'll do my best to make sure you get it. But I'm a realist, Grace. So, I want you to promise me that if anything untoward happens, you'll head straight for that motor coach. Anderson and Kennedy will take care of you.'

'I—' Grace tried to frame another question, but Jack's sombre expression prevented her.

Jack leaned closer and tilted her face to his. 'Promise me, Grace.'

She nodded her head. 'I promise.'

He gave her hand a reassuring squeeze. 'Now let's go eat and then we can see what secrets your husband was hiding in that safe.'

Thirty minutes later, Grace carried the tray containing their lunch into the office and placed it on the desk. She picked up her plate and a can of soda, and sat down in the chair opposite Jack.

'Found anything?'

'Apart for a few receipts from the local gas station and one to a cleaning service, the desk is pretty much empty.'

'That doesn't surprise me. Daniel never threw a receipt away, no matter how mundane the purchase. But when it came to cleaning he was barely house-trained. He didn't know how to vacuum or dust. What about the safe?'

'I was waiting for you before I tried it.' He picked up his sandwich and took a bite.

'Before you do, can I use the phone? I'd like to call Catherine, see if she's at home.'

Jack popped the tab on his can of soda and took a long swallow.

'I don't see why not. Mike's got a tap on the line. It will register the number, but won't interfere with your call.'

Grace lifted the receiver and dialled her sister's apartment, but all she got was Catherine's answering service. Next she tried Catherine's cell phone, but that too, ran into her voicemail.

'No answer?' Jack asked.

She shook her head. 'I'm worried, Jack. You'd think she would have been in touch by now.'

'Sounds like something serious is going on. Did you contact her through her employer?'

'I didn't think hearing about Daniel's death from some work colleague was a good idea. I've left countless messages for her to call me, but she's either ignored them, or just hasn't picked up her messages in the last couple of weeks.'

He shrugged. 'Maybe she's taken a vacation.'

'I suppose it's possible. Catherine can be fiercely independent when the mood takes her. Even so, I don't think she'd go off without telling me.'

'Are you two close?'

Grace's smiled faded.

'Not particularly. Catherine is your 'wild child,' whereas I'm—'

'Dependable?'

Grace smiled. 'I was going to say more staid. Catherine was always getting into mischief, and that hasn't changed. She lives life at full tilt, when she's not working she's dancing the night away in some club or other.'

Jack said nothing. Grace confirmed what he'd already surmised. Catherine was self-centred and cared for no one but herself.

'Do you have a picture of her?'

'Not with me. Why?'

'I just wondered what she looked like.'

'Catherine is the pretty one of the family. Long, wavy, blonde hair, and brown eyes. She's taller than me and thinner too. She's never been short of admirers, but so far she's remained single.'

Jack grunted, and wondered why Grace had such a low opinion of herself. He drained his soda and was about to throw the can into the trash, when he noticed someone had dumped the contents of an ashtray into it.

'Did Daniel smoke?'

'Only a pipe. I smelt his tobacco as soon as we entered the house.'

He picked a half smoked stub out of the trashcan.

'Whoever else was here, smoked Cuban cigarettes. I recognize the brand.' The same brand that Rosa smoked before she had Emilia. He dropped the cigarette in the ashtray on the corner of the desk.

'For all you know it might be the cleaner and he or she just forgot to take out the trash.'

'Could be.' Jack put the trashcan to one side. He'd bag up the rest of the stubs and give them to Mike. They might get lucky and find some DNA to link the smoker to a member of one of the known gangs. But he doubted it.

He crossed the room to where a large seascape hung on the wall, and ran his fingertips around the frame. Satisfied, it wasn't wired into an alarm he lifted it down and rested it against a bookcase. Then took a pair of exam gloves from his pocket and put them on.

'What are you thinking?' Grace asked.

'I was wondering why Daniel had a safe installed, yet didn't bother to set the burglar alarm when he left.'

'Perhaps he forgot or was in a hurry.'

'Or maybe he wasn't the last person to leave.' Jack looked at the old fashioned tumbler.

Grace opened her mouth and closed it. Jack had a way of getting right to the point.

'I don't know how many tries we'll get at this,' he said. 'But give me some birth dates.'

'Try ten, one, nineteen, seven, zero.'

Jack spun the tumbler and tugged at the handle. 'Locked. Give me another.'

'Three, seven, nineteen, seven, five.' Grace held her breath as he turned the dial.

'Nope. Anymore?'

'Twenty-eight, ten, nineteen, eight, zero.'

As he entered the last digit, Jack heard a telltale click as it was accepted. He turned the handle and the safe opened.

'Was that yours?'

'Catherine's. Did I mention that Daniel left her some money in his will?'

Jack kept his features composed. 'How much?'

'Not a vast amount, five thousand pounds. That's about seven thousand dollars.'

'Any idea why?'

'They thought the world of each other. I presume it was because Daniel was like a big brother to Catherine and helped pay for her education.'

Jack blinked. He had other ideas as to why Grace's husband might leave his sister-in-law money, but he wasn't ready to voice them, at least not yet.

He pulled a narrow spiral-bound notebook out of the safe, together with a small plastic box, a wad of cash, and a bundle of papers, and carried them over to the desk.

He showed Grace the notebook. 'Is this Daniel's handwriting?'

'Yes. I can tell by the way he writes a seven, with that little wavy line across the down stroke. And Daniel was left-handed. Whenever he wrote the letter 'g,' it looked as if he'd written it backwards.'

'I'll need to study the notebook to see if I can make any sense of it.'

'I doubt that you will. Daniel had his own version of shorthand. He tried explaining it to me once, but I never could understand. He uses a mixture of letters and numbers — it's a sort of code.'

Jack opened the box. It was empty. 'I wonder if this contained the disks your mysterious man was looking for.' The cell phone on his belt vibrated. He freed it and looked at the ID window — his SAC, Mike Zupanik.

'Hey, Mike.'

'Bad news, Jack. The police pulled Zachary Parous out of the Miami River an hour ago.'

'Shit.'

'His hands and feet were bound and he'd been systematically beaten. The medical examiner says it looks as if someone tossed him in then left him to drown. We'll know for sure after he's done the autopsy.'

'Grace and I saw Pete Jacobs again today. He regularly flew Elliott down to an island near Marathon Key. He said he didn't know who owned it, but I got the impression he knew more than he was saying. I've got the GPS co-ordinates. It's not enough for a search warrant, but I wondered about satellite surveillance.'

'I don't know, Jack. That's a big ask when we've got so little to go on. Let me think about it, talk to a few people.'

Jack signed heavily. 'Okay. What else do you know?'

'I only know one thing for sure,' Mike said. 'You'd better keep an even closer watch on his client's widow.'

CHAPTER TWELVE

Spanish was the only language spoken in the La Bodequita del Medio bar in Little Havana, Miami. The potent aroma of high-octane coffee fought with the smoky air and lost, while the heady rhythm of salsa music blared out from the radio above the bartender's head. Any tourists who entered expecting to find somewhere quiet for a meal and a drink, quickly left.

For Sergio Vasquez, it was his home and his office — the place where he ate and did business. Despite his slight, wiry build, his reputation as a hard man was known throughout the city. No job was too big or too difficult. What mattered was the money he earned, the kind of cash that was impossible to earn back in Cuba. In recent years many Nicaraguans and Hondurans had moved into the area. Those who frequented the bar knew to keep out of his way.

He ordered a plate of *ropa vieja* and a beer, and sat down at his usual table in the corner, the surface scuffed and scratched from years of use. While the other inhabitants of the bar wore the traditional, locally produced, linen *guayaberas*, the four-pocket men's shirt,

Vasquez preferred Armani or Gucci and hand-made thousand dollar loafers when he wasn't working.

Last night's hit had been easy. He'd followed the Yuma, his American mark, from his office to the underground parking lot. As soon as he heard the trunk of the Mercedes open, Vasquez had stepped out of the shadow, struck the guy over the head and tumbled him inside, along with his briefcase.

The Mercedes was a fine car. He'd driven one like it before. He'd thumbed away a smudge from its otherwise spotless white paint, hopped inside and nestled himself into the black kid leather driver's seat, and drove across town to the deserted warehouse that served as his private torture chamber.

It had taken a while, but he got the information he wanted. Disposing of the body was simple; he'd driven to one of the slipways and dumped it into the Miami River, leaving the tide and the fishes to do the rest.

Although it had pained him to abandon the lovely Mercedes, he'd done as instructed, but that hadn't stopped him from taking a memento of his night's work. He smiled, and straightened the sleeves of his shirt, pausing to admire the heavy gold cuff links and Raymond Weil watch on his wrist previously worn by his victim.

The bar girl brought his meal, along with another bottle of beer. Barely out of her teens, her hair was a sheath of black silk, her body ripe and firm, in a few years time she'd be stunningly beautiful. He gave her ass a squeeze, and was rewarded with a smile and an extra swing of her hips as she sauntered back to the kitchen.

He scooped up a forkful of shredded beef in piquant tomato sauce, and chewed. The word on the street was that some minion had skimmed money from the Banker's account. No one messed with the Banker, not if they wanted to live, and especially not attorneys who thought they were beyond the Banker's reach.

No one knew the Banker's identity for sure. Some said he was Juan-Carlos Fuentes, head of the Fuentes family, who were into drug trafficking and money laundering rackets, others said he was the head of a rival gang based in New York. Vasquez had tried to find out. But he was smart. He knew that if he asked too many questions he'd end up as alligator food.

Vasquez pushed his empty plate away. The bartender appeared at his elbow and placed a cup of *café Cubano* in front of him, then discretely withdrew. He leaned back in his chair, lit a hand rolled cigar, sucked hard, and blew out a plume of smoke.

His eyes shifted to three elderly men, their heads bent over the table as they concentrated on their game of dominoes, a dish of Chicharrones and half empty glasses within easy reach of their gnarled and arthritic fingers.

Life was good. He had money to spend on hookers and a decent set of wheels. He even had a condo overlooking the ocean. Not bad for a boy whose parents had arrived in America some forty years earlier with little more than the clothes on their backs.

The door opened, a man entered. He paused briefly to size up the bar, then impervious to the curious glances from the other occupants, hobbled over to Vasquez's table, dragged out a chair and sat down.

Short and stocky, he walked with a slight limp, as if he'd been born with one leg slightly shorter than the other. He wore a silk shirt tucked into Italian slacks, and carried a jacket over his arm. His pale, square-jawed face marked him as an outsider. Beneath the dark aviator sunglasses, his eyes were indiscernible.

The bartender appeared at the newcomer's shoulder and placed a bottle of beer on the table in front of him, then retreated to the bar and resumed polishing glasses.

The stranger crossed one ankle over the other, and withdrew a packet of *Cohiba* and a gold Colibri lighter from the pocket of his jacket. He stuck a cigarette in the corner of his mouth, lit it, and sucked in a hit of nicotine.

Vasquez watched the smoke trickle out from between the man's lips.

'How did you know I'd be here?'

'You're predictable, Vasquez. If you want to survive in this game, you should change your habits.'

Vasquez tried to place the accent, Italian or Portuguese, maybe Spanish, he couldn't be sure which. But no matter, this wasn't a man to be crossed. A cheer came from the table in the corner where the three old men played dominoes. Heads turned, but Vasquez kept his gaze on the man sat opposite him.

'I like it here. The food is good and no one bothers me.'

The man shrugged. 'It's your life.' He puffed on the cigarette and scrutinized the Cuban through the smoke. Vasquez wasn't smart, but he was ruthless and did as he was told.

Vasquez's brown eyes narrowed and his back became ramrod straight. 'What are you complaining about? I got the job done.'

'If I can find you, so can the cops.' The thick fingers of the man's left hand, the nails chewed down to the quick, kept time with the beat of the salsa playing on the radio.

'Everyone in Little Havana knows that if they snitch on me, I kill them, and that it will be a slow, painful death.'

'Tell me what the attorney said.'

Vasquez licked his lips and smiled. 'He thought he was a big man, but a few punches and he was screaming for his mama.'

'I didn't ask for the details. I just want to know what he said.'

Despite the impatience in the other man's voice, Vasquez forced himself to stay calm. 'The woman you asked about — the widow — she's gone to the island. She, and the man who accompanied her, paid a visit to the First Apopka bank before they left.'

'Did the attorney know why?'

'He said something about her transferring money.' Vasquez tapped the ash from the end of his cigar and studied the man. His face was pockmarked, and his hair cropped close, so close to his skull that Vasquez wondered if he wasn't bald, and it was actually a tattoo. He looked in his fifties, yet his body remained muscular, and he carried himself with sheer macho confidence that made lesser men slink away into the shadows.

'The man with her, did the attorney know who he was?'

'West, Jack West. He said she introduced him as a family friend, but he thought he looked like a cop.'

The stranger took the half-smoked cigarette from his lips, and ground the stub out on the table.

'A cop? Are you sure?'

'That's what he said. I can ask around if you want, see if anyone on the street has heard of him.'

'That won't be necessary. And the attorney's car?'

'A burnt out wreck.'

He nodded his head. 'You've done well. I have another job for you.' An envelope appeared on the table.

'The same fee as usual?'

'There's an extra five thousand for expenses. You'll be out of town for a couple of days.'

Vasquez's face twisted into what passed for a smile. He thought about his retirement plans - the house in the Cayman Islands was becoming a real possibility.

'You want me to take out West and the woman? I got my own gun.'

'Not yet. The details are inside.' The man tapped the envelope. 'This has to look like an accident, you understand?'

'Hey, I'm not stupid. I finished school.'

The envelope slid across the table. 'The balance will be transferred to your account when I read about this tragedy in the Miami Herald.' The man's chair scraped back. He settled his glasses more firmly on his nose, gathered up his jacket and left the bar.

Vasquez pocketed the envelope. He downed the last of his beer, then picked up the other glass, and swallowed the contents in one gulp.

CHAPTER THIRTEEN

Jack wasn't a mathematician, but the trick to breaking any code, he knew, was finding the key. He pulled the notebook across the desk and stared at the combination of letters and numbers. Instinct told him they were somehow connected to the amounts deposited in Elliott's Miami bank account, but it could be a shopping list for all he knew. What's more, there seemed to be no discernable pattern.

He compared the numbers on the slip of paper Grace had found with the passport to those in the notebook. None of them matched. He stretched and sighed, then settled deeper into his chair. He could ask the tech guys to run the entries through code breaking software or email it to one of Bureau's experts. And he still would if he couldn't decipher it.

Among the board games on the bookshelf was a box of Scrabble. He picked it up, and carried it back to the desk and emptied out the contents. He tried forming words by shifting the tiles around, but they made even less sense than the entries in the notebook.

Grace placed a mug of rich, dark coffee under his nose.
'If you study that much longer, your eyes will cross.'

'What do you mean will?' Jack said. He lifted his head and looked down at the tip of his nose.

'Ha, ha, very funny.'

He grinned. 'Just trying to lighten the mood.'

'Well, you've succeeded.' She indicated the Scrabble tiles with a nod of her head. 'Think you can put them aside for half an hour?'

'What did you have in mind?'

Grace smiled. 'After the events of last night, I don't think a walk on the beach is a good idea. But I can't stay cooped up in this house all day. I'll go mad. How about we take advantage of the pool?'

Jack took a sip from his mug and weighed up the risk. It would be dark soon and with Anderson and Kennedy taking turns watching the perimeter, and the coastguard cutter patrolling just offshore, the threat to Grace would be minimal.

He pushed his chair back from the desk and stood. 'Okay. I don't see why not.'

'I'll go change and see you by the pool.' She turned and left the room as silently as she'd entered.

Jack looked at his watch. He figured seven hours sleep was enough for any agent. He picked up his cell phone and keyed in Anderson's number. 'Get your ass out of bed. I need you and Kennedy to make a sweep of the garden and beach.'

'Why? What are you gonna do?'

'Cool off in the pool.' He cut the connection with Anderson's muffled curse ringing in his ears, and went to change.

By the time Grace emerged from the house, he'd checked in with Kennedy to ensure no one was loitering in the vicinity of Sand Dollars, and left his gun under a towel, within easy reach of the pool.

When she slipped out of her robe, he sucked in a breath. The one-piece jade suit she wore clung to her like a second skin, accentuating her full breasts and narrow waist. Unlike the local women, her skin was pale, almost alabaster white. His pulse quickened, as his gaze roamed over her face to her shoulders, then settled on her long and shapely legs.

Miami beaches were full of women who wore less, yet none, not even Rosa, stirred his blood the way Grace did. He watched her balance on her toes, dive in, and swim a length underwater. She surfaced, slicked back her hair, and offered him a broad smile.

'Are you going to stand there all afternoon, or are you going to join me? The water's warm.'

A rivulet of water ran down her neck to the triangle of skin revealed by her suit. Jack wondered what her reaction would be if he were to haul her out of the water and lick the droplets off one by one. Six months of hearing her voice in his dreams, imagining what it would be like to feel her naked body beneath his had been bad enough, but sleeping in the same room and being this close to her, was exquisite torture.

With a silent curse he looked away. Giving into temptation was a real bad idea and the only thing he could do was wrap the investigation up as soon as possible, then get her back on a plane to England and out of his life. He dove into the turquoise water, covered the length of the pool, not once, but three times, finally surfacing next to her.

Grace wasn't accustomed to seeing half naked men and couldn't help staring at Jack in nothing more than a pair of hip-hugging black Speedos. Powerful, tanned, well muscled, with a sprinkling of dark hair on his chest, he moved with ease. He was so compelling, his magnetism so potent, that her pulses suddenly leapt with excitement. A rush of pink stained her cheeks and she hoped he didn't notice.

She couldn't tear her gaze from his face. The sudden intensity in his eyes made her feel alive and sent heat chasing through her body. Goosebumps crawled over her skin; they had nothing to do with the temperature of the water.

Powerless to stop, she rested one hand on his shoulder, felt her thigh brush his, the gentle massage sending currents of desire through her.

Without thinking, she brushed her lips over his. The tension that had been building between them tumbled over into raw sexual desire. Jack's arm wrapped around her waist and pulled her hard against him, moulding her soft curves to the contours of his lean body. She felt her knees weaken as his lips met hers. Their kiss went from tentative to something primitive and demanding in the space of a heartbeat.

Her breath hitched. With a soft moan, she buried her hands in his hair, and kissed him with a passion she didn't know she possessed. She wanted him. She wanted to feel him sink into her softness until she forgot where she was and why she was here. Long forgotten sensations rippled through her until she was trembling, and whispering his name with every broken breath.

Jack dragged his mouth from hers.

'Grace, stop it,' he said breathlessly. He lowered his forehead to hers. 'Go and get dressed before I throw my good intentions out of the pool and do something both of us will regret.'

The roughness in his voice almost broke her heart. Her face burning, she blew out a breath, too stunned to say anything. Dear God, what have I done?

Humiliated, she turned and swam away, lest he see the tears in her eyes. By the time she reached the other end of the pool he'd climbed out, and disappeared inside the house.

She floated on her back and stared at the cloudless, blue sky. Her relationship with Daniel had been easy; he'd been more like a friend than a lover. Her relationship with Jack, if she could call it that, was anything but. She felt confused, one minute he was giving her sultry looks, the next he was pushing her away. Yet that one kiss stirred more emotion, more passion, than ten years of marriage to Daniel ever had.

The look in Jack's eyes had reminded her of the night she'd told him she was married. Disappointment, or was it hatred? At the time, she hadn't been able to decide which emotion she'd seen. But what she'd witnessed just now was something far more disturbing. He'd physically responded, but it was clear he didn't share her passion. From now on, she promised herself, she'd guard her heart until they uncovered the truth. Then she would turn away from him, close the wound, and think of him no more.

At least she would try.

Unsettled by the pulse beating in the pit of her stomach, she tried to relax. When her body refused, she set off in a fast crawl, determined to keep swimming until she forgot the ache and sexual hunger flooding her veins.

****

Upstairs, Jack stripped off his trunks and stepped into the shower. He reached for the faucet, turning it to its coldest setting. The desire he'd fought so hard to contain all those months ago simmered and bubbled inside until the physical need had outweighed reason. He leant against the tile and allowed the water to stream over his neck and back.

Grace's kiss had taken him by surprise. He hadn't thought of her as being impetuous, the one to take the lead in the sexual two-step. She'd always resisted him, kept her distance, but today it seemed as though she'd finally acknowledged the bond between them. His response had been so strong that he'd wanted to strip her naked and bury himself inside her until the sexual heat and need sent them both spiralling over the edge. His feelings for her went deeper than simple lust.

He knew it.

They both knew it.

The pain in her eyes had almost been his undoing. He hadn't wanted to hurt her, but it was the only way he could think of to stop from following through on her invitation. But it didn't prevent him from feeling like a first class heel.

He reset the faucet to hot. He'd waited six months to taste her lips, hold her close; he could wait another six or however long it took him to sort things out with Rosa. One thing was certain — he couldn't leave Emilia in Rosa's care, knowing that she cared so little for the child. He'd fight for sole custody, and hope that Grace would accept that he and Emilia came as a package, and that she'd help him raise his daughter.

But raising another woman's child was a big undertaking. What if Grace wasn't willing to take on a ready-made family? What would he do? He couldn't abandon his daughter. He closed his eyes, and pushed away the pain. He was an idiot for allowing his thoughts to race ahead like this.

He needed to sit down and talk to Grace, explain about Emilia.

But not yet.

He stepped out of the shower and grabbed a towel. He wasn't a rookie. He'd worked with confidential informants before and knew the rules. Returning Grace's kiss was downright stupid. But leaving her with another agent, someone she would have to learn to trust would be insane and far more dangerous than the situation she was in right now.

Through telling himself he was a fool for letting things get out of hand, he dressed quickly in jeans and a T-shirt, the agent once more in control. His priority was to find Daniel's killer, and keep Grace safe, not get her hot and have her come apart in his arms.

He strode out onto the veranda and looked down at the pool below. It was empty. His heart slammed into his ribs. Where the hell was she?

He drew his gun and crept out of the bedroom. He was halfway down the stairs when the door to the kitchen opened and Grace walked into the hall. He took a deep breath and holstered the weapon. He'd been so wrapped up in his own emotions he'd not given a thought to her whereabouts.

With an impatient curse at his own stupidity, he waited until she reached him. He looked at her. Her face was drawn and pinched, her lips pressed tight together, as if she was fighting pain. Pain he'd caused.

'Grace, I—'

She straightened her shoulders, and gripped the edge of the towel. 'I don't want to talk about it, Jack.'

'But—'

She marched passed him into the bedroom, the door slamming shut behind her.

He flinched, then continued downstairs to the kitchen and set about making dinner. A stack of CDs stood on the counter next to a compact stereo. It seemed that Daniel preferred opera to pop, but amongst the pile was a solitary jazz album. He popped into the player and turned up the volume. The mellow sound of a tenor saxophone filled the air.

He was busy mixing a marinade for the two twelve ounce steaks he'd already tenderized, when Grace joined him twenty minutes later. She carried the notepad and Scrabble tiles from the office.

'I thought we'd eat here,' he said.

'Fine, whatever.'

He slammed his fist down on the counter. He got enough of the cold shoulder treatment from Rosa without putting up with it from Grace too. He stormed across the room, and pulled her chair round to face him.

'Look, Grace. There's no point denying what happened out there. I'll admit I handled things badly, and I'm sorry if I offended you. But don't you see, we can't allow it to get in the way of uncovering the truth.'

His blunt words made her wince. She pushed him away, her blue eyes cold as ice. 'Don't worry, Jack. I know this is only a job to you. I promise it won't happen again. As soon as this investigation is over, I'll be out of your life, for good!'

'Damn it, Grace, do you have to be so—'

'So human? And stupid?'

'That's not what I was going to say. I've already told you my life is complicated; let's not make it any more so. We have to work together. If you don't think you can do that, then I'll ask Mike to replace me with another agent. Is that what you want?'

Grace looked away. When she finally answered her voice was bleak.

'I… No.'

'In that case, see if you can make any sense of that notebook, while I cook dinner.' He opened the microwave and put two potatoes into bake, then set about preparing a salad. He cast a glance over his shoulder at her. She sat slumped over the table with her head in her hands. Pain, anger, compassion and love all fought for supremacy. Only common sense won out. If he went to her now all he could offer was a night spent in a hot tangle of sheets, rather than the lifetime of love he craved.

He closed his eyes, but it didn't make his agony less. He'd pushed her away once before and never thought to see her again. This time he knew he'd lost her for good. He lit the gas grill and slapped the steaks down on top. He was an agent. He was required to be cold and emotionally unavailable. That was part of his job. And he'd always thought the words described him perfectly.

He flipped the steaks and checked on the potatoes, then uncorked the bottle of red wine he'd found in the garage. He placed a glass in front of Grace and tried to ignore the sadness in her eyes.

'Having any luck?'

'Some. The single digit that precedes each entry,' she tapped the page. 'What if you write the letters out as a number — 'A' is one, 'B' be is two and so on. Do you think it could represent another bank account?'

Without thinking, Jack rested his hand on her shoulder while he counted the letters. Nine. 'It could be, or it may be the number the ABA, the American Banking Association, gives to financial institutions over here. If it is, then the Bureau can find out which bank it is, but we'd still need a name for the account holder or the account number. The steaks should be done by now. I'll ask Mike to check it out and see if you're right.'

'Have you noticed,' Grace said when they'd finished eating, 'how the consonants are interspersed in groups of three throughout the page.'

'Yeah, what's your take on that?'

'I think they represent countries or airports within those countries. Look here,' her finger traced a line across the page. 'LHR is the code for London Heathrow. And this one MAD,' she said, tapping the page once more, 'is Madrid. I only know because I've seen it on Catherine's suitcases when she's returned from a trip abroad. But I don't know what the others are.'

Jack stared at the page. Now that Grace had made the connection he saw the codes for four other cities, Mexico City, Frankfurt, Miami, and AUA for Aruba.

'If Daniel was moving dirty money around Europe and the Americas he could arrange inter-bank transfers, but he'd have to go there to set up the accounts to begin with. But his passport only had entry stamps for the States.'

'There are no longer frontier controls between European Union countries, so your passport isn't stamped on entry. Something else has been bothering me, too.'

'Oh, yeah?'

'Pete Jacobs called me Mrs Lattide, yet neither Mr Parous nor Mr Cody at the bank did, although Mr Cody said he'd met me before. So Jacobs only knew Daniel by his other identity.'

'Jacobs must be involved in the scam and either knows where the money came from or who's running it.'

'Then I don't understand why Daniel didn't use the name Lattide when he purchased this house.'

'Perhaps Lattide and Elliott are just aliases, and Daniel had another passport in another name. They're easy enough to obtain if you know how.'

Grace carried her plate over to the dishwasher and placed it inside, then put the coffee maker on. She swung round and faced Jack.

'If Daniel had a third passport, he kept it someplace else. After the accident, Shaun cleared out Daniel's office and brought me all his personal papers. I went through everything, and I'm telling you there was nothing else.'

'What about the contents of his car?'

'The police returned his briefcase and MacBook after the inquest. But, his cell phone was missing.'

'Daniel had a laptop?'

'Yes, what about it?'

'Did you examine the files, his calendar? Was there anything to suggest he was up to something?'

'I-I don't know. I couldn't get it to work.'

Jack shot her a penetrating look. 'Why didn't you say something sooner? It might have saved us a lot of time.'

'How was I to know? I assumed it had been damaged in the accident.'

'Where is it now?' He held up his hand as she started to speak. 'Don't tell me, let me guess — back home in England.'

'Actually, it's upstairs in my suitcase. But I'm telling you it's useless.'

Jack bit back an impatient curse. 'Go and get it. Could just be the battery's dead. If not, I can turn it over to the Bureau's tech department. They'll scour the hard drive. If there's anything worth finding, they'll find it.'

Jack finished stacking the dishwasher while he waited for Grace to return. He couldn't blame her for thinking Daniel's laptop was useless.

'Did you ever see Daniel use it? Did he use a password?' he asked as she handed him the laptop.

'I've no idea. I went into his office once when he was working—' She shivered as the image of that evening focused in her mind. Subconsciously, she rubbed her cheek. 'But he threw me out, and told me never to enter again. He wouldn't even let me take him a cup of coffee.'

Jack laid the MacBook on the table. The case was battered and scratched. He didn't hold out much hope that it would work, but he pushed the power button anyway. One of the LED lights briefly flashed then died.

'Yep. Battery's completely dead. We'll take it to Miami tomorrow, after we talk to Jacobs again. One of the tech guys might be able to get it to work.'

He spooned coffee into the pot and filled it with hot water, just as someone knocked on the kitchen door. Reflexively his hand reached for his gun and flicked the safety off. Uncertain, Grace looked at him. He jerked his head, signalling that she should move away from the table.

'Go lock yourself in the bedroom and stay there until I come and get you.'

Unable to speak, Grace nodded her head and ran for the stairs.

With caution born from years of experience Jack stepped to the side of the door, and turned the key with his left hand. The handle turned and the door opened. A man stepped into the kitchen, his arms held away from his body.

'That's an easy way to get killed,' Jack said, holstering his gun.

Anderson's breath hissed between his teeth. 'Yeah. Who'd you think it was?' A tall man, with sun-bleached hair, Anderson had the body and weary eyes of a fighter. His clothes were typical Floridian garb — washed out T-shirt and cut off shorts. 'Where's the widow? I heard she's a real hot piece of ass. You sleeping with her yet?'

'Watch the mouth, Anderson,' Jack said. He glared at the other agent. The cool tone of his voice barely concealed his contempt. He reached for the coffeepot and helped himself to cup.

'I don't suppose there's another cup in the pot?'

Jack didn't move. 'You suppose right. What's so important that you had to risk blowing your cover?' Anderson was a decent enough agent when he wasn't ass kicking to get ahead, which was most of the time.

'I've been asking round. The word on the street is that Pete Jacobs has money worries. His wife filed for divorce last May and was granted interim custody of the kid. Since then, Jacobs has been struggling to make ends meet.' Anderson's gaze shifted to the notebook lying open on the table.

Jack snapped it shut. 'What about the family home?'

'Jacobs is behind on the repayments. The bank has threatened to foreclose if he doesn't clear the arrears and his business overdraft. He put it on the market three months ago, but so far no takers. The realtor's suggested he drop the price, but Jacobs has refused. According to the court records, he's behind on his alimony payments, too.'

'What about his office and seaplane?'

'The office is rented by the month. The seaplane is about the only asset Jacob's has. He had a run in with the FAA, Federal Aviation Association a couple of months back. They say he failed to file a flight plan, but Jacobs disagrees and says that he submitted the requisite document, but it was never received due to a computer malfunction. The FAA refused to accept his explanation and fined him a thousand dollars.'

'Any history of drug running?'

'He's not on the DEA's radar, but that doesn't mean to say he's clean. According to local gossip, he specializes in charters, mainly for fishermen, tourists and the occasional honeymoon couple. Although, the rumour circulating the island is that he'll fly anywhere for cash.'

'Check with the IRS. Find out whether he's filed his taxes and whether he owes anything. In the meantime, you'd better go and join Kennedy,' Jack said.

'Kennedy can manage. He's down on the beach, keeping an eye on a group of teenagers. They're having a barbeque and a few beers. I doubt they'll cause any trouble.'

'Even so, Anderson, I want you out there, doing your job.'

'But there's a storm front moving in. Nothing is likely to happen.'

'You don't know that. Now get your butt back out there.'

Anderson's mouth compressed into a tight thin line. He held Jack's gaze for a moment, then turned on his heel and left.

CHAPTER FOURTEEN

Small towns made Sergio Vasquez nervous. He preferred to work in the anonymity of the city. There he could duck down a darkened alleyway out of sight of prying eyes. Here on Gasparilla Island he felt exposed, as if everyone knew why he was here, and the crime he was about to commit.

Stealing a car and getting to the island was easy. He took the shuttle bus to the airport, and strolled through the long-term parking lot looking for a suitable vehicle. Nothing too flashy, just something that wouldn't seem out of place on an island full of snowbirds and millionaires. On the third level he'd spotted a black, late model Saab convertible. He'd been stealing cars since he was old enough to reach the gas pedal. Back then, it took him nearly half an hour to pull off a heist. Today it took less than two minutes to jimmy the lock and climb inside.

A quick search of the glove compartment revealed that the owner had conveniently left the parking ticket for him. This time there was no need for him to create an excuse to tell the attendant about losing the ticket. It was right there in his hand. He kissed the ticket and crossed himself, ever thankful to the Blessed Virgin for his luck.

Once clear of the airport, he drove to a vacant lot, switched the license plates with those he stole off a beat up old pick-up truck an hour earlier, and drove, at legal speed so as not to attract attention, to Boca Grande. The car loved the road. He didn't much care for Saabs, but he had to admit to himself this was one model he might even steal for himself one day.

About four blocks square, and located in the centre of the island, the small residential community of Boca Grande bustled with activity. He parked the car in a side street next to the local community centre and walked around the tree-lined streets. Every house was unique, the gardens full of flowering plants. There were no high rises or traffic lights. No blare of car horns to disturb the old gentleman sleeping peacefully in a chair on his porch.

Vasquez picked up a copy of the local paper, the Boca Beacon, along with a street map from the stand outside the post office. He crossed the road to the local eatery, and ordered a New York strip, rare with pepper sauce and fries, and a bottle of Bud. While he waited for his order to be filled, he studied the map, memorizing the layout of the town. He lingered over his meal, only leaving the restaurant when it closed for the night.

The air inside the Saab was hot and stale. Vasquez wound down the window and turned the A-C to full. He drove slowly past the building. No lights showed inside. He turned left at the intersection and went over a few blocks, before parking under the branches of a Banyan tree. He sat and watched the street, and listened.

No curtains twitched. No doors opened, and no lights came on.

Satisfied that if anyone had seen or heard him arrive, they didn't care, he grabbed the gym bag off the passenger seat, and stepped out of the car.

Dressed all in black, he strode confidently along the tree-lined avenues, his footsteps silent in the still of the night. Suddenly, a door opened, bathing him in light. A barrel-shaped middle-aged man appeared on the porch, two poodles yipping frantically at his heels. Vasquez bent down and pretended to tie a shoelace. The man paused for a moment as the dogs took turns doing their business on the sidewalk, then looked his way.

One heartbeat. Two heartbeats.

Vasquez could only tie his shoes for so long. He could kill him if he had to, but it would be messy out here. Besides, he liked dogs. He wouldn't want to drop their master right there in his yard. They might bark, and then he'd have to use his sleek black gun with the silencer on them too. That would be a shame.

He stood and pretended to answer his cell phone. The dog man stood still. Was he watching? Then suddenly, the dog man clapped his hands, and the little vermin scurried back inside the house. Their owner followed. Praying again to the Virgin for small favours, Vasquez continued on his way.

His instructions were very specific; deal with the target and then return to Miami. Vasquez thought about that as he scanned the surrounding houses. Most appeared empty, either second homes or rentals, and in such a quiet neighbourhood it would be easy to slip down a driveway unnoticed. Old habits were hard to forget, but petty larceny was a game for amateurs, not a seasoned professional like him.

He walked quickly along the deserted streets, but not so quickly so as to draw attention, should anyone happen to look out of their window. He looked back at the dog man's house. Nothing. Good.

He turned right at the intersection. The target building remained in darkness. Vasquez smiled. Snowbirds were predictable; nearly everyone was in bed by ten o'clock. Despite his earlier misgivings, perhaps working in such a small community wasn't going to be so difficult after all.

An intricate wrought iron gate and an equally impressive lock stood between him and the rear of the property. After a quick look around to make sure no one was watching, he took a ski mask out of the gym bag and pulled it over his head, then sprang over the gate like a cat, landing soundlessly on other side.

He waited. He listened. But there was only silence.

Confident that the occupants of the first floor apartment slept on undisturbed, he followed the path down the side of the building toward the rear. He inched his way past a couple of windows and a side door.

A light breeze rustled through the trees. Under the ski mask, Vasquez's skin itched and dripped with sweat. At the edge of the building he paused. Tied to a concrete dock, less than fifty yards away, and illuminated by a solitary light, was a single-engine seaplane.

A rush of adrenaline filled his body. He removed a pair heavy rubber gloves from the bag and pulled them on. It only took a few seconds to open the service panel and disconnect the electricity supply, plunging the dock and surrounding area into semi-darkness.

Under the ski masked he grinned. It was almost too easy, but he was too much of a pro to be complacent. He swapped the heavy gloves for a pair of lightweight exam gloves, gently easing the thin latex over his sweating palms.

Vasquez waited for a count of fifty. Satisfied that the sudden loss of light hadn't attracted attention, he sprinted across the dock to the plane. He dropped the gym bag down on the edge of the dock, took out a small flashlight then, using the wing as cover, stepped onto the float. When the plane sank slightly under his weight, he didn't worry.

Balancing on the float, and guided only by the narrow beam of light, he edged his way toward the propeller. He released the three engine cowling latches and pin locks. Whoever maintained the plane had done their job well, for hinges opened smoothly and silently. Vasquez rested the rubber-encased flashlight on top of the battery and reached blindly into the engine compartment. Fear of being discovered, combined with the slight swaying motion of the seaplane and the smell of high octane Avgas twisted in his stomach. He swallowed the bile and tried to keep his hands from shaking.

Concentrate. Concentrate.

The small wrench slipped from his fingers, the noise reverberating in the stillness.

He froze.

Somewhere off to his right a dog barked. If its owners noticed, they weren't bothered. He cursed his clumsiness. He shifted position and felt for the wrench. It was somewhere. He knew it. Finally, his fingertips touched it, but he couldn't get a grip on it. He stretched until he was standing on his toes. The float sank, submerging his ankles in cold water. Coño! With his left hand, he grabbed the edge of the fuselage and hoisted himself up until he could reach down and pick up the wrench. His body slick with sweat and shaking from the exertion, he worked quickly, aware that time and his luck were both dangerously close to running out.

CHAPTER FIFTEEN

By midnight, a slow-moving storm shimmied in from the Gulf of Mexico and settled over Gasparilla Island just as the weathermen had predicted. Grace lay in bed and listened to the rain lashing the windows. She loved storms — something about the violence and the ensuing calm and freshness fascinated her. It was if Mother Nature was renewing herself in a not-so-subtle way. A thunderclap rolled over the house like a slow drum solo. A flash of lightening briefly illuminated Jack's face as he slept in the bed across the room from hers. He stirred briefly, and then went completely still, his breathing once more deep and rhythmic.

Grace plumped her pillow and rolled onto her back. A soft sighed escaped her lips as she thought about her life. She was different now. Daniel's death had made her stronger, more determined to be her own person, other than just someone's wife and sister.

From the very first moment they met, she'd been swept along by Daniel's self-confidence and determination to get what he wanted, to give any thought to her own needs and desires. She'd been too young, too eager to provide a stable home for Catherine when she fell in love with him to realize that under all that charm he was arrogant, controlling, and manipulative.

Lightening lit up the room once more. She turned to look at Jack, his profile dark in the eerie light. He was so different from Daniel, and he made her all too aware what love between a man and woman could be. His very look held a promise of sultry heat and erotic secrets to be shared. She'd been totally unprepared for the emotions their one brief kiss had unleashed within her, the slow, sweet oblivion that made the rest of the world fade away.

The storm passed on, but Grace found it impossible to sleep. She rolled over, and deliberately shut Jack out of her mind, preferring instead to wonder if Olivia had her baby. But thinking of babies focused her mind once more on Jack, and made her question why he hadn't told her about his wife and daughter.

Outside, palm trees rustled in the lingering breeze, a sliver of moonlight filtered through the gap in the drapes. As her eyelids grew heavy with sleep, it was Jack she dreamed of, not Daniel.

The following morning, evidence of the ferocity of the storm lay all around. Two large planters had blown over spilling their contents onto the decking, leaves and palm fronds littered the footpaths.

Grace glanced at the pool, the surface covered with pink bracts from the bougainvillea.

'The garden's a mess. It will take months to recover.' She picked up a fallen rose and dropped the bruised and torn bloom into the trash.

'That was just a tropical storm,' Jack replied, as he followed her through the garden toward his car. 'You should see first-hand the damage a hurricane causes.'

'I'd rather not. Do you think Pete Jacobs will risk flying in this wind?'

'Those seaplanes are robust, but I guess it will depend on what it's certified for.'

The drive into town took only minutes. The local eateries, normally bustling with the early lunchtime crowd, were half empty, many of the tourists preferring to stay inside.

As they drove along Bayou Street past the island's public dock, Grace caught a glimpse of a white seaplane with red stripes slowly taxiing toward the mouth of the inlet and open water.

'Isn't that Jacobs' plane?'

Jack slowed just long enough to lean over and peer out of the passenger window. 'Sure looks like it. He's probably refuelled at the marina, and is heading back to the dock to pick up passengers.'

Grace continued to watch the plane. The rudder flicked from side-to-side. The wing flaps lowered.

'I think you're wrong. I think he's preparing to take off.'

Jack cast a glance at the ocean. There was a slight swell, but no white-topped waves. He hit the gas pedal and headed for the empty lot adjacent to the bridge on Harbor Street. Milliseconds later, the Explorer skidded to a stop in a cloud of dust. Grace threw open the door and leapt out of the passenger seat before Jack pulled on the parking brake. She hit the ground and ran to the water's edge.

But it was too late.

As the seaplane reached open water, Jacobs clearly visible behind the windshield, opened the throttle. The engine pitch increased, the plane gathered momentum, a small wake forming under the floats. As the nose tilted up, the floats lifted clear of the water, and the plane rose gracefully into the air. Grace shielded her eyes and watched it gain height, then bank to the right.

Suddenly, a blinding light burst from the engine compartment. An instant later, the fuselage shattered by a thunderous explosion, turned the small plane into a fireball. The concussion reverberated through the air until it faded into the distance like a retreating thunderclap.

Flocks of terrified pelicans and gulls took to the air in a screaming, whirling brown and white mass.

Immobile, Grace watched part of a wing spiral down and crash into the sea, followed moments later by a section of the tail. Jack ran across the empty lot, threw her to the ground and shielded her body with his, as pieces of the shattered seaplane rained down.

For a few seconds a tense silence filled the air.

Then people started streaming out of houses and the local inn to stare at the twisted, charred metal and burning aviation fuel floating on the ocean. In the distance, a fire truck's siren wailed.

'We've... got...' She swallowed hard against the fear and concentrated on breathing, her ears still ringing from the explosion.

Jack helped Grace to her feet and wiped the dust from her face. She tried to pull away, but he held her tight.

'Easy, Grace. There's nothing you can do.'

'But—' She turned away from him to stare at the ocean, its surface a burning caldron.

'Grace, don't.' He caught her face between his hands, forcing her to look at him. 'No one could have survived that blast, least of all Pete Jacobs.'

Horrified and helpless, she began to shake. 'Do... do you think it was an accident?'

'Even though his business was in financial trouble, by all accounts, Jacobs was a stickler for maintenance. I'm no expert, but I'd say that was an explosive device of some kind.'

Grace felt the colour drain from her face. Jack's words tore at her heart. She closed her eyes, but could still see the image of the burning plane. The world spun, her knees buckled. Tears streamed down her face.

'Oh my God. Jacobs. Parous. They'd still be alive if I'd stayed at home and sold the house.' She clamped a hand over her mouth to stop the scream begging for release.

'Jacobs knew what he was getting into, just as I'm sure Elliott did. And if you'd sold the house, whoever's behind this scam would still come after you.'

She was about to argue, but he was right. But that didn't stop her feeling guilty.

'I can't do this anymore, Jack. I can't be responsible for any more deaths.'

'None of this is your fault, Grace. You know that. I know you're having trouble believing that just now, but it's true. Focus on the one thing that matters, bringing Elliott's killer to justice before you become his next victim. Let's get out of here.'

Grace slept from Boca Grande to Miami. Empty and drained, fatigue settled in dark rings under her eyes. Every now and again a whimper escaped her lips and her body trembled, as she relived the images and sensations of the last few hours.

Jack ignored the speed limit and drove in the outside lane of the freeway. Once they reached Miami, he adjusted his speed to match the heavy traffic where every driver jostled for position in the usual stop-go chaos.

Aroused from the numbness that weighed her down; Grace yawned and looked out of the window at the skyscrapers glinting in the late afternoon sunlight. She felt hot and dirty, and longed for a shower to cleanse her body and soul of the death and lies that had become her life.

'I thought you were asleep,' Jack said.

'The change in momentum woke me up. Where are we?' she asked, straightening her shoulders and finger combing her dishevelled hair.

'About five minutes away from headquarters.'

Grace's hands clenched.

'Stop worrying. Mike isn't going to blame you for Jacobs's death.'

Her head snapped round to look at him. 'How can you be sure?'

'Because he's a good agent. He examines the facts, all of them, before making a judgement.'

Grace looked at him for a long moment. Nothing he said made her feel better.

He drove into the parking lot reserved for Federal employees, and took his ID out of his jeans and slipped it, badge out, in the pocket of his shirt.

'Ready?' he said to Grace as they entered the building.

'You make it sound as if I'm about to be arrested.'

Jack smiled. 'Don't be scared. Mike's only going to ask you some more questions. Just be honest with him.'

'I have been honest with him and look what's happened. There's nothing more I can tell him, Jack.'

He took her hand and gave it a reassuring squeeze. 'Then there's no need to feel apprehensive.'

They found Mike Zupanik in his office, but he wasn't alone. 'Jack. Grace. Take a seat. I've asked Agent Diego to join us. He's come up with some interesting information.'

'Mike, you ought to know that Pete Jacobs died this morning.'

'Jesus, Jack. How'd it happen?'

'His plane exploded on take-off, and it didn't look like an accident.'

'What makes you say that?'

'We were there.'

Mike switched his attention to Grace. 'Seems folk have a habit of dying after you meet them. Makes me wonder if you've come here to clean up for whoever's behind this scam.'

Grace jumped to her feet. The look on her face said she was scared.

And angry.

'How dare you accuse me of… what exactly are you accusing me of, Mr Zupanik?'

Mike met her cool stare. 'Sit down, Grace. I'm merely making an observation, that's all.'

Grace glanced at Jack, but his face was unreadable. She'd asked for his help, but she didn't have to sit here and be insulted by his boss. She could walk away whenever she wanted.

Or could she?

Images of Pete Jacobs' burning plane filled her mind. If she left now his death would remain on her conscience for the rest of her life. She slumped down into the chair and buried her face in her hands. It took her several minutes to regain her composure. When she lifted her head it was to find Mike Zupanik regarding her with impassive coldness.

'Parous and Jacobs deaths are more than a coincidence.'

'Explain, Jack.'

'There are three possibilities. Either Grace was followed here; someone was worried that Parous and Jacobs would talk, and is sending a message to everyone else involved, or someone inside the Bureau is leaking information.'

Mike glanced at Diego. 'Have the airlines come up with the passenger manifests yet?'

Diego shook his head. 'We're still waiting on them.'

'Then start kicking butt. I want them on my desk within twenty-four hours. In the meantime, nothing said here goes beyond these four walls. Understood? Now, Diego, why don't you fill Jack and Grace in on what you've found out so far?'

Diego consulted his notes. 'Until eight months ago, Lionel Lattide didn't exist. There's no record of him owning property or filing taxes, and he's never been issued with a drivers' licence. I'm waiting to hear back from the banks regarding any accounts he may have held. And so far, there's no record of him owning a cell phone.'

'So the passport is a fake,' Jack said.

'Almost certainly,' Diego replied. 'But the details on Elliott's passport are legit, but here's the kicker. He died when he was six months old.'

'That's impossible, you're lying,' shouted Grace. Icy fear slid down her backbone. 'I've seen photographs of Daniel as a child with his parents.'

'They may have been his parents, but their name wasn't Elliott. The British authorities checked the birth certificate Elliott produced with his passport application against death certificates and found that Daniel Elliott died in February 1971.'

Diego handed Grace a sheaf of papers. She knew her hand trembled, but there was nothing she could do about it. She carefully read the contents, not once, but twice.

'Then I don't understand how his passport can be authentic.'

'It's a common ruse used by criminals. They trawl through graveyards until they find the headstone of an infant who died when they were only a few months old. They order a copy of the birth certificate. Once they've received that, they can apply for a social security number, drivers' licence, passport — anything to make them appear a bone fide citizen,' Jack told her.

Biting her lip, Grace looked away. Jack had confirmed what she already suspected. Her marriage, like everything else about her life of the last ten years was nothing but a lie. When she turned and faced the three men in the room none of them mentioned the tear tracks on her face.

'If Daniel Elliott is another alias, just who was my husband?'

'We don't know,' said Mike, 'which leads me to my next question. Did you identify Elliott's body following the accident?'

Grace shuddered. 'Daniel was badly disfigured, so Shaun, his business partner did that.'

'Any chance he could have been mistaken?'

'Daniel and Shaun were partners. They'd worked together for over ten years. Besides, Daniel's briefcase was found in the car, along with his wallet.'

'That doesn't mean the body in the car was his.'

Disconcerted, Grace crossed her arms and looked away. 'But if it wasn't Daniel, who was it?'

'That's what the British police are about to find out. They've applied for an exhumation order.'

Barely able to control her gasp of surprise, Grace turned to Jack. 'Did you know about this?'

Jack's hand closed over hers, his thumb gently stroking the soft skin at her wrist.

'No. But it makes sense. It's the only way to find out Elliott's true identity.'

Grace wanted to argue. She couldn't. 'Do you think the order will be granted?'

Mike relaxed. 'I think there's sufficient evidence.'

'In that case, tell me what you need me to do,' said Grace.

'Nothing, we don't even need your permission, Grace. The undertaker can identify the body, so you don't need to be present. The pathologist will take samples of DNA for analysis, and compare his findings with samples on national and international databases. That could tell us who Elliott really is and whether he had a previous criminal record.'

Jack handed Mike a paper bag containing the cigarette stubs. 'These might help. I found them in the trashcan in Elliott's office. It might be possible to extract DNA from the saliva to enable us to identify who smoked them.'

Mike leaned back in his chair. 'It's worth a try, I guess. What else have you got for us, Diego?'

'Elliott made regular calls to Parous and Associates from both his office in England and the house on Gasparilla Island. He also called the First Apopka Bank on the first Thursday of each month. His calls were routed through the switchboard, so we have no idea who he spoke to, but my guess is Cody, the guy handling his account.'

'What about the calls from Parous' office?' Mike asked.

'We're still checking the numbers,' replied Diego. 'Parous had a gambling habit, and frequented the 'Golden Dollar' owned by José Mendez. Word on the street is that Mendez is a front man for the Fuentes family, but we've been unable to confirm that.'

'Did Parous owe any money?'

'A few grand. I checked with the Bar Association, one of his clients made a complaint recently about misappropriation of funds. The allegation was dismissed for lack of evidence.'

Mike inclined his head toward Jack. 'Anything you want to add?'

'Elliott's MacBook, and a list of his clients.' Jack placed it on the desk, along with a copy of the fax he received from Daniel's secretary. 'Grace couldn't get it to work. The battery is dead.'

'Diego, get this over to the computer analysis response team. Let's see if they can recover anything from the hard drive. Anything else I should know about?'

'I found a notebook in the safe, but it's written in some sort of code. Grace has come up with a few theories about what it contains, but I'd like to hold on to it for the time being.'

'Any particular reason?'

'I'm betting sooner or later someone will come looking for it.'

'In that case, let's get it copied, and get the rest of the team working on it. Then I want you and Grace to return to the island tonight.'

Jack and Grace stood to leave. They got no further than the door, when Mike called out. 'Diego, get Grace some coffee, I need a word with Jack in private.'

Grace cast a glance at Jack, as if seeking his consent. When he made no movement, she followed Diego out of the office.

Mike waited until the door shut behind them. 'Go and see Rosa before you leave Miami.'

'There's no time, not if you want us back at Sand Dollars tonight.'

'Chrissie called at the condo. She's worried about Emilia, doesn't think Rosa is coping very well on her own.'

'And you think seeing me will make a difference?'

'Can't do any harm.'

'I don't know, Mike. We didn't part on the best of terms, and if Rosa catches sight of Grace she'll freak out. There's no telling what she might do.'

'Then leave Grace here. Diego can show her some mug shots. Just an hour, Jack, that's all I'm asking, otherwise I'll pull you off the investigation.'

Jack stared at the wall above his SAC's head, his brows drawn together in a frown. Emilia was his daughter, his responsibility. Grace needed his protection. Yet he couldn't in all consciousness leave Emilia with a woman who cared little for her wellbeing.

'All right, Mike. I'll go and see Rosa.'

CHAPTER SIXTEEN

The family room in the condo looked like the inside of an abandoned crack house. Plates bearing the congealed remnants of half eaten meals covered every conceivable surface. Bottles and glasses lay on the floor, their contents either drunk or spilled, ashtrays overflowed. Jack threw open a window and picked his way through the debris to the kitchen. Unwashed dishes and pans filled the sink. He wrinkled his nose at the rich stink of rotting food coming from the overflowing trashcan.

'Rosa!'

When she didn't reply, he walked down the hall to the bedroom. The air smelt stale. An empty bottle of tequila and a half eaten sandwich lay on the bedside table. The comforter formed a tangled heap on the bed with the pillows. The wardrobe door stood open, clothes strewn across the floor.

Heart pounding, he ran down the hall to the nursery. The door was closed. The muscles of his forearm hardened beneath the sleeve of his shirt as he turned the handle, and rushed inside.

Snuffling sounds came from the crib.

Emilia lay on her back, her face puckered and puce from crying.

Alone.

'Oh, my God,' he murmured. His hands trembled as he lifted her up and cradled her in his arms. 'Shush little one, Daddy's here. Where the Hell is your mother?'

The baby blinked and screwed up her tear-filled eyes. Jack clutched her small hand in his. It felt cold, her fingertips almost blue. He looked around. How long had Rosa been gone? Hours? All day?

He wanted to snap the woman in half. Instead, he quickly wrapped Emilia in a blanket and carried her into the bathroom. Equal amounts of fear and anger tore at him as he filled the baby bath with water.

'Damn you, Rosa. How could you do this to our daughter?'

He laid Emilia on the changing mat and deftly inched the yellow romper suit over her tiny arms and legs. Her soaking wet diaper stank and he felt the bile rise in his throat. He quickly removed it. Her bottom was red and dotted with blisters.

He looked down into his daughter's eyes. Despite the rash, the filth, and the loneliness she smiled at him. She smiled at him. His eyes filled with tears.

He tested the temperature of the water with his elbow, and satisfied it wasn't too hot, lowered Emilia into the bath, and began to soap her tiny shoulders and chest. When she kicked her legs and gurgled, he breathed a sigh of relief.

He rinsed off the suds and dried her in a fluffy towel and dabbed her blistered bottom with diaper rash cream. Once more warm and pink, and dressed in a fresh diaper and romper suit, he scooped her up and carried her into the kitchen. The refrigerator contained a single bottle of formula. He warmed it in the microwave, then sat down at the table and popped the nipple into Emilia's mouth. Her rosebud lips instantly fastened round it and she sucked hungrily.

The bottle was half empty when the door to the condo opened and Rosa stepped into the hallway.

'Welcome home,' spat Jack.

She stood motionless in the doorway. 'Christ, Jack. You scared the shit out of me.'

'I don't care,' he said. 'How could you, Rosa? How could you abandon a baby like this?'

'I've only been gone for a few minutes.' Her gaze drifted to the clock above the sink.

'Don't lie to me,' Jack murmured, keeping his voice down for the baby's sake. 'It's been a whole lot longer than that.'

'Thirty minutes—an hour maybe. I'm not sure. She was asleep when I left. You're making a big deal out of nothing.'

Jack placed the empty bottle of formula on the table, and then rubbed Emilia's back until she burped. 'Bullshit. Anything could have happened to her. She could have choked, or died from crib death.'

Rosa gave an impatient shrug. 'She's all right, isn't she? All's well that ends well.'

He shot her a withering glance. 'Ends well. Aptly put. What kind of mother are you, anyway, Rosa? You think you can just put a baby to down sleep and go out to do God knows what? You make me sick.'

'You can talk, you bastard!'

'Stop shouting, Rosa. The baby—'

Rosa kept howling. 'Three days! Three days you left me with that screaming, snot-nosed little shit. You don't have a phone? You can't call me? You make me sick!' She turned on her heel and lurched toward the family room.

Jack stood, but rather than follow Rosa, he carried Emilia into the nursery and settled her down in the crib. Despite Rosa's yelling, the baby's eyelids fluttered drowsily. He covered her with a blanket then crept out of the room.

'Where have you been, Rosa?' he asked as he shut the door to the family room.

Rosa sat on the sofa, a half smoked cigarette dangled between her bright red fingertips.

'Like you care. I needed to get out, get away from her.'

He reached out and hauled her off the sofa. His fists shook with rage as he clamped them around her wrists.

'Emilia's your daughter; she's not something you can put down when it bores you. You have a responsibility. Where were you?'

'Let go of me, Jack.'

'Not until you've told me the truth about where you've been.'

'I needed a drink, so I went to a bar in Little Havana. Hung out with a few friends, where's the harm in that? You're hurting me!'

Jack pushed her away, and she landed in a heap on the sofa. 'You're not fit to be a mother.'

'That's probably because I never wanted the damned baby in the first place!'

'So what did you want?'

'I wanted an abortion, but my brothers told me to keep it, that you'd give me a home, nice clothes, money, maybe a car.'

'So now the truth comes out. You assumed I'd owe you a bunch of stuff.'

Rosa raised her chin and glared at him.

'You callous bitch.' Jack slammed one fist against the other. 'God knows what I ever saw in you.'

She leapt to her feet. 'Jodete y aprieta el culo! I don't want to be fat and old before my time. I'm pretty, Jack. But who ever sees it? Not you. You're never here. I'm young! I want to have fun. And—'

'And what, Rosa?'

She bit her lip. 'Nothing.'

Jack grasped the collar of her blouse and pulled her toward him until her face was inches from his.

'Tell me.'

'Jorge said having the baby would be good for business.'

'What sort of business, Rosa?'

She flattened her palms against his chest and pushed hard. Nothing came of her effort.

'Family business. Importing, exporting, you know. That sort of thing.'

'Importing what? Drugs, cigars, people?'

'You figure it out, Mr FBI! You know everything, anyway, don't you?'

Rage overwhelmed Jack. He fought the urge to slug her. Instead he relaxed his grip. She staggered backwards.

'You used me, Rosa. You used my child. You're nothing more than a whore. Pack your bags and get out.'

'You can't throw me out of my own home. I'll call Child Services. They'll arrest you. I'm the kid's mother.'

'You forget who you're dealing with. I can arrest you myself. Right here, right now for child neglect,' Jack said. 'Or you can leave. Your choice.'

Rosa stiffened at the challenge, a sudden icy contempt flashed in her eyes. 'I'll go. But be careful, Jack. The next bullet could have your name on it. You never know.' She stormed out the door.

Twenty minutes later, Jack lifted Emilia and the baby carrier out of the Explorer, shouldered his gym bag full of her paraphernalia, and climbed the steps of the Cutler Inn. For the first time in his life he felt unsure of his welcome. He turned the brass handle and pushed open the door. Frank and Maisie Davis sat watching the evening news on TV.

'Hello, Jack. Brought the little 'un for a visit?'

'Not exactly. I'll come straight out and say it. I need you to look after Emilia for a few days. Please.'

'Where's Rosa?' Maisie asked.

'She left. That's because I threw her out.'

Maisie's smile faded. 'Oh. I'm sorry, Jack. I thought the two of you were trying to make a go of things.'

'Not any more. Look, I haven't got time to explain. I'm sorry, guys. I need your help like I've never needed it before.'

'What about your friend, Grace? She seems like a nice lady, can't she help?' asked Frank.

Jack grit his teeth as he lifted Emilia out of the carrier and cradled her in his arms. 'Grace is part of an on-going investigation into her late husband's affairs. Two people connected to him have died already. Grace is in danger. I can't put my daughter at risk too.'

Maisie looked at Frank. 'I don't know, Jack. We've got the inn and we're getting a little old for this kind of thing. Maybe we could call your sister—'

'I don't have time to take Emilia to Buffalo,' said Jack.

'Now, Maisie, can't you see the boy needs our help. We've never let him down and we're not about to start now.' Frank said, taking Emilia from Jack. 'Don't you worry. Maisie and I'll take good care of Emilia while you finish up your investigation.'

'Thanks, I really appreciate all you've done for me. But I need one more favour. In case anything happens to me. I'd like to name you as Emilia's guardians along with Charlotte. I don't want Rosa to have access to her under any circumstances. I know that's a lot to ask.'

Maisie took a quick, sharp breath. 'But Rosa's her mother. Besides, nothing is going to happen to you, Jack.'

'Promise me, Maisie. Promise me you won't let Rosa near Emilia.'

'But—'

'We'll do as you say, Jack,' said Frank. 'You're right to make provision for Emilia. Cops and agents face death every day. Why, just last month, I saw on TV that the number of cops being shot on duty was up twenty-four per cent from last year.'

'Thanks, Frank,' said Jack. 'I feel loads better knowing that.'

Maisie nodded. 'You don't need to remind me of the risks Jack takes. I worry about him all the time. Jack, we'd be honoured to be Emilia's guardians.'

Jack hugged her. 'Thanks. I feel happier knowing she's with people who love her.' He took out his wallet and removed a wad of bills. 'I packed what clean clothes I could find, but she'll need formula and diapers. This should cover it.'

Maisie pushed his hand away. 'No need for that, Jack. I'll see she gets everything she needs.'

'Take it, please.'

'All right,' Maisie said, tucking the bills into her apron pocket. Now, how about a cup of coffee, and a slice of pie before you leave?'

'I'm sorry, Maisie, gotta go.' He kissed her cheek. 'I have to pick Grace up from headquarters and drive back to Boca Grande this evening.'

'Here, Maisie,' Frank said, and carefully handed the sleeping infant to his wife. 'You take our little sweetheart while I walk Jack to his car.'

Frank put an arm round Jack's shoulders as they walked down the drive. 'Is Rosa likely to turn up with an attorney?'

'That'd be the last thing she'd turn up with. She couldn't get away from Emilia fast enough. She'll be back though. For me. With reinforcements. She's just that kind of girl.'

'In that case, do your best to sleep with one eye open and never lose sight of your weapon.'

'I'll do my best.'

CHAPTER SEVENTEEN

Rosa paced the living room of her brother's home, chain smoking as her mind raced through the events of the previous day. She wasn't cut out for motherhood, so what? Jack could afford to employ a nanny to look after the child, so there was no reason why she couldn't enjoy life as she had before the birth, seeing friends, shopping, dancing until midnight.

She poured a measure of tequila into a shot glass and downed it one, then snorted a line of cocaine, just enough to give her a little buzz.

Maybe she was too hasty in giving into Jack's demands that she move out of the condo. He had the child, which was what he wanted, but what about her? Surely she was due some recompense for all the pain and discomfort she went through carrying the brat and giving birth. She refilled the glass, and sipped the contents. A familiar voice snapped her out of her semi-trance.

'What in Hell's name are you doing here?'

Rosa regarded her brother Ramon with impassive coldness. Short and thin, with jet-black hair and dark brooding eyes, he was the baby of the family and the most handsome.

'If you must know, Jack threw me out.'

'You stupid bitch! Jorge will be furious. Why couldn't you do as you were told for once?'

Rosa whirled round to face him, walking calmly toward him. 'I'm sick of Jorge giving me orders. I had the brat, didn't I?'

Ramon stepped back. 'Jack gave you a home, money. You must really have pissed him off. Where's the baby?'

'I left the screaming brat on her own for a while, okay? Jack found out, we argued, and he threw me out. The baby's with him. End of story.'

'The cousins are going to be real upset when they learn they won't be getting green cards.'

Rosa ground out her cigarette and took another out of the packet on the table, but didn't light it.

'This isn't about the family, money or green cards. This is about me!'

Ramon ran a hand through his hair. Rosa had a volatile nature and arguing with her was getting him nowhere.

'You're so damn selfish.' He turned and walked toward the kitchen, but Rosa grabbed him by the throat and pinned him hard against the wall.

'You just don't get it, do you?' she screamed.

'Then explain it to me,' he said hoarsely.

'I didn't have the baby because Jorge told me to. I did it for revenge.'

'Revenge for what?'

'Christ, were you born with no brains? Do you take no interest in family business?'

'Whose fault is that? You and Jorge ignore me most of the time.'

'Is that surprising, given the way you behave? You'd rather be out playing baseball than taking an active role. Do you have any idea the effort Jorge and I put into providing you for and the rest of the family?'

'The store—'

Rosa's dark eyes narrowed. 'Provides nothing! You really believe that's how we make our money? You're more stupid than you look!'

'I'm not stupid.'

'Then prove it! Go out there and help your brother.'

'With what?'

'Why do you think Jorge spends most of his day down at the docks?'

Ramon's eyes widened in surprise. No longer able to breathe, he shook his head from side to side, trying to free himself from her vice-like grip. His lungs felt ready to burst. His world darkened. Just as he was about to lose consciousness, Rosa relaxed her hold. His body sagged, he slumped to the floor, chest heaving.

'You're such a coward. You're not worthy of the name Nuñuz.'

Ramon put a hand to his throat and massaged the bruised muscles and tendons. 'But what has that got to do with Jack and the baby?'

'Eighteen months ago, your second cousin, Estefan, suspected someone had infiltrated his organization. It took a while, but he found out who this person was, and ordered them killed.' She lit another cigarette, drew in smoke, and held it, before letting it out in a steady stream. 'But, it was too late. The man had already passed the information to the FBI. Estefan was arrested and charged with drug trafficking.'

'So?'

'Jack was on the task force. He was the agent the informer passed the information to. Jack set up a meeting with your cousin, offering Estefan a foolproof way to bring a shipment of cocaine into the country. Only it was a trap, which is how Estefan came to be serving twenty-five years in the state penitentiary.'

'Face it, Rosa. A few drinks and you'll spread your legs for any man. If you hate Jack so much, why did you let him get you pregnant?'

She ran at him then, her nails raking down his cheek, drawing blood. 'How dare you! Jack West ruined my life. Having his baby was my way of getting revenge for what he did. I loved Estefan. He loved me. We planned to marry, and would have done, if Jack hadn't arrested him and given evidence at his trial.'

'And now you've failed because you couldn't keep your mouth shut and behave like a mother.'

Rosa laughed. 'But I haven't.'

'What are you planning to do? Blackmail Jack into handing back the baby?'

Rosa's lips twisted into a cynical smile. 'Oh, I've already taken care of Jack. He won't be seeing his daughter ever again.'

CHAPTER EIGHTEEN

'Are you sure you don't recognize him?' asked Agent Diego.

Grace rested her chin on her hands and studied the picture, just as she had every other photograph on every other page.

'I'm sorry, Agent Diego. I don't recognize any of them.'

'Well, thanks for trying, Mrs Elliott. Can I get you some more coffee?'

She wrinkled her nose. 'No thanks. That stuff is strong enough to keep every insomniac on the planet awake for two lifetimes.'

Diego laughed. 'It is kind of potent. The computer geeks like it that way. They say it helps them concentrate.'

'Do you have any idea what's keeping Jack?'

Three men and two women filed into the office, dressed in cookie cutter black suits. They nodded at Diego and the other agents in the room.

'Shift change,' Diego said by way of explanation. 'Jack — I expect he's doing something for Special Agent Zupanik.'

Grace gave him a slicing sideways look. 'What sort of something? Is it connected to my husband's death?'

Diego held up his hands. 'Hey, I'm guessing. I have no idea what goes on in the SAC's office when the door is closed. Are you sure I can't get you another coffee? Or how about a Coke or a sandwich?'

'No. I'm fine.'

She drummed her fingers on the desk, and was about to ask Diego to call Mike Zupanik when the door to the office swung open and Jack walked in.

'You finished here, Diego?' he growled.

The other agent leaned back in his chair. 'Yeah, we're through.'

'Grace, grab your things and let's go.'

She clenched her hands together then forced herself to pick up her purse. She shook hands with Agent Diego then walked slowly across the room.

Jack motioned for her to hurry. 'Come on, pick up the pace!'

'Do you have to be so rude?' she hissed.

He clutched her hand and pulled her down the hall toward the exit. 'I've had my fill of this town for one day and Mike wants us back on the island tonight.'

Grace matched her steps to his. 'But that doesn't explain where you've been for the last three hours.'

'Not now.'

'What in Hell's name does that mean?'

'It means I don't want to discuss things.' They crossed the parking lot to his car.

'Whatever you were doing, it has something to do with Daniel's death, doesn't it?'

'No,' replied Jack. He helped her into the passenger seat, then walked round to the driver's side and climbed in behind the wheel.

'I don't believe you.'

He stared at her, expressionless. 'I've never lied to you, Grace.'

Twin stains of scarlet appeared on her cheeks. She took several long deep breaths. 'Diego wouldn't tell me where you'd gone and I—'

'It's personal, okay? I didn't expect it to take so long.'

'Then why didn't you say so?'

Jack ran a hand through his hair. 'It's been a rough day for both of us. What do you say we go see if there's any mail waiting for you at the Island Palm, and then grab something to eat before heading back to Sand Dollars?'

'If you're sure we can spare the time.'

Jack fought through the heavy downtown traffic and crossed the bridge into South Beach and onto Collins Avenue. The hotel parking lot was full, so they left the SUV on a parking meter and walked the short distance to the entrance.

The lobby felt cool after the late afternoon heat. The concierge looked up from his book and smiled as Grace and Jack approached the desk.

'How can I help you?' he asked, laying the book aside and reaching for the computer keyboard.

'Are you holding any mail for Mrs Grace Elliott?'

'Just a moment.' The concierge consulted the computer.

Grace looked into the large gold-framed mirror that covered the wall behind the desk. Reflected in it were two men, their faces creased with concentration, as they examined documents spread out on the table in front of them. The thinner faced of the two looked up, as if conscious that he was being observed. His gaze locked with hers. One corner of his mouth twisted upwards. Heat rose in Grace's cheeks. She cast her eyes downward. But like a honeybee seeking a flower, her gaze was drawn to the mirror once more.

'You look great.' Jack touched her arm, his words a buzz in her ear.

She started. 'What did you say?'

'I said, you look great. There's no need to check your make-up.'

She'd been so busy observing the thin man she hadn't noticed the concierge had left his post. 'I wonder what's keeping him.'

'They store the mail in the hotel safe. He went to ask the manager for access.'

Grace glanced in the mirror again. The man was still watching her. Embarrassment turned to uneasiness. Her heartbeat thundered in her ears, cold sweat trickled down her spine. She couldn't breathe. For a moment, she was back in the graveyard, standing under the lych-gate being threatened by the nameless man with the darting tongue.

The buzzing in her ears grew louder. Panic snapped at her throat. Stop it, she told herself. You're not at the graveyard. This man has nothing to do with the one who was there that day. You're imagining things.

Disgusted with herself, she tore her gaze away from the mirror and noticed a stand of visitors' brochures. She snatched a leaflet advertising trips to Key West. She'd hardly had time to admire the photographs when the concierge returned.

'I'm sorry for the delay, Mrs Elliott,' he said, pushing a large envelope toward her.

Grace stuffed it into in her purse. 'Thank you,' she said and handed him a ten-dollar bill, hoping it was an appropriate tip. Jack raised one eyebrow, evidence that she'd given the man too much. She backed away, turned on her heel and marched toward the exit leaving.

'Whoa! Slow down,' he said, placing a gentle hand on her elbow.

'Hurry up — slow down. What do you want me to do, Jack? You said we had to be back on the island tonight.'

'It's only seven-thirty. There's a great seafood restaurant close by. Best Grouper for miles.'

Grace matched her pace to his. 'Would you mind very much if we skipped dinner?'

Jack drew his brows together. 'I thought you were hungry.'

'I've lost my appetite.'

'If you're thinking about Pete Jacobs, don't.'

'I can't help it.'

Jack unlocked the Explorer and helped her inside, but rather than closing the passenger door, he cupped her chin tenderly in his warm hand.

'Talk to me, Grace. Tell me what's really bothering you?'

She slowly removed his hand from her chin, and then ran her hands restlessly up and down her arms. 'I feel as if I'm being stalked. That whatever I do, wherever I go someone is watching me.'

'How'd you mean?'

'The thin-faced man in the hotel; he never took his eyes off me.'

Jack tipped his head back and laughed. 'Yeah, I saw him. He probably thought I was a lucky son-of-a-bitch to be with such an attractive woman.'

'It's no joking matter,' Grace said evenly.

His expressive face changed and became almost sombre. 'You're right. I shouldn't make fun of how you feel.'

'And I'm scared. I'm scared for me, for you, and for—' She couldn't say the words 'your daughter.'

'Don't worry about me, Grace.'

His fingers slid round her neck and gently brought her face to his until there was only a breath between them.

'I get frightened too. Every time I put on my badge and strap on my holster, and step out the door.'

'I'm so scared I feel physically sick. Yet you seem so calm and focused. Aren't you afraid that things are spinning out of control?'

'There are times when I've looked down the barrel of a gun and thought 'this is it, my life is about to end,' but training takes over, and you do what's necessary to stay alive.'

'You mean you shot the person aiming the gun at you?'

'I've fired my weapon. But you don't need to hear about that. Trust me. The FBI will do everything to protect you while you're here in Florida.' He let his hand fall away, and without another word she clicked her seatbelt into place.

Grace bit down hard on her lip. Nerves quivered just below her skin. She closed her eyes and released a long breath. Her face was still warm from where he'd touched her. She'd been so sure he was about to kiss her. Disappointment mingled with emptiness and guilt. The look in his eyes reminded her of the night he had taken her to dinner, the night they had said goodbye never expecting to see each other again. Now her heart ached under her breast for the man she wanted but could never have. When she opened her blue eyes again, they were full of pain and unquenchable warmth.

Sultry air billowed through open passenger window. Her fingers shook as she closed it.

'How do you remain so detached?' She asked after a while.

'I've got no other choice. But that doesn't mean that some things don't get to me, they do. I just try not to dwell on them too much.'

'And what if you can't — can't stop thinking about them?'

'Then that's the day I retire. Look, Grace, you're just a pawn in this game. You're not responsible for what happened to Parous or Jacobs. Remember that.'

She shuddered. 'You make it sound so cold, so clinical.'

'The world of crime and corruption often is.'

The bright lights of the city fell behind. Ever since Daniel's funeral she'd been forced to confront a world she knew nothing about, seen things she didn't want to see, and accept that the man she'd married was a stranger to her.

'What happens next?'

'We wait. Whoever is behind this is getting desperate. I'm betting they'll make contact in the next twenty-four to forty-eight hours.'

Grace didn't want to think about how she would react when that happened, but she knew it would destroy the fragile control she had on her life.

Jack patted her knee. 'I know it's not easy, but try to relax. We'll be back on the island in a couple of hours.'

They drove on in silence. Something bad was in the air. Grace could feel it. It was more than the suffocating humidity. She tilted her head from side to side to ease the tension in her neck and stared at the tall sawgrass swaying in the moonlight.

Without warning, the SUV careered sideways across two lanes of the freeway. Jack swore and fought the wheel.

Grace stared at him wordlessly.

'Punched a hole in the tyre. Don't panic.' He lifted his foot off the gas, and struggled to bring the vehicle under control. Suddenly, the driver's wing mirror shattered showering him in glass. Blood trickled down his face from a cut on his cheek.

'Shit!' he cried, and dashed it away. With one hand he released Grace's seat belt and shoved her head first towards the foot-well. 'Get down and stay there,' he commanded.

'But—?'

'Just do it, damn it!'

Grace reached beneath her seat for the lever, released it, and pushed the seat as far back as it would go. Her heart pounded uncomfortably, as she huddled down in the narrow space.

The muscles in Jack's arm corded as he threw the wheel first to the right, then the left. The tires screamed in protest. A bullet rebounded off the doorframe inches above his head. He dragged the wheel back to the right, using every one of the evasive driving manoeuvres he'd learnt. The car skidded savagely, the headlights careened dizzily across the highway. For a moment Grace thought he'd lost control, but the swaying vehicle remained upright.

'The son-of-a-bitch is driving without lights. I don't know how long the tyre will last, but I'm going to try and lose the bastard in the marsh. Hang on!'

The engine roared as the Explorer veered off the freeway and raced down a steep bank. The suspension growled as if in pain as the underside bounced off a rock and the car took flight. It smashed down, the wheels spinning as they fought for grip on the grass.

Shots bounced off the tailgate in a spray of sparks. Grace screamed. She fisted her hands, digging her nails into her palm as they careered down the dirt track in the Everglades with no visible means of escape.

Please, God. We're too young to die! Please don't let Jack die. His baby daughter needs her Daddy!

Thin, flat bladed leaves of sawgrass swayed and rustled in their wake. Occasionally, she caught a glimpse of a cypress tree rising up out of the marsh. She squinted up at Jack, his brow creased in concentration as he fought for every yard of progress.

A hail of bullets gouged the bodywork as they crested a small rise. Grace knew Jack was driving as fast as he dare, but it wasn't fast enough. The pursuing vehicle was closing on them, its headlights flooding the passenger cabin with dazzling, white light.

The track suddenly petered out and they were driving through a slough, a free-flowing channel of water. The offside wheel hit a submerged mangrove root throwing Grace against the door with such force that pain shot down her right arm and across her neck. She bit back another scream and tasted blood.

The wheels found firm ground, as the first drops of rain fell on the windscreen. The Explorer lunged forward at the same wicked pace. They'd barely covered half a mile when Jack put it into a power slide that had them turning right onto another track.

The interior was plunged into darkness as the other vehicle missed the turning, but Jack kept his foot hard on the gas. The Explorer bucked and bounced over the dry earth, dust and grit boiling in its wake.

Grace braced herself as best she could, but her back slammed into the dashboard, forcing the air out of her lungs, leaving her bruised and gasping for breath.

'We've lost them for now. But it won't be long before they back track and find the turn-off. We'll have to ditch the car.'

'Are you crazy?' she gasped. 'There are snakes and alligators out there!'

'The rear tyre is finished and we're out gunned. We'll stand a much better chance if we hide out in the sawgrass until morning.'

Cold sweat snaked down Grace's back. She clamped down on her fear and peered over the top of her seat. Headlights circled the night sky. 'Can't we call for help?'

Jack tapped the cell phone on the dashboard. 'There's no signal. Trust me. We're better off on foot. The Everglades are criss-crossed with dirt tracks. Once we've lost our tail, we can make our way to a Ranger station, and I can use their phone to call for back-up. Either way, it's our only chance of surviving.'

Grace felt like a cornered animal. Her breath was almost as rapid as her heartbeat. It will work out, she told herself. We'll still be alive tomorrow. Won't we?

Ahead, rising out of the darkness, stood a dense patch of trees and low-growing bushes and palms. Jack put the Explorer into a skid, the wheel kicked like a bronco, and dust mushroomed up in a cloud. He switched off the engine and took out his gun and checked the clip. It was full.

'Ready?'

'I… can't… do… this.'

'Yes you can. It's less than ten yards to that stand of trees.'

Grace took a long gulp of air. No matter how hard she tried she couldn't get enough. Her vision blurred. She fought the panic, made herself breathe in, breathe out, slow and deep.

Jack rested a hand on her shoulder. 'Stick close to me, okay?'

Despite her fears, she forced herself to answer. 'Okay.' Her knees buckled as she climbed out of the vehicle. Using the bodywork for support, she inched her way round to the tailgate into time to see Jack unlock a metal box in the trunk.

'Here hold this.' He handed her a flashlight, then removed two spare clips of ammunition from the box.

Headlights flared on the track. She tugged at his shirt. 'Jack—'

'What?'

'I think they've found us.'

Jack swung round and glanced at the approaching lights. He pocketed the spare clips, stuffed an old jacket and a bottle of water into a duffle bag, along with Grace's purse, his cell phone and the Sat-Nav. He grabbed her hand and pulled her into the river of grass.

The moon vanished, swallowed by clouds. Within minutes, the rain turned into a deluge, plastering Grace's shirt to her skin. Water seeped into her shoes and soaked the bottom of her jeans as they moved deeper into the marsh. She lost all sense of direction as she blindly followed in his footsteps.

Jack kept up a relentless pace, but she couldn't ask him to slow down or stop, not when there was a chance they could outwit their pursuer. Sweat mingled with the rain, and trickled down her face and neck and between her breasts. She pushed her wet hair out of her eyes and stumbled on. Sawgrass rattled in the breeze. Fox? Turtle? Man? She strained to pick up the slightest sound. But all she could hear was her own rapid heartbeat.

Suddenly, a sharp cracking sound came from her left.

'What was that?' she hissed.

'Probably a gator eating dinner. Keep moving.'

She envisioned those huge jaws ripping into her flesh. Her mind froze. Panting in terror, she thrashed at the sawgrass, impervious to the pain from the sharp-toothed blades as it sliced at her skin.

Jack caught her in six strides and clamped his arms around her waist. She screamed and kicked out.

'Stop it, Grace. Do you want to give our position away?'

She tried to remain calm, but the panic attack had taken hold. Her lungs burned as she fought for breath. A roaring sound filled her ears and blackness threatened. Shuddering, she buried her face in his shoulder.

Jack gentled his hold and stroked her back. 'We've got to keep moving.'

'I-I know. I'm sorry,' she said in between shallow quick gasps. 'The thought of an alligator—'

'Understandable. Can you manage without your medication?'

Gradually the tightness in her chest eased and her heart rate slowed. She rubbed a hand over her eyes. Gathering her strength, she forced herself to step back.

'I think so.'

Jack took her hand and guided her through a small pond and up the bank on the other side into a hardwood hammock. Here the air was damp and smelled of peat. Southern live oak, royal palm and palmettos grew in dense clumps, blocking out the moonlight.

Bushes sprang up to block their path. Sharp leaves tore at clothes and flesh. The deeper into the Everglades they went, the more difficult it became to penetrate. They forged on for what seemed like hours until Grace was tired, so tired her feet dragged with every step.

'We should be safe here until morning,' Jack said.

Grace sank to her knees, and rested her head in her hands. Under the canopy of trees, the surrounding vegetation was so thick that Jack melted into the undergrowth, until he became just a voice in the night. At least the bushes offered some shelter from the rain, but they couldn't stop the shivers that racked her body. Nor could she stop the tears. They merged with the rain that ran down her cheeks.

Jack settled her against his chest, covering them with his jacket, but not even his re-assuring warmth could dispel the overwhelming sensation she had of being helplessly trapped.

CHAPTER NINETEEN

Catherine Peterson straightened the jacket of the business suit she wore, then strode up to the glass booth, and handed her passport to the immigration official. Her gaze never wavered as he compared her to the photograph on the back page, and passed it through the barcode reader. The passport was new and she'd been assured it was good enough to pass close scrutiny. It had cost enough — the last of her savings and the gold watch that had been a gift from her lover.

'How long are you staying in the United States?'

'Two weeks, possibly three.'

'And what is the purpose of your visit?'

'I'm here on business.'

The official flicked through the pages, examining each one for signs of tampering. He flipped forward… backward… looked at the front and the back… glanced up at her. Then he said, 'I'll be right back.' And left.

Oh shit, she thought. Other officials waved people behind her to their booths. What was so suspicious about her for God's sake? A family of Muslims, women draped in black burkas walking dutifully behind, was ushered through without incident.

A minute ticked by. Two. Perspiration gathered on her forehead.

The bearded passport agent returned. He looked her in the eye for what seemed like forever. Then, wordlessly, he stamped the visa page, added a squiggle, and then handed it back. Catherine let out the breath she she'd been holding and nearly ran away.

Once clear of customs, she entered the first ladies room she came to. She slipped into an empty stall and locked the door. After travelling non-stop for the last seventy-two hours, she was so jet-lagged that she struggled to remember where she was supposed to be let alone stand. Rome, Dublin, London, Amsterdam, and then Paris, she'd lost track of time and places, but had finally made it to Atlanta without being followed. Even now, she knew she couldn't afford to take chances.

When Grace started leaving messages on her cell phone, she knew something was wrong. She'd ignored her sister's numerous calls, and gone to work as normal, attending a conference for a group of surgeons in Rome. As soon as it finished she checked out of the conference hotel and into a small, inexpensive guesthouse near the Vatican City. But with her money fast running out, she needed cash and there was only one place to get it.

She opened her small overnight bag and pulled out a short black skirt, a bright pink ruffled necked blouse, and a pair of killer heels, the sort of clothes a high-class hooker would be proud of, and quickly changed. The smart business suit and low heels she'd worn to travel from London, along with the trilby she used to conceal her blonde hair, went into the bag. She'd find somewhere to dump it once she got out of the airport and onto the open road.

She placed an ear to the door but could only hear the sound of a running tap. Cautiously, she slid back the bolt and opened the door a fraction. The room was deserted. She grabbed her case and wash bag, and crossed to the basin. Leaning toward the mirror, she opened a small box and removed a blue contact lens and a small bottle of eye drops. Her hands shook so much it took three attempts to insert the lens into her right eye. She blinked, and then repeated the process for the other eye, adding some drops of artificial tears from the bottle. Satisfied her eyes were dry enough for re-touching, she pulled a mascara wand out of her bag and gave her long lashes a quick brushing.

When she looked at herself in the mirror; she doubted anyone, even her sister, would recognize her. She reached for her oversized purse and removed the chin-length black wig she'd purchased in London. It was a tight fit and would make her scalp itch, but it was easier and quicker than using hair dye. She took her time applying the rest of her make-up, accentuating her now blue eyes with a brown shadow and eyeliner. A last coat of mascara and her transformation from a brown-eyed blonde to blue-eyed mystery woman was complete.

The door to the ladies room swung open. Her heart leapt, and she spun around. A small, dark-haired woman with two young children entered and rushed past her, chattering to them in some strange, guttural tongue. She quickly gathered her belongings and left, merging into the crowded concourse, full of families heading home for Christmas.

Home.

Quiet nights in, boring television and Sunday roast dinners; the place she'd run away from at the first opportunity and had no intention of returning too — ever. She wanted to enjoy life, see the world, and not settle for anything other than a five-star lifestyle.

And no one was going to stand in her way.

Especially not her sister.

She pushed her way through the crowds towards the car rental desk and adopted what she hoped sounded like an American accent. 'I'd like to rent a car, please. Nothing too big or flashy.'

The pink-faced young man behind the desk offered her a stunning smile. 'Let me see what we've got. Are you on vacation?'

Catherine tapped her fingers on the desk, and looked anxiously over her shoulder. 'What? Oh, a vacation… yeah, that's right.'

The clerk clicked keys brightly. Suddenly he hit the space bar. 'Sorry. The system's kind of slow today. So where you from?'

Great. A nosy one. Think, Catherine. Where am I from? 'Kansas,' she said, knowing no more about it than any other state.

The clerk scratched his chin. 'Never been there myself.'

Thank you, God. 'So do you have anything available?'

'Ah… yes. We're up and running now,' he beamed. 'Yep. I've got a compact. A real steal. I have a two door Chevy Aveo for $110 a week plus insurance. That is unless you've already got a car. We can tag it on your policy, so that reduces the weekly rate somewhat.'

'No. I don't. Does it have air conditioning?'

He looked stunned. 'Yes… well, of course, ma'am. We don't rent cars without A-C. I don't believe anyone does, come to think of it.'

'Oh, sure. Guess I'm just a little tired — jet lagged, you know how it is. And I don't rent cars often.' She mentally counted the hundred dollar bills in her purse, renting the car would take most of her cash, but driving was the quickest way to get to Miami. 'I'll take it.'

'Of course,' he said. 'I'll need to see your drivers' licence and a credit card please.'

Heart pounding, she turned away. Breathe slow and deep, this is the easy bit compared to getting through immigration. 'I'd prefer to pay cash.'

'I'll still need to see a credit card.'

Her hand trembled as she slid back the zipper on her purse and pulled out her wallet. She let out another long breath and placed her licence and the fake credit card on the counter.

The clerk tapped the pink licence with a fingertip. 'This is a British Licence.'

Catherine forced herself to remain calm. She squared her shoulders and looked directly at the clerk, giving him a radiant smile.

'Is that a problem?'

'You said you were from Kansas.'

Anxious to escape from the clerk's probing questions she settled for half-truths. 'I've been working in London for a couple of years. I'll re-apply for a US licence once I get settled in my new job.'

'Just checking. You'd be surprised how many people try to rent cars with false or out of date documents.'

Color flooded her cheeks, but thankfully the clerk was too busy tapping away at his keyboard to notice.

'Sign here.' He pushed the rental agreement across the desk. She hastily added her signature.

'Okay, you're all set. Enjoy your stay in Atlanta.'

'You can count on it.' Catherine snatched up the keys and marched through the terminal to the parking garage.

Outside the rental agency, she doubled over and took a few deep breaths, feeling like an exhausted long-distance runner.

Another hurdle overcome.

Too many more to go.

She jogged down the lanes until she spotted her rental. It was small, grey, and entirely uninspiring. She opened the right side door and slid in, only to realize her mistake. Hoping that no one had seen her gaffe, she squeezed over the hump in the middle, including the gearshift, tucking her long legs under the steering wheel.

Her skin felt clammy, and her body ached. Exhausted, she pressed both hands over her eyes and tried to scrub away the weariness. The relentless travel had taken its toll. All she wanted to do was stretch out in a king-sized bed and sleep for a week, but she had to reach Miami by morning.

She opened her purse and took out a small bottle of pills. Working as a sales executive for a pharmaceutical company meant she had access to all sorts of drug samples. She flipped open the top with her thumb, shook out one of the pills, and rolled it in her palm.

One tiny capsule would keep her awake for another twenty-four hours. But she already taken two and swallowing another one would be risky. She popped it back into the bottle and replaced the cap.

Reluctantly, she inserted the key into the ignition and stepped on the accelerator. The little engine responded with a tinny growl. She put the car into gear and drove out of the parking lot.

An accident on the slip road of the interstate leading south cost her thirty minutes while she waited for a tow truck to clear away the damaged vehicles. Once free of the accident, she kept rigidly to the speed limit. No point drawing attention to herself this late in the game.

After five hours, her body screamed with pain, her eyes burned with fatigue. Ahead lay miles and miles of near empty highway. She leaned back against the headrest and felt her neck muscles relax, the rhythmic hum of the tyres strangely comforting. Her eyelids slowly drifted lower and lower.

A truck roared by, the blare of its horn startling her awake. She threw the wheel to the right, the Chevy swerved out of the truck's path. A few more inches to the left and she would have been killed instantly. Body shaking and covered in sweat, she pulled on to the shoulder, and rested her head on the wheel.

Five minutes passed before her heartbeat returned to normal, and she felt able to move. She fumbled in her purse, and took out her cigarettes, dropping them twice before she finally stuck one between her lips. Her hand trembled so much that it took her several attempts to light it. She shuddered the smoke into her lungs.

The clerk at the rental agency had given her a map. She unfolded it and tried to work out exactly where she was. She remembered passing a gas station some miles back, but didn't recall seeing any houses. Two cars roared by, rocking the small rental, making her gasp. One thing was certain, she couldn't stay where she was.

Catherine stepped out of the car. She rubbed her arms unsure whether it was the cool night air making her shiver or her near death experience with the truck. Empty and drained, she knew that eight hours sleep, in a comfortable bed, would lift her weariness.

With a long sigh, she climbed back behind the wheel. She cranked the A-C up to full with the hope that it would keep her awake and set off once more. Half an hour later, she crossed the state line, and drove into a small town. A cluster of houses lined one side of the main street, the other bordered the railroad. A quarter of a mile further on, she came across a billboard advertising the name of a motel.

She pulled in and drove up to the manager's office. Greasy haired and unkempt, the woman behind the desk was huge. Catherine instantly regretted her decision to stop, but with so little cash in her purse she had no choice but to stay in this run down and seedy motel.

'I'd like a room, please.'

The woman tapped the sign on the wall. 'No hookers here.'

Momentarily rebuffed, Catherine lowered her gaze in confusion. 'I'm not… Oh! You mean my clothes. I've been to a party and I'm too exhausted to drive home,' she lied. 'I'll be gone in the morning.'

The fat woman looked her up and down and grunted. 'Just one night, but that's it. Number four. Down the drive, second block on your left.'

Catherine counted out five ten-dollar bills and collected the key. If the outside of the motel looked run down, the inside of the room looked as if it hadn't been touched in over fifty years. She dragged her suitcase inside and locked the door. A single light bulb hung from the ceiling, casting a yellow glow on the peeling walls. The scent of damp, filthy carpet and old cigarettes pervaded the air. The carpet stuck to her feet, and in places appeared threadbare, while the floral comforter on the bed smelled of mothballs and made her think of old ladies and charity shops. She pulled it back to reveal yellowed wrinkled sheets.

A deep rumble rocked the room as a train ran along the track behind the building. Smothering a sob, Catherine freed her blonde hair from the black wig, dropping it in the trashcan, then kicked off her shoes and collapsed onto the bed. How had she come to this?

She gulped hard and wiped her eyes. Too tired to undress, she dragged the quilt over her body and was asleep within minutes.

CHAPTER TWENTY

'How long do we have to stay here?' Grace whispered.

'Long enough for whoever is out there to assume we're gator food. Thirsty?'

She nodded and shifted position. Jack offered her the bottle of water from his backpack. She took a few sips. Lukewarm, it did little to quench her thirst.

'Kennedy and Anderson will contact Mike when we don't show up at Sand Dollars,' said Jack. 'He'll organize a search as soon as it's light.'

'You can't be sure of that.'

'I'm sure.'

Grace bit down on the inside of her cheek. The pain kept the confusion roiling inside of her from spilling out. She didn't know whether to believe him or not. The night closed in around them. She'd never been afraid of the dark, but hemmed in by palmettos and willow bustic, every branch and leaf seemed to threaten her very existence. Would this nightmare never end? Would help ever arrive?

She lost all track of time. Water dripped and plopped through bushes, ran down leaves, soaking her skin. Her blood ran cold, her teeth chattered uncontrollably. The moonlight cast crazy shadows on the ground. Apart from the sound of rustling leaves and creaking branches, there was silence.

Something slithered over her leg. She clamped her hands to her mouth to hold back a scream, as the cold, lithe body of a snake wrapped itself around her foot.

Jack hissed in her ear. 'It's a corn snake — non venomous. The heat must have brought it out of hibernation. Don't move.'

'Get it off me! Get it off me, now!' Heart booming in her ears, she watched, mesmerized, as the snake paused to taste the air before unwinding its sinuous body, and gliding through the undergrowth toward a dense thicket of palmetto.

'It's okay, it's gone.'

Grace relaxed, sinking into Jack's cushioning embrace. His hands cupped her face. His lips brushed her temple, her cheek.

'It's okay,' he repeated, and then his lips found her mouth in a kiss that made her senses spin.

All the fear that she'd worked hard to control flared into passion. The need that rose up in her so strong, so unlike anything she'd ever felt before, that all she could do was let the moment spin out around them.

Breathless, Jack dragged his mouth from hers. He ran a fingertip over lips. She didn't move. One of his hands slid into her hair. And he leaned in until his lips were almost brushing hers.

'I shouldn't have done that. But damn it, Grace, I want you.'

'You do?'

'I want you so much it scares me.'

'But now's not the time or the place?'

Jack shook his head. 'There are things we need to talk about. Things I need to explain.'

'Later?'

'Promise.'

She saw the light, then—a narrow beam, swinging from side to side at the edge of the trees. Every nerve in her body tensed.

The light grew brighter.

The leaves of the palmettos and bustic crackled as their pursuer came within yards of their hideaway. The surrounding bushes convulsed as something heavy thrashed down through the branches.

Moving silently, Jack came to his knees, arms outstretched, gun at the ready, a lethal calmness in his eyes.

Grace stuffed her knuckles in her mouth to suppress a scream. Bile rose in her throat. She willed the sickness away. Rigid with fear, she crouched in the bushes, certain she was about to die.

After moment, their pursuer moved off to the left.

Water rippled and bubbled.

Suddenly, the light swung in a semicircle and settled back on their hiding place.

Grace's instinct was to spring to her feet and run, and keep on running, but whoever was out there would kill her then Jack. She couldn't allow that.

Jack shifted position, his gun following the narrow beam of the light as it danced through the branches.

A shadow stepped out of the trees.

'It's no use hiding. I know you're there,' a male voice shouted.

The ground in front of Grace exploded in a hail of bullets. She scooted backward into the head-high scrub, ignoring the sharp leaves of the palmetto that scratched and tore at her skin.

Jack yelled, and waited until the light focused on him, then returned fire. The gunman cursed, but let off another round. A bullet slammed into the tree next to Jack's shoulder, sending bark chips flying.

Jack fired again in rapid succession. Grace lost count of the shots.

The shooter screamed, sank to his knees, a hand clutched to his chest as he crumpled to the ground.

'Grace, stay here until I tell you it's safe to move,' Jack called. He edged forward, his gun trained on the spot where the man lay face down in the dirt. He kicked the man's weapon away, then leaned down and felt for a pulse.

Grace crawled out from her hiding place. 'Is… is he dead?'

Jack lowered his gun, and spun round. 'Yeah, he's dead.' He stood and walked over to her and helped to her feet. Smothering a groan, she fell into his arms and pressed her face to his shoulder.

'Do you think he was alone?'

'We'd have known by now if he weren't. Think you can hold the flashlight for me? I need to check for ID.'

Grace picked it up from where it lay on the ground and shone it toward the body. She tried not to look at the rapidly growing stain covering the man's shirt. The world spun and she swayed. She closed her eyes against the nausea that rose in her throat.

'You okay?' Jack said.

'I feel—' She quickly turned away and bent over.

Jack locked an arm around her waist and held her steady until she was done. When she turned around and looked at him, her face was shockingly pale.

'Don't feel embarrassed. I hurl every time I walk into an autopsy.'

Grace wiped her mouth with the back of her hand. 'I didn't realize there'd be so much blood,' she said through clenched teeth, her body shaking.

'Here, rinse out,' Jack said, offering her the bottle of water.

Grace did he suggested, then poured some into her hands and splashed it on her face.

'Feeling better?'

She nodded, head down, eyes focused on her feet.

'Go and stand by that tree while I finish up here.'

Taking a deep, unsteady breath, she tottered away, her hands clenched stiffly at her sides. Jack dropped to his knees next to their assailant, and went through his pockets.

'Do you recognize him?' she called over her shoulder.

'No, and there's nothing in his pockets except a book of matches and a set of keys. We'll need fingerprints and dental records to make a formal identification.' He pocketed both, picked up the assailant's gun, and strode over to where she stood. He lightly touched her elbow.

'Let's get out of here.'

Grace looked at the body with distaste. 'What about him?'

'In the morning the medical examiner can collect what the alligator's leave behind.'

Her energy drained, every footstep became an effort. Several times they were forced to backtrack almost to the edge of the slough before they finally found their way out of the marsh onto a dirt track.

Grace hunched over, her arms resting on her thighs. 'Which way now?'

Jack turned to his left and walked a little way down the track, then walked back, stopping in front of her. The ground was damp from the rain, but he could still make out faint tyre tracks.

'That way,' he said pointing to the right.

'Are you sure?'

'There's a stand of trees up ahead. I reckon that's where we left the car.' He shifted the backpack into a more comfortable position on his shoulder. 'You ready?'

Grace pushed back her tousled hair, and straightened. Used to the sounds of the night and the shifting shadows, her hand slipped into Jack's as they walked quickly, guided only by the silvery moonlight.

They rounded a bend, and there, parked in a small clearing was Jack's Ford Explorer, and next to it a Dodge Ram pickup.

Jack placed a restraining hand on her arm. 'Wait here while I check things out.' Without taking his eyes off both vehicles, he crept forward, gun in hand. The driver's door was open, but the cab was empty. He holstered his weapon then did a quick search of the interior, but found nothing more than an empty Coke bottle.

He slipped the keys he removed from the shooter's pocket into the ignition and started the engine, then reversed back down the track to where Grace was waiting.

'Get in.'

Grace dropped the backpack onto the floor between her feet, and fastened the seatbelt. Glancing at the dashboard clock she saw that it was just after midnight. She wrapped her arms around her chest and peered at Jack.

'What happens now?'

'According to the GPS there's a Ranger Station about three miles from here. There'll be a phone. We can call Mike, fill him in, and have him send help.'

They fell into silence disturbed only by the sound of the pickup's engine. Gradually, the trees thinned out and marsh and sawgrass took over. She stared out into the darkness, and felt only fear.

So much had happened in so little time, that she no sooner came to terms with one event, when she was knocked sideways by another. And then there was Jack. Tonight the agent had taken charge, cool, efficient, yet at the same time gentle and protective.

Rain lashed the windows, overwhelming the wipers, misting the windows. Jack leaned forward and scrubbed a hand over the glass.

'There!' Grace said, pointing to a single story log cabin rising out of the darkness. 'It looks deserted.'

'Probably closed for the Christmas holidays.'

Jack manoeuvred the pickup into position in front of the building and cut the engine. A single light illuminated the door. Grace could make out a series of birdfeeders hanging from the eaves. A row of pots, filled with a variety of plants and flowers sat under the porch. What appeared to be an observation tower of some description stood off to one side.

'Bring the backpack,' Jack said and got out of the car. He lifted a tyre iron out of the toolbox in the back of the pickup and used it to jimmy open the shuttered door. An alarm sounded, filling the air with a high-pitched wail.

Grace clapped her hand over her ears. 'Can't you stop it?'

'Sure.' He swung the tyre iron at the control panel, smashing it to pieces then flipped on the lights. An interactive display covered the back wall; to the left of the entrance there was a retail area, selling guidebooks, videos, and clothing.

Jack strode over to the cash register. A cordless phone lay on the counter next to it. He picked it up and listened for a dial tone.

'Take some clothes off the rack, and see if you can find anything to eat and drink. I'm going to call Mike.'

Grace grabbed a sweatshirt and fleece jacket from the rack, and a pair of hiking socks from the stand, then followed the signs to ladies room. Once inside she stripped off her T-shirt and used it, along with a whole pack of paper towels to dry herself off as best she could. The sweatshirt was three sizes too big, but at least it was warm and dry. There was nothing she could do about her wet jeans, or shoes.

The staff kitchen was small and well equipped, but the cupboards and refrigerator were empty.

Jack hung up the phone as she returned. 'Mike's sending a helicopter. It should be here within the hour.' He pulled a T-shirt off the rack and changed into it. 'There's a sofa over there. Why don't you lie down and get some rest? Here use these as a pillow.' He tossed her a couple of thick fleece jackets.

'What about you?'

'I'm okay.'

Grace stretched out. Weariness swamped her, yet something troubled her. 'That guy… how did he know where to find us?'

'He must have followed us.'

Grace shook her head. 'All the way from Sand Dollars to Miami and back? I don't think so.'

Jack opened his mouth to say something, but she was right. He would have noticed the vehicle tailing him, which meant that someone had to have tipped the guy off. But who?

He slid off the sofa and started to pace. Grace heard a fluttering in the distance. It grew louder.

'Helicopter,' Jack said. 'Thank God for Mike.'

After that things moved quickly. Jack relayed information regarding the location of the shooter to the police and medical examiner. Grace sat on the sofa watching. It was bad enough that she'd witnessed the incident, without hearing Jack recant the events again and again.

People came and went. Minutes became hours. Someone wrapped a blanket round her shoulders and offered her a hot drink from a flask. The sun was an orange and gold glow on the eastern horizon when Jack's shadow fell over her.

'Cops and medical examiner will be here for hours yet. It's time to go.'

Grace stood and followed him out to the waiting car. She was too tired to enquire where it had come from. Instead she sank gratefully into the leather passenger seat. Every bone in her body ached. She longed for a long soak in a hot tub, and eight hours solid sleep.

The digital clock on the dashboard flashed eleven fifty-five am, as they drove across the causeway to Gasparilla Island. Somewhere along the way she'd drifted off to sleep, lulled by the drone of tyres on tarmac. She sat up and rolled her neck, yawning.

'Another few minutes and you can crawl into bed.'

Grace shook her head, gazing his face the whole time. 'Tea, a shower, and then bed.'

He raised an eyebrow. She seemed steadier than he expected. 'The great British cure-all.'

'Don't mock it. Many a crisis has been averted over a pot of tea.'

'You've changed, Grace. You've been threatened, shot at and yet you seem so… I don't know… resilient.'

'Perhaps I've always been this strong, but Daniel's domineering personality overwhelmed me. I've had time to accept that he was involved in something illegal. He exerted control over me during our marriage; I won't allow him to control my life from the grave.' She stared straight ahead. 'I wonder who he really was.'

'We may never find out. Does that bother you?'

'It did at first, but not anymore. Who do you think tried to kill us?' she asked as they entered the house.

'Someone who thinks we're getting too close to the truth,' he suggested.

Grace went straight to the kitchen. Wearily, she filled the kettle but didn't switch it on. Instead, she rested her back against the counter. 'The truth about what?'

'Daniel Elliott's true identity. The mastermind behind the scam. I'm not sure which.'

She didn't answer right away, but thought carefully about his suggestion. 'But if they kill me, how will they get the money?'

'I don't know, Grace. Maybe the money isn't that important to them, but the information contained on the computer disks is. I think it's safe to assume there's a connection — a common denominator between Elliott, Parous, Jacobs, and you. I just don't know what or who it is yet.'

'It can't be anything else because I've told you all I know.'

'I'm not so sure. There's something we're missing, a vital piece of information, an overheard conversation perhaps, that links the three of you. I think you should let me put you into the witness protection scheme.'

'Why now?'

His expression was tight with strain. 'Because we got lucky tonight. I just don't want you to get hurt.'

'I'm not going to run away, Jack.'

He gathered her into his arms. 'You wouldn't be running away, you would be protected.'

She smiled at him. 'You protected me.'

'And a damn poor job I did. Look at you. You're covered in cuts and scratches.'

Grace smiled, touched by his concern. 'They're not your fault. I'll put some antiseptic cream on after I've showered,' she said and traced the line of the cut on his cheek. 'Your face—'

'Is fine.'

'At least let me put a dressing on it.'

'Stop worrying about me.' He captured her right hand and kissed her fingertips. Her breath hitched. It was the most seductive thing she'd ever experienced. He turned her hand and tasted each one of her fingers before his lips moved across her palm to the sensitive flesh at the base of her wrist.

'What are you doing?'

'What I've dreamt of doing every night for the last six months.'

Grace's eyes widened. She started to say something, but the words never formed. His mouth covered hers hungrily, his tongue gentle and probing. Currents of desire rippled through her. Instinctively, her arms went around his neck, her lips parted as he gave her what she wordlessly sought.

Heat chased through her body, and settled in her groin. She could feel his heart thudding against her breast and felt the answering beat of her own. His hand slipped under her sweatshirt, and explored the soft lines of her back, waist and hips, his fingers teasing and arousing her. Shivers of delight followed his every caress, flooding her body with desire.

When he finally ended the kiss, Grace rested her cheek on his chest with a sigh of pleasure, her breathing almost as ragged as his.

'I meant every word I said earlier. I want to make love to you, Grace. I have done since the day we met. But—'

'But you're married and you have a daughter.'

Jack closed his eyes for a moment hiding the guilt and the pain. 'Who told you?'

'Frank. But I don't think he meant to.'

'Emilia is seven weeks old. Rosa, her mother, and I aren't married and never will be. In fact, Rosa doesn't want anything to do with the child.' An inexplicable look of withdrawal came over his face, yet he didn't physically move. He lifted his hands and cupped her face. 'If you can't accept that Emilia and I come as a package, then this ends now.'

For several heartbeats Grace remained silent. When she finally spoke there was a gentle softness in her voice.

'Emilia is such a beautiful name. And I'd very much like to meet her.'

His whole face spread into a tender smile. 'You're sure?'

Her emotive blue eyes held his gaze. In answer, she drew his face to hers and kissed him, lingering, savouring every moment.

With a husky murmur of pleasure, Jack pulled her hard against him and returned the kiss as deeply as she gave it. He took her hand and led her upstairs to the bathroom. He turned on the shower and checked the temperature. And then he kissed her, teasing and tasting her until she moaned and moved against him in a haze of hunger.

Taking hold of her sweatshirt, he pulled it up until they had to break away from each other so that he could get it over her head. Underneath she wore a rose coloured bra, the lace cupping the creamy swell of her breasts. He undid the zip on her jeans and slid them down past her hips until they pooled around her ankles. She stepped out of them, at the same time kicking off her shoes.

He trailed feather-light kisses down her neck and shoulders, his warm breath searing her skin. His every caress filled her with desire and anticipation until all she could think of was him.

Watching her intently, Jack flicked the front hook of her bra freeing her breasts, fondling them in slow, sensuous circles, skimming his thumbs over her nipples, teasing them into hardness.

Grace inhaled sharply, her body hungry with desire. When his hands stroked her thighs, and pushed aside the lace of the thong that covered her soft, moist centre, she arched helplessly, and cried out.

He quickly discarded his own clothes, stepping out of his jeans and shedding his sweatshirt, then pulled Grace into the shower stall. Standing behind her, he began to lather her entire body with a bar of citrus-scented soap. Fragrant steam swirled around them. His hands moved gently down the length of her back, then over the swell of her hip to the taut and sensitive flesh of her stomach.

Grace felt her knees weaken. The pleasure was pure and explosive, and her cries, soft at first, became wild and demanding. His hands sought her breasts again, his fingers soaping the swollen nipples. Waves of desire coursed through her leaving her aching for the sweet release she knew only he could give.

She turned in his arms. Her fingers wove into the crisp dark hair on his chest, luxuriating in the wealth of sensations flooding her body as his erection pressed against her thigh. His hands, more urgent then, stroked and teased until she writhed against him.

Jack lifted her out of the shower and wrapped her in a towel, the fabric soft as it moved over her skin. He carried her to the bed and lay down beside her. His tongue continued the exploration his hands had begun, teasing and sucking until the need grew and she could take no more. His body moved to cover hers, her warm moist folds sheathing the hard length of his penis. There was nothing languid about their lovemaking then. His hands held her hips, as he thrust deeper until the desire and passion overwhelmed them as they sought release.

Heat pulsed through Grace. She wrapped her legs around his, crossing her ankles, driving him deeper until her breath came in long, surrendering moans, and she trembled as the first wave of her orgasm washed over her.

CHAPTER TWENTY-ONE

It was eight-thirty when Catherine woke. Her movements stiff and awkward, she headed for the bathroom. Water trickled out of the showerhead. With a muttered curse, she stepped inside the stall. Barely tepid, it was sufficient to wash away the last of her tiredness. Once dry, she pulled on fresh underwear, a pair of jeans and a check shirt, and finger combed her hair. She longed for some coffee, but she'd most likely catch salmonella poisoning if she drank the burned tar from the ancient coffee machine in the motel reception.

Catherine carried her suitcase out to the car and placed it in the trunk. She started to back out, when a car screeched to a halt directly behind her. It was black, and she could see nothing through its darkly tinted windows.

Two suited men in sunglasses leapt out. One came to her window and tapped on it.

Her mind turned over a thousand scenarios in the second before she rolled down the window. Immigration? FBI? MI6? Something darker?

At the end of the longest second in history, she chose to fake indigence. 'Who the hell do you think you are and why are you blocking my car?'

Expressionless, the first man pulled his blazer away to show the butt of a gun.

'Get out. Move slowly and keep your hands where we can see them.'

Catherine's mouth worked, but words were slow in coming. 'I need... I need some identification.'

'Step out of the vehicle, ma'am and I'll show you some.'

Panic like she'd never felt before welled in her throat. She fought hard not to scream. Moving slowly, she slid gracefully out from behind the wheel. Before she had chance to say a word, she was spun round and shoved up against the side of the car. Then the man roughly patted her down. Crimson suffused her face, as she seethed with anger and humiliation. When he finished, he turned her round to face him and thrust a shiny gold badge under her nose.

'Agent Lowell. This is Agent Purcell,' he said nodding at the red-haired man standing next to him. 'DEA.'

'DE... what?'

'Drugs Enforcement Agency. Now let's see your ID.'

Catherine felt her knees buckle. 'In... in my purse, behind the driver's seat.' She chewed on her lower lip and stole a glance at the other agent as he grabbed her purse and tipped out the contents. It didn't take him long to find her passport. She shook as he thumbed through the pages, comparing her to the photograph on the back page.

'My name is Catherine Peterson. You've made a mistake. I'm no drug dealer.'

The first agent said nothing. The other agent pulled out his cell phone and read the details off her passport to some faceless individual.

Silence stretched.

Finally, he turned to the guy holding her and said, 'Name checks out. Visa was issued in Atlanta yesterday. Photo ID matches it.'

The agent restraining her stepped back. 'Looks like our information was wrong. You're free to go.'

She glared defiantly. 'Gee, thank you. How kind.'

Only when the men climbed back in their car and disappeared from view did she slump down into the driver's seat. The fear that clutched at her stomach turned to nausea. Catherine whipped open the door and vomited onto the tarmac. A few moments later when the worst of the gut wrenching spasms had passed, she raised her head and looked in the driver's mirror. Her face was chalk-white and pinched. She pulled a tissue from her jeans pocket and wiped it roughly over her mouth.

Christ! That had been close.

Still shaking, she threw the car into gear and reversed out of the parking lot, and drove down Main Street at a steady pace. Sandwiched between a grocery store and the local bank was a coffee shop. Like the motel, it too appeared to had seen better days, the sign above the door announcing 'M y b th's offe hop'

Lured by the thought of food and a hot drink, Catherine stopped the car and grabbed her purse. Once inside, she ordered an Americano with an extra shot and a cinnamon bagel to go. While she waited for the waitress to fill her order she took a seat at the counter next to a middle age woman.

The woman's purse sat open on the floor, her wallet in clear view. Catherine glanced around at the other occupants, but they were too busy eating breakfast to notice her. Casually, she angled her knees so the napkin slid off her lap and over the woman's purse. She bent down to retrieve it, her hand tightening around the wallet, wrapping it in the napkin.

She waited for a count of ten, hoping the woman wouldn't look down or pick up her purse. When she didn't move, Catherine stuffed the wallet and napkin into her own purse, then paid for her order and left.

Back in the car, she sipped her coffee, and ate the bagel, then examined the contents of the wallet. Ten, crisp twenty dollar bills were tucked in the billfold. She crammed them into her purse, then opened her door and flung the wallet as far as she could under the car.

Re-energized, she tossed the Styrofoam cup into the passenger foot-well and checked her cell phone. There were two messages, both from her sister, both saying the same thing.

It's Grace. Call me as soon as you get this message. It's important that I talk to you.

She deleted both, and then switched off the phone to conserve the battery.

Traffic on I-75 was heavy with people rushing home for the holidays. Towns and cities came and went in a blur. Outside, the sun rose in a cloudless sky with the promise of another hot day. The drone of the car's air conditioning drowned out the hum of the tyres. She tried the radio again, but found all the advertisements irritating and switched it off, preferring instead to drive in relative silence.

A thoughtful smile played at the corner of her mouth, another four or five hours and she'd be able to live her life, her way. Everything would be different from now on. No more scrimping and saving. No more taking orders from her greasy haired boss with the wandering hands or chaperoning hospital consultants at conferences and listening to their ribald jokes.

North of Miami, she stopped at one of the service areas for a bathroom break. The restroom was empty when she entered. She twisted her blonde hair into a tight knot and removed a chestnut coloured wig from her oversized tote, then inserted the blue contacts into her eyes. Her transformation complete, she examined her reflection in the mirror, tilting her head to the left, then to the right. A derisive grin settled on her features.

She gathered her things and left, stopping briefly to purchase a burger and Coke, before climbing back into the car and continuing her journey.

Weariness enveloped her as she negotiated the traffic in downtown Miami. She rubbed a hand across her aching temples and tried to remember exactly where the bank was located. Catherine circled for a while until she had no option but to leave the rental in a parking garage. She shouldered her purse and head bowed, walked quickly toward the heart of Miami's financial district.

The streets were full of city workers busy grabbing a late lunch or cigarette on an all-too-short break from the office. It took her a while to find the right building, but finally she passed under the bank's signage and stepped up to the ATM machine.

A quick glance over her shoulder ensured no one was watching as she slipped the bankcard out of her purse and into the machine. She tapped in the security code and waited while the bank's computer system compared the information she'd inputted to that held in its databank.

Seconds ticked by.

Catherine's fingers tapped restlessly against the side of the machine. She took off her sunglasses and peered at the screen. Account closed. Please contact your bank.

Her fist hit the wall, drawing blood. 'That's impossible!'

Shock yielded quickly to fury. She stormed into the bank, ignoring the queue at the counter, strode over to the information desk.

'I've just tried to use my bankcard, but the stupid machine says the account is closed. Can you check?' she said in a lower voice than normal.

The poker-face young woman behind the desk looked up. 'Take a seat. Do you have your account number and some identification?'

Catherine lifted her chin and struggled to maintain an even, conciliatory tone. 'The number is 295636190. But

I'm not sure I have my drivers' license with me.' She made a pretence of looking in her purse.

The clerk entered the number into her computer and studied the details on the screen. 'Are you related to the account holder?'

'Yes, how else would I know the number of the account?'

Closed circuit security cameras monitored the banking hall. Catherine forced herself to remain calm, praying she would not betray her agitation. The wig made her head ache, irritated her scalp, and her eyes burned from the contacts, forcing her to blink repeatedly. She crossed one slim ankle over the other to prevent her foot tapping nervously against the marble floor, as she watched the hands of the clock move from the half to the quarter hour.

What's taking her so long?

Catherine stirred uneasily in the chair. She studied the security camera and wondered if it was trained on her. Across the hall, the queue for the tellers lengthened. A security guard paced up and down its length watching for any suspicious movement. His attention focused on her. Fear slammed through her. Her hands, hidden from sight by her purse, twisted nervously in her lap. The guard leered at her and winked, then turned his attention back to the line.

Shaken, Catherine glanced at the clerk with a frown, sorely tempted to ask the woman to call someone more senior.

'There's no mistake. The account has been closed and the money transferred.'

At first, the words didn't register. She wavered, trying to comprehend what she'd heard. Adrenaline and ice flooded her veins. Shock yield to fury. Transferred? What in God's name was the clerk talking about?

Her heart was beating too fast, making her head spin, her palms damp. She clung to the desk for support. 'What! I mean when was this?'

'Two days ago. Mr Cody handled the arrangements. Would you like me to see if he's free?'

Part of Catherine wanted to scream. Part of her wanted to take the woman by the collar and shake her until she admitted there was some mistake.

Swallowing hard, Catherine tried to keep the anger from her voice. 'No, no, it's all right. No need to disturb him.'

She turned away. She felt trapped, helpless. Betrayed.

'You look pale. Are you feeling okay? Would you like some water?'

Catherine barely heard the personal remark. Think. Brazen it out. Don't run. Whatever you do, don't make the security guard suspicious.

She took several long, deep breaths, and forced herself to meet the clerk's gaze. When she spoke, her voice was flat, calm. 'I'm fine. Just a little tired. Thank you for your time. I'm sorry to have troubled you.'

Catherine hurried back to the car. She slammed the car door and dragged off the wig. This couldn't be happening. Not to her. Not after all her careful planning.

She'd been duped. There was no other explanation. For the first time in her life, she understood what it felt like to want to kill someone.

Her knuckles tightened on the wheel. While being angry felt good, it wouldn't lead her to the money. Think! Damn it, think!

She forced herself to sit up. Her body vibrated with tension as she stared out of the windscreen at the row of parked cars. Then the realization hit.

There was only one place she could go. The place that only she and one other person knew about.

Some of the tension ebbed away from her body, but she remained physically tired. She fumbled in her purse and took out the bottle of pills. One would give her enough of a buzz to keep her alert for hours, but last time the drug had been slow to take effect. She shook two into the palm of her hand and popped them into her mouth, washing them down with the last of the Coke.

The sun was an ochre crescent hovering on the horizon as she turned onto the Interstate, heading west. Euphoria bubbled in her laugh and shone in her eyes. No one double-crossed Catherine Peterson and got away with it.

CHAPTER TWENTY-TWO

Jack's cell phone rang just as he and Grace were getting up. He grabbed it off the bedside table, checked the digital display, and then punched answer.

'Hi, Mike. What do you have?' He rubbed a hand over his eyes and swung his legs over the side of the bed.

'The airlines finally came through. Elliott sat next to a woman on every flight he took. It may be a coincidence, but there's a strong possibility she was travelling with him. The name on the manifest is different for each trip, but that doesn't mean a thing. Chances are its same woman and she used a false passport like Elliott. Homeland Security is looking into it.'

'Anything from the airport security cameras?'

'I've got a team reviewing the tapes, but it will take time. We're also trying to track down the flight attendants. One of them might remember Elliott and the woman, and be able to give us a decent description of her.'

Jack looked at Grace. Fully awake now, she stretched and yawned. He stood and carried his cell phone over to the window.

'How did they pay for the tickets?'

'Elliott always paid cash.'

'Smart. Obviously didn't want any record on his credit card or bank statements in case Grace saw them.'

'Yeah, that was my thinking too. The woman used a credit card in the same name as her passport. We're checking to see if it was stolen or a counterfeit.'

Grace threw back the covers, and walked naked to the bathroom. Jack waited until he heard the taps running then asked, 'Any news from the British police on the second autopsy?'

'It's underway. The DNA results should be available within the next twenty-four hours. We'll run them through CODIS - the Combined DNA Index System, although there's no guarantee we'll come up with a positive ID.'

'What about his car?'

'Diego's been through the accident report. There was no sign of any mechanical failure. The tyres were fully inflated, so the idea that someone tampered with them doesn't fly. Likewise, the brakes; there's no sign they were interfered with. It's just as Grace said. Elliott lost control and slammed into a wall. The car burst into flames on impact. If it hadn't been for another driver dragging Elliott's body clear of the wreckage, he would have been burnt to a crisp.'

Jack frowned. Every break they got turned up more questions than answers. 'Does the autopsy say anything about toxicology screening?'

'There's no mention of it in the report. Why do you ask?'

'Call it a hunch.'

'You think Elliott was drugged?'

'According to Grace, he was a careful driver. The road conditions were good at the time and you've just said there's no evidence to support the theory another car was involved or his car was tampered with. Something caused him to lose control.'

'I don't know, Jack. He could have had a momentary lapse of concentration. Besides, the body's been embalmed, so a blood test is impossible, but I guess a hair sample might tell us something.'

The bathroom door opened, Grace emerged in her underwear, her hair damp from the shower. Jack watched her pull on her jeans and a clean sleeveless shirt, then stand in front of the mirror to comb her hair.

'What… did you say, Mike,' he said into the phone.

'The computer lab techs got Elliott's MacBook working, and there's still no identity on the shooter from last night. We've run the plates on the pickup he drove. The owner reported it stolen from outside a Target store in North Miami Beach late yesterday afternoon.'

Jack stifled a yawn. 'Right now, I'm more concerned about how he found us, than who he was.'

Mike didn't take one second to get to the bottom line. 'You still think there's a leak within the Bureau?'

'It's the only explanation.'

Mike's voice was tight with strain. 'All right, Jack. From now on, you check in with me or Diego, every four hours. You miss a call, and I'll have the local SWAT team on your doorstep before you can blink.'

'Understood.'

'One more thing. Does the name Joaquin Vicente Alzua mean anything?'

'Never heard of him.'

'Not sure. His name crops up regularly on Zachary Parous' appointment calendar, but as yet, we've no idea why. If anything else breaks, I'll be in touch.'

Jack broke the connection and turned round. Grace sat on the bed watching him.

'That was Mike. They've started the second autopsy.'

'So I gathered.'

'He'll call as soon as he hears anything,' Jack said, and got dressed.

Grace followed him downstairs to the kitchen. She filled the coffee maker and waited for it to brew. 'So where does that leave us?'

'Hip-deep in shit.'

'Tell me something I don't know.'

'How about we order some food and go over what we know so far?'

'I don't see what good it will do, but if you think it will help, why not.'

'A morning hug and a kiss help me think,' Jack said, making a grab for her, and nuzzling her neck.

Grace tried not to grin but couldn't help it. 'In case you hadn't noticed, Agent West, it's ten after five, almost time for dinner.'

'So?'

She stepped back. 'Morning usually starts with the sun rising, not setting.'

'Yeah, but kissing, that's good at any time.' He ran a fingertip down her cheek and tilted her head. His other hand slid round her hips, pulling her close. His kiss was heat and fire. When he lifted his mouth from hers, they were both breathing hard.

Grace blew out a breath and looked at him from under her lashes. 'Is that one of the skills the Bureau teaches its agents, because I'd hate to think you used the technique to get your suspects to confess?'

Jack's laughter was low, throaty. 'That's one I acquired all by myself.' He watched Grace run her tongue over her lips, tasting his kiss. His libido kicked. He closed his eyes and ignored the blood pumping in his groin. When he opened them again, the agent was back in charge.

'You think the coffee is done yet?' he asked.

'Pot's probably boiled dry by now. I'll make some fresh while you order a pizza. I think I saw a number for a delivery service pinned to the cork board by the refrigerator.'

Jack picked up the phone and punched in the first three digits, then hung up. Hunched over, he studied the assortment of business cards and telephone numbers pinned to the board. One in particular caught his attention. He took it down and tucked it into his pocket.

'You want anything special on yours?' he called over his shoulder, as he placed the call.

'Tuna and anchovies. No salami.'

'The guy said twenty minutes.' He took a sip from the steaming mug Grace had placed on the table in front of him. The coffee was rich and dark, just how he liked it. He pulled a yellow legal pad and pen toward him, along with the photocopied bank statements and notebook.

'Tell me more about Elliott's business partner.'

'I've told you as much as I know already.'

'Tell me again. How did he and Elliott meet? What's his speciality?'

Grace wanted to bang her head on the table, and tell him it was futile. Instead, she pulled out the chair opposite his and sat down.

'Shaun's surname is Dixon. He and Daniel spent a year working for the same firm, before setting up the partnership. They've been in business together for nine years. Shaun deals with personal taxation, UK investments, and company audits.'

Jack started doodling and making notes on the pad. He reached for his mug, draining the contents.

'What about other members of the firm.'

'There are two junior accountants and an auditor. But I've only ever met Liz Shelton, Daniel's secretary. She joined the firm about eighteen months ago, straight from college.'

'Could she be Daniel's mistress?'

Grace was silent for a few moments before she finally shook her head and said, 'No.'

'You sure about that?'

'Liz is a sweet girl. She lives at home with her elderly, disabled mother. There's no way she would leave her mother on her own and accompany Daniel on a business trip.'

'Okay, strike her from the list of suspects. That leaves Daniel's clients. Did any of them ever call him at home?'

'Not that I recall, although… now that I think about it, there was one guy who called a few times.'

Jack looked up from his notes. 'Can you remember his name?'

She sighed, and rubbed her temple. 'John… John Vance… Vickers… Vines… I'm sorry I can't remember his surname. He came to the house once, too. But he should be on the list of clients.'

Jack ran his finger down the list. 'Nope, there's no one with a name like that. Do you know which company he worked for?'

'I've no idea.'

Jack walked to the counter and re-filled his mug, and carried it back to the table. The doorbell rang just as he was about to sit down.

'That'll be dinner. Wait here.' He opened the door with one hand and paid for the pizza, then kicked the door shut with his foot.

'Tuck in', he said, and placed the box on the table, helping himself to a slice in the process. While he chewed, he read through the notes he'd made.

'There's always a pattern to any crime, especially a money laundering scam, but I just don't see it here.'

Grace spun the pad around, and read through his notes before flipping to a new page. 'If the electronic files were so important, why didn't Daniel just hand them over?'

'Because they were his insurance; so long as he had them in his possession, he was safe.'

'So you think someone stole them.'

'Despite what the accident report and initial autopsy say, I don't believe Elliott's death was an accident. So either he gave them to someone for safekeeping or whoever killed him has them. It would also explain why his attorney was murdered.'

'You think Daniel gave them to Mr Parous?' Grace asked.

Jack reached for another piece of pizza. 'There was no sign of a break-in at the attorney's office or home. If Parous had them, he must have handed them over to his killer.'

Grace drew a question mark between each name on the page. 'There's another possibility — Daniel's could have given them to his mistress.'

He hesitated, not wanting to cause her any distress. But there was no polite way to ask, other than come straight out with the question.

'When did Daniel make his will?'

'Shortly after he purchased this house, why?'

'If he didn't want you to know of its existence, why include it in his will? It doesn't make sense, unless—'

'Unless what?'

A muscle quivered at Jack's jaw. 'Unless he planned to change it at a later date.'

'You think Daniel was going to divorce me?'

'It would be one way of preventing you from inheriting his property. The other would be to kill you.'

Shock siphoned the blood from her face. 'Don't be absurd. Daniel wouldn't stoop to murder.'

'With you out of the way, legally or otherwise, he could leave his property to anyone he liked. And if my hunch is right, and Daniel was murdered by someone else involved in the scam, it would also explain why someone tried to kill us yesterday.'

Grace shuddered deep inside. Somehow the suggestion made Daniel sound like a hardened criminal, not the man she had married.

'What if the man who threatened me at the funeral also owns the island Daniel visited, the one Pete Jacobs told us about? He wanted the electronic files; why not assume the money was his? He could have followed me here.'

'That's a lot of 'if's' and there's only one way to find out if you're right.'

Grace ignored the chill running down her spine. She sipped her coffee and waited. When he didn't say anything she asked, 'Are you suggesting we visit the island?'

Jack swore under his breath. 'Your ass is already in the firing line. Going there—'

'Would be suicidal?'

'I was going to say too dangerous.'

She shrugged. 'Well, I can't be in any more danger than I already am. When do we leave?'

'Even if Mike agreed, I wouldn't let you do it.'

'But—'

Jack jumped to his feet, and strode round to round to Grace's side of the table, pulled her chair back with a jerk.

'Damn it, Grace. It's a job for a SWAT team, not an innocent civilian. Do you have any idea what I went through last night, knowing that I might not be able to protect you, prevent you from being killed?'

Her breath lodged in her throat at the fear and passion reflected in his eyes. She didn't move.

His fingers slid into her thick auburn hair. He leaned in until their foreheads touched.

'I love you, Grace. I think I always have. But you have to trust my judgement on this.'

Before she could form an answer, his lips brushed hers. Her own mouth responded, and a familiar shiver of wanting stirred deep inside her body. She lifted her head and saw the heart-rendering tenderness of his gaze and said, 'But—'

'No argument. That idea gets shelved under 'last resort.' Agreed?'

She put a hand to his cheek and let her fingers rest there for a moment. 'Agreed.'

'Anyway,' he said taking his seat again and grabbing another slice of pizza, 'that just leaves the notebook.'

'I've been thinking about that. What if it's not written in code?'

Jack frowned. 'How'd you mean?'

'We never compared the entries in the notebook, to the dates of the deposits on the bank statements. It might explain where each deposit originated.'

'You think it could be that simple?'

'What's that saying about hiding things in plain sight?'

Jack rubbed his beard. 'You have a point. I'll mention it to Mike when I call him. And find out if the tech guys have come up with any suggestions.'

Grace twisted the platinum band on the third finger of her left hand. It meant nothing to her now. She pulled it off, along with the matching diamond engagement ring, and slipped both rings into her pocket. When she returned home, she'd sell them and give the money to Cancer Research or some other charity. She stood, and picked up the empty pizza box and dropped it into the trash, then helped herself to the last of the coffee before taking her place at the table once more.

'Something else has been bothering me.'

'Go on,' said Jack.

'Mr Cody said that all bank customers are issued with an ATM card, yet there was no such card in Daniel's wallet when it was returned to me by the police.'

'What about his British bank and credit cards? Were they missing too?'

'No, and what's more, his wallet contained a considerable amount of cash.'

'How much are we talking about?'

'Three hundred and fifty pounds.'

Jack looked up, his face grim. 'That's a lot of cash to carry around. Someone close to Elliott had to know he was skimming cash from the money laundering scheme. When he refused to hand some of it over, they killed him, then stole the ATM card.'

'It's certainly a possibility.'

'Check the bank statements. Were any withdrawals made after Daniel's death?'

Grace shuffled through the statements until she found the one for November. She ran a finger down the page 'It only goes up to the fifteenth of the month. I wonder—' She pushed back her chair and ran upstairs only to return a few minutes later with an envelope. 'I didn't get chance to look at this yesterday.'

She quickly tore it open and tipped out the contents. 'Check book, ATM card, and yes, there's another statement covering the account up to the date it was transferred into my name.'

Jack reached for it. She pushed his hand away.

'There have been eleven withdrawals since Daniel's death on the seventeenth, each for small amounts — twenty-five dollars or less. The last one was four days ago.'

'Here' let me see that.' He took the statement and began reading. 'You don't need a pin number for such a small sum. Just walk up to the cash register, swipe it through the machine and get a receipt. A person could survive on small purchases such as those for quite some time and it's one way of determining whether the account is still active.'

'Then whoever has the card is in for a surprise.'

'That's one way of putting it.'

'So all the FBI has to do is arrest them when they try to use it again.'

Jack looked at his watch. 'Make some more coffee while I call Mike, and ask him to check a few things.'

'What things?'

'I'll tell you if and when they pan out.'

CHAPTER TWENTY-THREE

Mike Zupanik closed his files and locked them in the cabinet. He clutched his briefcase tightly and headed out to the parking lot. Already dark, a gentle breeze blew in off the ocean. His workday over, he paused to loosen his tie, and unbutton the top button of his shirt. For the first time in a week he was looking forward to being home in time for dinner.

He smiled, unlocked his car and slid into the drivers' seat, tossing his briefcase onto the seat next to him. He planned on stopping at the local supermarket on his way home to pick up some flowers and chocolates for Chrissie, his wife.

It had been a long week, and he could sure do with spending some time with his grand kids, but Jack's assertion that someone within the Bureau was leaking information bothered him.

Only six people, excluding the forensic accountant examining Elliott's records and the computer tech dissecting the MacBook, knew what case Jack was working on.

Apart from Jack and himself, only Diego, Mancuso, Kennedy and Anderson had access to all the relevant information and were directly involved.

He paused at a set of lights to allow a mother with a young child to cross the road. He grinned as the small boy tugged at his mother's hand, urging her to hurry along. He reminded Mike of his grandson, David, always rushing ahead, eager to get on with life. Another seven months until he retired, then he and David would pack up the RV he planned to purchase, and take off into the backwoods for a summer of camping and fishing.

The car behind tooted his horn. Mike lifted his foot off the brake and set the car in motion, his mind once more on his problem.

Alejandro Diego was the newest member of the Miami office. A dedicated career agent, he'd undertaken some tough assignments while working for the DEA, and was the last person Mike would suspect of taking a bribe from a criminal gang. Joel Mancuso had been with the Bureau for ten years, and while he might not have Diego's quick wit or knowledge of the Cuban Drug trade, he was conscientious, polite and had an impressive record for solving cases.

That just left Bill Kennedy and Seth Anderson.

Mike scrubbed a hand over his temples. It was no secret that Anderson despised Jack. Mike had never understood why, and put it down to a clash of personalities. But now he wondered if it wasn't something more serious.

Jack and Anderson had completed their basic training at the Academy at the same time. Anderson had done his two-year probationary period with the Anchorage office, while Jack had completed his in Boston. Their paths hadn't crossed again until three years later, when they were both assigned to the Detroit office. That was the last time they'd worked together until fourteen months ago when they became part of his team.

Mike could never figure out why Jack and Anderson hated each other. He was dimly aware of the decade-long feud and had been told to watch for it. But years of experience told him that was where he was going to draw the line. Now he wondered if his non-involvement had been the right course of action.

From day one, the animosity between the two of them had been palpable. Jack visibly gritted his teeth in Anderson's presence and Anderson balled his considerable fists whenever Jack walked his way. Mike had seriously considered having one or both of them transferred, but then the case Jack had been involved in crossed international borders and he'd gone to work in London.

Jack was a damned good investigator, did everything by the book, and his record for solving cases was solid. However, Jack wasn't averse to voicing his opinions and had been on the wrong side of more than one SAC during his time with the Bureau. But for all that, Mike trusted Jack's judgement implicitly, and had put him forward for promotion to Assistant Special Agent in Charge.

Anderson, on the other hand, was somewhat of an enigma. He never discussed his family or socialised with his co-workers after work or at weekends. Lately, he'd been even more withdrawn than usual, as if there was something troubling him. More than once Mike could have sworn a flicker of sadness interrupted Seth's perennially stony expression.

Mike spun the wheel and sent the car spinning through three hundred and sixty degrees. The tyres screamed in the dusk. It wouldn't hurt to check the personnel files of those involved in the case. He punched three on his cell phone's speed dial — home and Chrissie.

'Hey, beautiful,' he said.

A woman sighed on the other end of the line. 'When I'm 'beautiful', that generally means you're gonna be late.'

'You know me so well.'

225

'Thank God our marriage vows didn't include showing up for dinner… which you're not going to do, are you, Mike?'

'Sorry, pet. Got a hot date with a big problem.'

'Good thing I made a casserole. It'll be in the microwave whenever you happen to show up.'

Mike pursed his lips. 'I love you, you know.'

'I love you too. Probably more than I should.'

The phone went dead in his ear. It was unlike her not to say her usual 'bye'. He felt a sudden chill. Too much air conditioning, he rationalized. So she didn't say goodbye. It was really nothing.

Wasn't it?

The FBI building was in darkness save for the lights illuminating the security desk. Mike showed his pass to the agent on duty, and then jogged his way upstairs to his office. Once inside, he flicked on the desk lamp and dropped his briefcase onto the sofa in the corner of the room.

Mike wasn't the type of SAC who rode his agent's backs. Normally he trusted them implicitly, but something about Jack's concerns resonated with him. He spun the dial on his safe and pulled out a stack of brown folders.

According to Anderson's file, after he'd graduated college he'd done a short stint in the US Army before applying to become an agent. He'd passed all the intensive background checks and the physical, but had failed to be selected first time around. There was nothing unusual in that — often applicants were weeded out on the grounds that too many had applied that year. Not to be deterred, Anderson had reapplied twelve months later and been accepted onto the fifteen week training course at the Academy. Since graduating, his career had been unremarkable. He was a steady worker. Showed up when he was supposed to. Reported his cases just the way he was taught. Mike rubbed his chin. He'd never really realized it before, but with Anderson, it was as if this was just a job to him. Nothing more.

Mike turned the page. Anderson had been investigated for misconduct—once for passing on information to a reporter, although nothing was proven, and on the second occasion, for making derogatory sexual remarks to a female agent. He knew the agent in question. She'd done very well at the Bureau, and held an exceptional rank for someone her age. This explained why Anderson been turned down for promotion on more than one occasion. In the Bureau, memories were long.

Mike leaned back in his chair. Ordinarily, Jack was a fair man and always looked at the bigger picture, but could the stigma attached to Anderson's misconduct be the reason for Jack's animosity?

Agents had an unspoken code of honour and wouldn't hesitate to turn a fellow agent in if they knew he'd done something illegal. Did Jack have something on Anderson — something that would link him to criminal activity?

Mike shook his head. There was nothing in the files to support Jack's supposition that Anderson had anything to do with leaked information. He checked his watch, nine thirty- five. Jack would be calling shortly. He stood, and rubbed the back of his neck and rolled his head from side to side.

So Anderson was out. That left Bill Kennedy. Fifteen years into his twenty, he was marking time until retirement. Divorced twice, he'd been with the Miami office for seven years. Kennedy was by far the most serious bastard Mike had ever met. How many times had he looked into those steel coloured eyes and wondered what Kennedy was thinking? And how many times could he claim he knew? He used to tell himself that inscrutability was the mark of a good agent. But now Mike had other thoughts... had Kennedy been hiding something all this time?

The squad room was empty, the computers silent. Mike picked up his empty mug. On the way to the coffee machine he paused at Kennedy's desk. It looked as if the man had just moved in. There were no photographs, nothing of a personal nature to indicate whose workstation it was. He reached to open the top drawer, but, feeling like an intruder, withdrew. If he couldn't trust members of his own team, then Chrissie was right, it was past time for retirement.

The cell phone on his belt vibrated. His stomach growled as he propped a hip on the edge of the desk, reminding him of the casserole waiting for him at home.

'Zupanik.'

'Sir, this is Agent Baker from the computer forensics laboratory. That piece of paper with the numbers on, the one Agent Mancuso copied to me, I've finished running it through the computer and it turns out that it's an IBAN number.'

'A what?'

'An IBAN number - an International bank account number, used by the European Banks clearing system. IBAN numbers identify accounts at banks all over the world. They're used to speed up the transfer of funds.'

'That's fine, but can you identify the bank and country where the account is located?'

'Yeah, I can. The twenty four digits represent the country code, the clearing bank and the account number.'

'I don't need an explanation. Just tell me the name of the bank and the account number. You can put the rest of the details in an email.'

'The Suisse Bank, in Lausanne. Account number 0C1024502871CH.'

'Any news on the laptop or notebook?'

'Cryptology is still working on the notebook. As for the laptop, the hard drive has been re-formatted.'

'You can't salvage anything?'

'When you format a hard drive, the software writes over the previously stored data. We've been able to reconstruct a virtual drive and re-create some of the files.

Most of them are connected with Elliott's accountancy clients, but three are encrypted. We're working on those.'

'Thanks for the update Agent Baker. Keep me informed.'

'One more thing—'

'Yeah?'

'Agent Mancuso sent us some videotapes from Miami International. We managed to enhance the pictures and pull off a picture of a woman who looks like she was travelling with your guy. She appears twice; once chatting to Elliott as they wait in line at immigration, and later walking through the terminal building. Homeland Security is trying to match her face to a name and passport, and trace her seat allocation with the airline. In the meantime, I'm faxing over some still shots.'

'As soon as you get a positive ID let me know.'

Mike cut the connection. Finally, they were getting somewhere. The fax machine in the corner of the office buzzed and whirled into life. Slowly, the image of a woman appeared. He lifted it off the tray and stared at the grainy photograph. Apart from her shoulder length blonde hair, her features and eye colour were indistinct. He swore and wished that airports would replace the videotapes in their security cameras more often instead of re-using them.

He started to punch in Jack's cell phone number then thought the better of it. This information he would deliver in person.

Back in his office, he returned the files to the safe and locked it, then picked up his briefcase and turned out the lights. Twenty minutes later, he turned into the drive of his home.

Lights showed through the gap in the curtains covering the large bay window of the family room. Mike climbed out of the car and rubbed the left side of his chest, just below the ribcage. His ulcer was playing up again, and he hoped Chrissie had gone easy with the peppers in the casserole.

He always enjoyed coming home. No matter how badly the day had gone, Chrissie always welcomed him with a smile and a hug. He unlocked the door and stepped inside. The house was silent. He stood his briefcase on the hall table. Chrissie's Cairn terrier, Briar, came running up to greet him, jumping up at his side for a pat and tummy rub.

'In the kitchen,' Chrissie called.

Mike ruffled the small dog's head then went in. Chrissie sat at the counter drinking her customary bedtime cup of hot chocolate. He planted a kiss on her cheek.

'Sorry for being late.'

Chrissie stood, and took the casserole out of the fridge.

'You're never home on time, Mike. It comes with the job, something I accepted years ago. I just wish you'd been around more when the kids were growing up.'

Mike sighed. They'd had this argument almost weekly for the last thirty-one years. 'I know. At least I can do right by David and Angie.' He watched his wife spoon casserole on to a plate and cover it with film. The burning sensation in his chest hit a new high. His breath caught and he winced.

'You get off to bed, I'll see to that,' he said taking the plate from her hand.

'You're sure?'

'I know how to work the microwave. Go on, I'll be up in a minute.' He kissed her cheek and waited until she left the room, then took the jug of milk out of the fridge and poured some into a glass. The cold liquid soothed the burning in his stomach. He drained the glass and went back for a refill.

Pain, unlike anything he'd experienced before, tightened like a vice around his heart, and pulsated down his left arm. The glass slipped from his grasp spilling its contents on the floor. Sweat popped on his brow; the room spun. Nausea rose in his throat as he struggled to breathe.

He staggered across the room into the hallway. His outstretched hand gripped the banister, but the effort was too much. His semi-conscious body slumped to the floor; his wife's name an unspoken whisper on his lips.

CHAPTER TWENTY-FOUR

Grace woke with a rush of adrenaline. Muffled sounds came from downstairs. Wide-awake, she lay still, hardly daring to breathe. A rustle from the other side of the bed told her that Jack had heard the noise too.

His lips brushed her ear. 'Stay here,' he breathed, and reached for the gun he'd left on the bedside table. 'I'll check out the house. Call Anderson — speed dial two on my cell phone — and tell him we have an intruder.'

Grace bit back her scream, and watched him pull on his jeans. She wanted to protest, but knew she wouldn't win the argument, so merely nodded her agreement.

Semi-naked, Jack flipped the safety off his weapon, then crossed silently to the closed bedroom door and listened.

Another muffled thump came from below.

Sweat slid down his spine. His pulse kicked. He opened the bedroom door a mere inch and peered out. The light in the hall was on.

He hadn't left it that way.

Jack weighed up the risk of staying put versus facing the intruder and decided he didn't like the odds either way. He glanced briefly over his shoulder. Grace sat on the side of the bed, her arms folded across her chest, her breathing ragged. He gesticulated toward the bathroom, hoping she'd take the hint and lock herself in, do anything except sit there waiting for whatever fate would befall them.

He put his ear to the door once more.

Silence.

He opened it a fraction. When no one slammed it into his face, he stepped onto the landing. His fingers tightened around the stock of his gun. He leaned over the banister and peered down into the hallway below.

Empty.

Keeping his back to the wall, he crept down the stairs. The marble floor tiles felt ice cold under his feet as he moved stealthily through the hall to the kitchen. Another muted noise came from inside. His heart rate picked up, sharpening his senses.

The door was ajar, a thin ribbon of light showed through the crack. A suitcase stood on the floor next to the counter. He rammed into the door with the full weight of his body. 'FBI,' he shouted. 'Don't move!'

The woman stood next to the sink screamed. The glass slipped from her fingers, and shattered into vicious shards.

'Keep your hands where I can see them, and turn around slowly.'

For a long moment, Jack stared at her. Slender, and of medium height, with wavy blonde hair and brown eyes, she held her hands out by her side. As he approached, she lifted her chin, and boldly met his gaze.

'Let's see some identification,' he ordered.

The woman stiffened at the challenge. 'In my purse on the table. I'm—'

Grace appeared in the doorway, eyes and mouth wide open. 'Catherine? Catherine! Oh, thank God!' She rushed forward and seized her sister in a shuddering embrace. 'I've been worried sick. Didn't you receive any of my messages? How did you know where to find me?'

Catherine almost sobbed with relief, hating herself for being pleased to see her sister.

Jack put his gun on safety and tucked it into the waistband of his jeans. 'I'd still like to know how you got in here.'

Catherine turned her mind over and over, struggling to remember the name of her sister's friend, the one Grace always confided in.

'Olivia,' she said at last. 'I phoned Olivia and she told me you were here.'

'Then you know about Daniel,' Grace said, her face sombre.

There was silence, during which Catherine sucked in a breath. Every nerve in her body erupted with spasms of alarm. Something was wrong. Horribly wrong. She jerked free of her sister's arms and gripped the edge of the counter for support.

'What... what about Daniel?'

'You'd better sit down, Cat,' Grace said, using her sister's childhood nickname.

'I don't need to sit down. Just tell me what you mean.'

'There's no easy way to say this — Daniel's dead.'

'Oh, God, no! No! You're lying. It's not true.' Catherine covered her face with her hands. Her heart was beating too fast, making her head spin, her skin damp. She would have fallen had it not been for the counter supporting her back.

'Daniel's fit, healthy, and young. He can't be dead. Why are you saying this?'

'Because it's the truth.'

Catherine's brown eyes showed the tortured dullness of disbelief. She sank to her knees. 'H-how did it happen?'

Grace slid a supporting arm around her sister's shoulders and helped her to her feet. Catherine staggered across the room to the table, and flopped down in a chair. Nausea churned in her throat, tears streamed down her face.

'Jack, fetch the brandy,' said Grace.

Jack thrust a glass into Catherine's hands. She tossed it back and held it out for a refill.

Grace handed her sister a tissue and waited for her sobs to subside, then explained how Daniel had died.

Jack leaned against the kitchen counter, and watched the interaction between the two sisters.

When Grace finished speaking, Catherine dug into her purse for her cigarettes. Her hand shook as she struck the match. She drew in smoke, the nicotine made her lightheaded, adding to the side effects of the drug she'd taken hours before. Confused, she struggled to concentrate.

'Dear God.' Catherine blinked hard and gulped, fighting the tears. She lifted a hand to her sister's cheek. 'I'm so sorry. I'm so sorry I was away at a sales conference when you needed me most.'

Grace squeezed Catherine's hand. 'You're here now, that's all that matters. Hearing about Daniel's death like this must be a shock. I know you loved him too.'

A quick glimpse at Grace's dishevelled state and heightened colour made Catherine think there was more to her sister's relationship with Jack. Maybe, just maybe she could turn that to her advantage. She drew a long breath and chose her words carefully.

'I can't believe my brother-in-law was some sort of criminal. He provided a home for me after Mum and Dad died. He paid for my education, taught me to drive. He paid attention to me. Yet the man you describe, he seems so alien, so different, to the Daniel I knew.'

'He deceived us both. Did you know he kept a mistress?'

The blood siphoned from Catherine's face. 'I—Are you sure?'

Jack and Grace looked at each other.

'Yeah, we're sure,' Jack said.

A muscle flicked at Catherine's jaw. She bowed her head and swallowed hard. Jack's eyes seemed to bore right through her. 'Do you have any idea who she is?'

'We're working on it.'

Catherine ignored Jack and looked directly at her sister.

'The son of a bitch. You must be devastated, poor darling.'

Grace ran a hand through her hair. 'Not any longer. Now, I just hate Daniel for all the lies he told.'

'At least he left you this fabulous house.'

Jack's dark eyebrows rose. 'How do you know that?'

'Which thing do you mean,' asked Catherine, 'that it's fabulous or that it now belongs to Grace?'

The right corner of his mouth tilted up. He'd met some confident liars in his time, and this woman was right up there with the best.

'That it belongs to Grace.'

'Olivia told me.'

'This conference you were at… where was it?'

'Rome. Why?'

'Grace was pretty messed up that she couldn't find you. How long were you there?'

Catherine's eyes narrowed. 'Five days. I played host to a group of consultant surgeons. I can give you their names and the addresses of the hospitals where they work, if you want.'

'Maybe later. After the conference ended, then what did you do?'

Grace whirled round to stare at Jack. 'Stop this! Catherine hasn't done anything wrong.'

'Two people connected with Daniel are in the morgue. Someone tried to kill us last night. Next time they might succeed. I think that gives me the right to ask your sister a few questions.'

'It's all right, Grace.' Catherine rested a hand on her sister's arm and then turned to face Jack. 'I had some leave due, so I stayed on for a few days. Do you have a problem with that?'

'No, but that doesn't explain why you didn't return any of Grace's calls.'

Sudden anger flashed in Catherine's brown eyes. 'My cell phone was stolen, along with my purse.'

'Which would also contain your passport. In that case, how did you get here?'

Catherine's features remained composed. 'I went to the British Embassy. They replaced my passport and organized a flight back to London. When Olivia told me Grace was here, I got on the first available plane.'

'That still doesn't explain how you got in the house.'

'Well, obviously I didn't break in. And as I don't have a key—'

Jack held her gaze. 'Nothing is obvious. All the doors were locked.'

Catherine's brown eyes glared up at her inquisitor. 'Are you implying I'm lying?'

'That's enough, Jack. Catherine isn't a suspect,' Grace said, and turned to her sister. 'You must be tired. Come on upstairs. I'll show you where the guest room is.'

Jack watched the two women leave the room arm-in-arm. He glanced at his watch — close to midnight. With any luck, Mike might still be awake. He tapped in the number and waited for his SAC to pick up the call. Surprised when no one answered, he cut the connection and dialled Agent Diego's cell phone instead.

'Jack West,' he said when Diego answered. 'Sorry for the late call, but Mike's not picking up and this is—'

'Mike had a heart attack. He's in a critical condition.'

Jack's hand tightened on the phone. 'Jesus. Which hospital is he in, Diego?'

'Jackson Memorial. Chrissie found him slumped in the hallway. It doesn't look good, Jack. If he can get through the next twenty-four hours then he's in with a chance.'

'I'll be there as soon as I can.'

'There's nothing you can do, Jack. And if he were able, Mike would tell you to continue with the investigation. I'll let you know as soon as there's any change in his condition.'

Deep down Jack knew Diego was right, but it still cut to the bone. 'In that case, can you run a background check on Catherine Peterson — thirty, Caucasian, five feet ten, with brown eyes? She's a British Citizen, so you'll need to contact our friends across the pond. I want to know her movements for the last three weeks, and in particular whether her passport has passed through Immigration anywhere on the east coast. Oh, and check out her employers, Ross Pharmaceuticals. She's one of their sales representatives.'

'What's her connection to Elliott?'

'She's Grace's sister. Turned up at Sand Dollars an hour ago. Walked straight in; claims the front door was unlocked. She spun some story about losing her cell phone and passport while chaperoning a group of surgeons at a conference in Rome. So check with the British Embassy there and see if they issued her with a replacement.'

'Anything else?'

'Yeah, compare her photograph to the videotapes from the airport to see if she matches any of the women who arrived on the same flights as Elliott.'

Diego made a strangled sound. 'Do you have any idea how many women were on those flights?'

'Just do it.' Jack interrupted. 'And make sure you keep me posted on Mike's status.'

Jack cut the connection before Diego could tell him what he thought.

CHAPTER TWENTY-FIVE

'If Daniel's death was an accident, how did the FBI become involved?' Catherine asked as she and Grace climbed the stairs.

'I asked Jack for his help. He took me to meet Mike, his boss, after we'd been to see Daniel's attorney in Miami. Mike decided to investigate.'

'So you've known Jack for a while?'

'We met earlier this year.'

'That was lucky. Are you two involved?'

Grace stopped and turned to face her sister. 'No, we aren't. And, no we weren't. Unlike Daniel I kept my wedding vows. Jack and I were… are good friends.'

'No need to get defensive. What will happen when the FBI finishes its investigation? Will you be allowed to keep the house?'

Grace tried to ignore the curiosity in her sister's glance and took another step. 'It's complicated. I may not have any choice but to hand it over.'

'But if Daniel left it to you in his will, then surely it belongs to you.'

'Not if the money used to purchase it was obtained illegally. Besides, I'm not sure I want it.'

'Good grief, Grace. You can't just give a house like this away! I mean, prime beach front location; it must be worth a packet.'

'It probably is. But I could never be comfortable living here knowing Daniel scammed countless people out of their money. Besides, Jack believes that Daniel planned to divorce me and change his will in favour of his mistress.'

Catherine tripped on a stair and staggered onto the next. Regaining her balance, she asked, 'And… and do you believe him?'

'It makes sense when you consider that Daniel bought this house without my knowledge.'

'Perhaps he wanted to surprise you,' Catherine suggested.

Grace laughed. 'Oh, he did that all right. When a man buys his wife a new house, he doesn't usually install his mistress in it first.'

Catherine managed a choking laugh. 'I guess not. Even so, it is stunning. There are what, four or five bedrooms?'

'Four. The master suite and room I'm in overlook the beach. The other two are on the side of the house. You can have one of those.'

Grace turned right at the top of the stairs. As they passed the first door, Catherine pushed it open and stepped inside. Clothes and shoes were scattered everywhere — on the king-sized bed, the pale blue carpet and dainty dressing table chair.

'My God. What happened here?' she asked, stunned and sickened at the sight of a delicate peach silk and lace teddy that had been torn in two.

Grace's cheeks burned in remembrance. 'It's Daniel's room. The one he shared with his mistress. I felt so betrayed when I found her clothes, I couldn't control my anger. I'll get some sacks tomorrow and clear up the mess.'

'You can't just throw everything away,' Catherine said, plucking a silk Missoni jacket off the floor and placing it with infinite care on the bed.

'I don't want them. Do you have any idea how I felt finding her clothes here?'

'It can't have been easy. But at least let me look through them first. I mean, these are all designer labels, and too small for you. Why, these shoes are Jimmy Choo's and just my size. There are thousands of dollars worth here.' Catherine held a sapphire blue cocktail dress against her body and paraded in front of the mirror.

'Thousands of ill-gotten dollars.'

Catherine continued to admire herself, smoothing creases out of the fabric.

'You don't know that for sure.'

Grace stared at her sister, a vague memory floating in the back of her mind. She snatched the dress out of her sister's hands and threw it down on the floor.

'How else did Daniel pay for this house? And where do you think the money in the Miami bank account came from, Disneyland?' she yelled.

Catherine stiffened in shock. 'He left you money too?'

'Whether he intended to leave it to me or not doesn't matter. The question is where did he get two million dollars? He certainly didn't earn it.'

'Two million? Jeez, I had no idea he'd siphoned off so much.'

Sudden anger lit Grace's eyes. 'It's nothing to be proud of. After all, he was your brother-in-law. This way, your room is down the hall.' Frowning, she ushered her sister out of the master suite and along the hallway.

'Two million, plus this house; no wonder Jack's sniffing round you like a dog on heat.'

Grace thrust open the door to the guest room. It slammed against the wall, denting in the plasterwork.

'You've not listened to a word I've said. I don't want the house or the money. And Jack is not 'sniffing round' as you put it. He's doing his job.'

'Great speech,' Catherine said, and flopped down on the bed, 'pity I don't believe the bit about Jack. Use your imagination for once, and think of the life you could have with all that cash. I'm telling you, Gracie, if I was in your position, I'd take the money and run.'

Weariness swamped Grace. Her shoulders sagged.

'If I keep the money it makes me a thief, just like Daniel. I won't stoop to his standards.'

'You always have to do the right thing, don't you? God, you must have driven Daniel mad. No wonder he lost control of his car and slammed into a tree.'

Grace balled her fists, fighting the urge to strike her sister. 'How—how dare you! Daniel and I loved each other. We had a good marriage.'

'Really? Then why did he need a mistress? Daniel was too good for you, Grace. He was dynamic; he should have married someone more outgoing, someone—'

'More like you?'

Heat suffused Catherine's cheeks. She paused to catch her breath. She had to stay calm.

'I'm sorry. I shouldn't have said that.'

'No you shouldn't have!'

'I said I'm sorry. Forgive me, please?'

Grace ran a hand through her hair. 'Why did you come here, Cat?'

'I was concerned. I thought you might welcome my support.' Catherine stood and wrapped her arms around her sister.

Grace shoved her away. 'I needed your support the day Daniel died, not three weeks after. And especially not after you've spewed all that bile!'

'I already told you, I'm sorry I said that stuff. I'm sorry I didn't get your message. I'm even sorry my phone was stolen.'

'You really expect me to believe that when you're so dependent on a cell phone? You of all people would have had a replacement within hours.'

Baffled, Catherine stared at Grace. She'd changed. In the past Grace had done everything to avoid confrontation, but here she was fighting back.

'What is this, an inquisition?'

'Daniel's been dead for nearly a month. You've accounted for two weeks. What were you doing the rest of the time?'

'Sorry, big sister. I don't have to report to you anymore.'

'I guess not. But you have unconscionable gall coming to my house — yes, that's right: my house — and speaking to me like this. And you better have some answers ready for Jack, because I guarantee he'll check everything you've said is true.'

'I came here to help you and you treat me as if—'

'I'm treating you as if you're cruel and selfish and as if your sister means nothing to you. I'm also trying to understand why it wasn't important to you to return my calls.'

Catherine drew a long breath and yawned.

'Look, we've both said things we don't mean tonight. You're tired; I'm tired. Let's let bygones be bygones and stop fighting like children. Then we can catch up properly in the morning like two long lost sisters should. All right?'

Grace paused at the door. 'What name did Olivia and Tom give their baby?'

Catherine's mind spun. 'Well. I... I never thought to ask.'

'You didn't think to ask?'

'Oh come on, Gracie. Give it a rest. We only spoke for a few moments, just long enough for her to tell me you were here.'

Grace scowled at her. Maybe it was the light. Maybe it was the time. Maybe it was Florida and Jack and Daniel's death and the house and all the things she never wanted conspiring against her thought processes. Catherine was a stranger to her tonight. Maybe she'd always been a stranger. Grace regarded her for a long moment, looking for bits of the freckled little girl she'd nearly raised, the college student she'd supported, the eager young career woman she'd cheered on. Nothing of them remained in the flinty gaze that met her own.

'Never mind,' she said sternly. 'I'll call Olivia myself in the morning. I'm sure she'll have plenty to say. Goodnight.'

CHAPTER TWENTY-SIX

Bill Kennedy squeezed his barrel-chested, six-foot frame into an empty booth at the back of the all night diner and ordered a black coffee. The bored looking redhead who waited on him was clearly counting the minutes until her shift ended so she could close up for the night.

The place wasn't to his liking. Whoever owned it was a cheapskate. Half-burned out fluorescent lights buzzed overhead. Tears in the old red plastic seats, tables partially cleaned, it was clearly a hangout for truckers and a few tourists desperate to use the bathroom. Only one other booth was occupied. A couple of truckers sat drinking coffee, presumably before spending the night in their rigs in a dark corner of the parking lot.

The glass door opened and a short, stocky man in a trench coat, limped inside and down the aisle to the booth at the rear of the diner. He wiped the seat with a paper napkin from the dispenser on the table before sliding into the booth opposite Kennedy. He grimaced when his left knee struck the table leg, and shifted into a more comfortable position.

Kennedy gestured at the coat. 'Kind of warm for these parts, isn't it?'

'I can't get used to your weather,' the little man coughed. 'I don't know how you stomach it.'

Kennedy nodded. 'Doesn't matter. You made good time.' In the background the two truckers argued over the quickest route to Miami, the I-75 or the Tamiami trail.

'You said it was urgent.'

'It is,' Kennedy replied.

The man grunted and waited while the waitress slapped two mugs of coffee down on the chipped Formica table, and then shuffled back to the counter. He took a swallow, grimaced, and pushed the mug aside.

'If this is so urgent,' the stocky man said, 'then how come you had to drag me all the way out here? I've got people to see, things to do.'

Kennedy raised an eyebrow. 'A girl, no doubt.'

The other man shrugged. 'What's so important that you couldn't tell me over the phone?'

'I've found the woman you were asking about.'

The stranger picked up a knife and ran the blade under his fingernails. 'And?'

'She turned up at Sand Dollars a couple of hours ago.' The waitress re-appeared at the table. Kennedy waved her away.

'My information alone has to be worth at least five grand.'

'Five grand,' said the little man evenly. 'So, both sisters are at the house, along with West. How many other agents are present?'

'Me and one other.'

'Armed?'

Kennedy glared at the man. 'What do you think?'

'I'm guessing standard issue Glocks. What about the house?'

Kennedy straightened his back. 'The doors and windows are fitted with an alarm. Control panel is just inside the door.'

'Can you get the code?'

'You don't need it.'

The stranger's mouth took on an unpleasant twist. 'What about the local cops?'

Kennedy laughed. 'Predictable. They do a drive by every hour, on the hour.'

'Anything else I should know?'

'The security lights surrounding the house are on sensors and light up when anything larger than a cat passes by. Tell me when you plan on visiting and I'll make sure they're de-activated.'

'Very well. I'll arrange for five thousand—'

'My fee's just doubled,' hissed Kennedy.

'—to be transferred to your account in the morning.'

Kennedy shook his head. 'Ten thousand. Five's not enough.

'Still the greedy one, aren't you, Mr Kennedy?'

'Think of it as an investment. I'm the one who's taking all the risk. You'll make a lot more than that, if you pull this off.'

'You mean when I pull it off, which I will do whether or not you are involved in the enterprise.' The stranger leaned forward and motioned for Kennedy to do the same. 'If you'd dealt with things properly in the first place none of this would be necessary,' he whispered conspiratorially. 'As it is, I've had to hire someone to clean up this mess. Five thousand, Mr Kennedy. Not a penny more. Take it, and be grateful you're still alive.'

Disgruntled, Kennedy eased his large frame out of the booth and headed for the door.

The stocky man remained seated, his gaze fixed on the retreating bulk of Kennedy as he crossed the parking lot to his car. He pulled a cell phone from his pocket and punched a number on his speed dial.

'The man getting into the Ford Taurus,' he said to Vasquez. 'Tall, overweight, blue jeans and a white sport shirt. Kill him.'

'That'll cost more,' Vasquez replied.

'Don't worry, you'll get paid.'

'When do you want it done?'

'Tonight, before he returns to the island. Make it bloody and brutal. I want the cops to think it's a revenge killing.'

'No problem.'

'When you're finished, call me. I have another job for you.' He snapped shut his phone and glanced at his watch — plenty of time to keep his next appointment. He slapped a ten-dollar bill down on the table. The bored waitress' eyes flew open in surprise. Before she could speak, he shuffled toward the exit, a satanic smile spreading across his thin lips.

Kennedy drove his Government Issue car out of the parking lot and headed west. Thirty seconds later a silver Ford Escape pulled in behind and followed the Taurus onto the highway.

He smiled, and thought about the addition to his retirement fund. Five thousand wasn't much, but small payments could easily be passed off as gambling wins and wouldn't draw the attention of the authorities.

He laughed out loud. Fifteen years chasing criminals, risking his life day and night, and what did he have to look forward to? A government pension that wouldn't keep his two ex-wives and daughter in shoes!

So he'd started his own pension scheme, one that would allow him to lead a comfortable life in whichever tax haven he chose. But he'd been careful, never jeopardizing the major cases; just a word in the right ear now and again ensured small, but regular payments into his account in the Cayman Islands. There was nothing like working the system, especially when you knew how.

A flash in the driver's mirror caught his attention. He straightened his shoulders and wondered what the asshole behind him was playing at. The lights flashed again. Kennedy swore. Perhaps he'd picked up a flat at the diner. He applied gentle pressure to the brake pedal, no point in ruining the tyre, and steered to the side of the road. The Ford pulled in behind.

Kennedy stuffed the keys of the Taurus into his jeans pocket and eased out of the car. As he bent down to examine the rear wheel, two feet appeared at his side. He looked up at the man standing next to him.

'What the—'

Two bullets slammed through his chest into his heart. He collapsed to the ground, shuddering, his last thoughts of his daughter, fearing, as the blackness took him away, that someone would tell her the truth about how he died.

CHAPTER TWENTY-SEVEN

Jack pushed his chair back from the table as Grace entered the kitchen.

'Pancakes or waffles for breakfast?' he asked, as he took eggs and milk out of the fridge.

'Neither thanks. I'll just have a bowl of cereal and a banana, and a cup of that delicious smelling coffee.'

Jack placed a mug under her nose, slid the jug of milk across the table, and sat down in the chair opposite.

'You and Catherine have an argument last night?'

Grace shrugged, and took a sip of coffee. 'Just the usual sisterly difference of opinion. I sometimes think I expect too much of her,' she said bitterly.

'How so?'

'I wish Cat was more dependable and considered her family, instead of always thinking of herself. Perhaps I shouldn't have indulged her so much after our parents died.'

'She was young. She had to grow up quickly.'

'That's the trouble. I don't think she did. Whatever she asked for, I gave her, but it was never enough. I never asked for anything in return. But it would have felt good if she'd put my needs above hers just for once.'

'Don't you believe the story about her cell phone being stolen?'

Her face clouded with uneasiness. The spoon paused halfway to her mouth. 'I'm not sure. A cell phone is like a fashion accessory to Cat. I just don't see her being without one for very long.'

Jack glanced at her pale cheeks and dark-ringed eyes, and wished he could scoop her up and take her some place far away. Instead, he settled for wrapping his arm around her shoulders and giving her a hug.

'From what I understand, Rome is a pickpocket's paradise. But yeah, it does seem odd that it took so long for her to get in touch with you.'

Suddenly, the door to the garden creaked open. Jack leapt to his feet and reached for his gun.

'Shit! What is wrong with you? Are you determined to get yourself killed, Anderson?' He slipped the gun into the holster at the small of his back.

'Sorry to disturb you, Jack, but I thought you should know Kennedy is missing. He asked me to cover part of his shift last night; said he was meeting an informant and would be back in a couple of hours. He never showed up.'

'And you waited until now to tell me?' Jack stared at Anderson. He'd never seen him so worried. There was nothing of his normal calm, easy-going manner.

'I followed protocol and kept the house under surveillance.'

'What the hell was Kennedy thinking following up a lead at that time of night? Have you tried his cell phone?'

Anderson looked down. 'It just runs to voicemail, so it's switched off or the battery's dead, or—'

'—Let's not go there right now,' Jack said, casting a glance in Grace's direction. 'Did he give any indication who this informant was or where they were meeting?'

'No. But he seemed jumpy, on edge.'

Jack blew out one long breath. This went against Kennedy's reputation for being ice-calm in any situation.

'Here's how we'll handle it. You get a trace put on his car. Could be he got tired and pulled off the road for a nap, so make sure they check the parking lots at the state parks.'

Anderson cleared his throat. 'You know, the night before Pete Jacobs died, a couple of residents saw a black Saab drive past Jacobs' office a few times. Unfortunately, none of them got details of the license plate. But one resident, an old guy with two poodles, recalls a young man in black, carrying a gym bag at around ten-thirty. He thought it was strange because the community centre gym closes at six. Then we got a report on a black Saab convertible being stolen from Miami airport that same afternoon.'

'Where is it now?'

'Abandoned the next morning in Tampa. You think there's a connection?'

Jack nodded slowly. 'Good work, Anderson. Contact the local cops; see if they managed to pull any prints off the Saab. Then get some rest.'

Anderson turned to leave. 'Okay. Any news on Mike's condition?'

Jack shook his head. 'Still in intensive care, last I heard.'

Anderson left, and Grace looked at Jack for a long moment. 'You think something bad has happened to Kennedy, don't you?'

Jack laid a hand on her shoulder. 'I won't lie to you, Grace. I think the bad guys are escalating their efforts, hoping to scare you into handing over the money. This is exactly why you should let me put you on a plane to Hawaii with a couple of muscle-bound bodyguards.'

Grace covered his hand with hers. 'We've been through this before. I'm not going anywhere, Jack. I will not be bullied by these people.'

'Not even if your life is in danger?'

'Daniel put me in danger the day he died. Maybe even before then, come to think of it. It doesn't mean I'm not afraid. I am. But I don't see that Kennedy's apparent disappearance makes any difference, do you?'

Jack's eyes narrowed. 'I could force you—'

Grace smiled thinly. 'But you won't, for the simple reason you'll be by my side twenty-four/seven.'

'You got that right.' He cupped his hands around her face and lowered his mouth gently to hers intending the kiss to be reassuring, but something primitive coursed through his veins. He deepened the kiss, his tongue tangling with hers, devouring its softness. He lifted his mouth from Grace's and smiled.

'How about we continue this upstairs?' He nuzzled her neck, tasting her skin. Then his phone rang.

'Are you going to answer that?' Grace mumbled.

'I'm trying to ignore it.'

'Is it working?'

'Unfortunately not,' he sighed. He snatched his cell phone off the table and examined the screen. 'It's Diego. I'll take this in the office.' He strode out of the room before answering the call.

'I checked with Homeland Security like you asked,' Diego said. 'Catherine Peterson passed through immigration at Atlanta three days ago. But get this: her passport is Irish, not British.'

The last of Jack's good humour vanished. 'You sure?'

'Absolutely. What's more, she used the same passport to rent a grey Chevy Aveo.'

'Can you fax over a copy?'

'Sure. Anything else?'

'Any luck with the video from the airport?'

'Yeah. The tech guys pulled an image off the tapes. They faxed a copy to Mike. Chrissie found it in his briefcase and handed it over this morning. I'll fax it, along with the passport. The number on the piece of paper - turns out it's a Swiss Bank Account. I've contacted the Swiss Authorities and asked them to investigate.'

'And speak to Cody at the First Apopka Bank. Elliott had an ATM card. It wasn't with the items returned to Grace. I want to know if it's been handed in or whether anyone tried to use it recently, and if so, where.'

'And there's another thing,' said Diego. 'The medical examiner finished the autopsy on the guy in the Everglades and managed to get pretty clear prints. We also pulled some prints off the pick-up he was driving. Forensics ran them through AFIS — the automated fingerprint identification system. We've got a match for a Hector Suárez.'

Jack's gut clenched. 'Suárez?'

'Yeah. His brother, Estefan is serving life for the murder of a rival gang member and drug trafficking. There are two other brothers and a sister, all of whom are known to us.'

'Shit. I worked on that task force.'

'He wouldn't be pleased to see you then, Jack.'

'Not likely.'

'But you think he's got nothing to do with this investigation?'

'Not a chance. Any news on the second autopsy on Elliott?'

'Nothing new so far.'

'Okay, Diego. Keep pushing the crime lab. I want to know the name of the woman who got off the plane with Elliott. In the meantime, Grace and I will pay a visit to Pete Jacob's secretary and see if we can access his files. Find out who owns that island.'

'You be careful, Jack. Stay alive. We count on you.'

'I'm not dying yet, Diego. I've got loads to live for. Just one of the many reasons you want to grow up to be just like me, right?'

The voice on the other end gave a dry chuckle. 'See you around, Jack. I'm counting on you.'

'Me too,' said Jack. Snapping the phone shut. Lost in thought, he stared out of the window at the trees swaying in the light breeze. He wasn't worried about the Suárez family or the fact that one of their number had chosen now to come after him. He was more concerned with the lies Catherine had told and what it would do to Grace when she found out.

Pain showed in his eyes and in the tight lines around his mouth. The fax machine in the corner whirled into life. The cover sheet informed him the contents were privileged information. He flipped the page. The tech guys had done their best to enhance the photo taken from the airport security cameras. Even so, the image was very poor quality. He folded the fax and tucked it into the back pocket of his jeans.

No time to waste.

Game on.

CHAPTER TWENTY-EIGHT

Catherine tossed her blonde hair out of her eyes, and padded over to the coffee machine. 'What time is it? My watch has stopped,' she asked, and helped herself to a cup of coffee.

'Eight-thirty.' Grace looked up from the slice of toast she was buttering. She arched an eyebrow, and skimmed her gaze over her sister. Her thin pink T-shirt clung to her curves and barely reached the top of her thighs.

'My God, is that all? My body clock must be really screwed. Where's Jack?'

'Right here,' he said, entering the kitchen.

Grace burned Catherine with a look that said aren't you the slightest bit ashamed of how you're dressed? Catherine missed the admonishment, or ignored it. Instead she smiled broadly at Jack, clearly inviting him to see what she wasn't wearing. She leaned back against the counter and crossed her long, shapely legs at the ankles.

'Don't mind me. Just carry on as if I'm not here.'

Grace buried her head in her hands. 'My God, Catherine...'

'What?' said her sister, feigning innocence. 'I was just saying good morning. What's wrong with that?'

'It's just — look at you — not what you're saying but how you're saying it.' She crumpled her napkin and turned away.

Jack laid a hand on her shoulder and addressed Catherine, his eyes never leaving Grace. 'Grace and I have to go out. Stay in the house, away from the windows.'

'What for?' said Catherine.

'There's an agent posted outside. You'll be quite safe.'

'You could at least tell me why. Anyway, it's a pity you're leaving. I was hoping you'd demonstrate the finer points of close protection to me.' She laughed, and slanted Jack another look from under her lashes.

'Thanks. But no.'

Catherine gave him a long smouldering look, then smirked. 'Your loss. But if you change your mind, you know where I am.'

Grace frowned. 'Stop it, Cat!' She collected the breakfast dishes and dropped them on the counter, smashing a plate in the process.

'I'm only kidding. You know that, right, Jack?'

Grace slammed her hand down on the table. 'You are not kidding and you don't give a damn about me, do you? I should have seen this before. I've been so blind.'

'Oh lighten up, sister dear. I'm just playing—'

'Life's one big joke to you, Cat. You don't understand how serious this situation is.'

'Oh for fuck's sake, Grace. I'm sick to death of your righteous sister act. Look, I'll be out of your way in a few days, and then you can go back to your boring life.' With that, she stomped out of the room.

Grace slumped against the counter, head bowed.

'Don't let her get to you,' Jack said.

'We used to be the best of friends years ago, but now — she's changed. I hardly know her anymore. I don't know her anymore.'

'She travels a lot. Even family can grow apart.'

'It's more than that, Jack. It's as if Cat's jealous, not that she has reason to be. After all, she fulfilled her dream to go to university and have a career, while I'm just a dreary housewife.'

His hand tightened over hers. 'No you're not. Catherine takes you for granted, which is a really shitty thing to do. Let it go for now, Grace. We have to get going. I want to have another chat with Jacobs' secretary.'

'You mean Mercy?'

'Yep. I need to see if I can get access to his files. We can't lose sight of our mission, Grace. I know you're upset — you have a right to be upset. Just not right now. Put it on a skyhook. Know what I mean?'

Grace died her eyes with her napkin and nodded. 'Sometimes, Mr West, you actually make sense.'

He grinned. 'I'll try not to make a habit of it.'

The drive into Boca Grande took less than five minutes. He turned off the ignition and looked across the sidewalk to the front door of Seaplane Charters.

'It doesn't look as if anyone is home,' Grace said.

'The office is at the back, remember?'

'And if Mercy's not there?'

'Then we'll ask around. Find out where she lives.'

'You can just ask? Won't people say no?'

'It's the way you ask,' Jack said as he got out and opened the passenger door for Grace. 'I can be very persuasive. Trust me.'

'I do.'

His hand rested lightly on her back. 'Ready?' he asked.

She smiled and nodded.

They walked around the back of the building. He turned the doorknob, but it was firmly locked. He rapped sharply on the wooden frame. A loud bang came from within followed by a curse. Jack tensed, ready to push Grace to one side. The rear door opened and Mercy slowly shuffled out.

'Hi, Mercy, may we come in?' said Jack.

'Hi, Mr West, Mrs Lattide. What can I do for you?'

'I'd like to ask you some questions,' he said showing her his ID card and shield.

Mercy's eyes widened. 'FBI? Why are you interested in Mr Jacobs?'

'Pete Jacobs' and Mr Lattide's death are somehow connected. I'd like to see Pete's flight logs.'

Mercy played with her hair. 'He was such a nice man. He didn't deserve to die like that.' She wiped her eyes. 'The files belong to Mr Jacob's wife now. I guess you could say she's still his wife. They had some problems. I don't know if I should even be saying that.'

Jack drew in a breath. 'Mercy, listen to me. I can get a court order, but that will take time. Three people are dead, including Jacobs. Do you really want to be responsible for putting more lives at risk?'

Mercy stiffened. 'Well, no of course not.' She glanced at Grace, her brown eyes full of sadness. 'Come on through to the office. Pete's filing system isn't what you'd call organized.'

Jack patted her forearm. 'Thanks, Mercy. You're doing the right thing.'

Jack and Grace followed her along the corridor to Jacobs' office. Two tall filing cabinets stood on the back wall opposite the large window that overlooked the bayou and Charlotte Harbor.

Jack tested the handle of the uppermost drawer. 'Locked. Can you get me the key?'

Mercy nodded and opened the top drawer of an old, battered desk and handed him a small key ring. 'The chrome key opens both cabinets. The brass one is for the safe, but there's nothing in there.'

'Thanks, Mercy. We'll take it from here. If we need anything more we'll come and find you.' She nodded and shuffled away, eyes cast down.

The drawers were full of loose papers. 'Mercy was right about the filing system. It looks as if Jacobs just tossed everything in.' He pulled out a sheaf of papers and spread them over the desk. 'See if you can find anything that mentions or corresponds to Elliott's visits to Sand Dollars.' He dumped the contents of the second drawer on the floor and crouched down, sifting through the documents.

'Do you really think Jacobs kept a record of the times he flew Daniel down to the island?' Grace asked.

Jack thought for a moment. 'The FAA requires all planes to file a flight plan. Jacobs had to comply otherwise he'd lose his pilot's licence.'

'Oh, I see,' said Grace. She started sorting papers into piles. 'These all seem to be credit card receipts going back for years, mainly for Avgas purchased at the marina and spare parts for the plane. Don't you think that's strange?'

'How?' Jack asked.

'Well most businesses set up an account for such thing as gas and servicing. You fill up at the pump, sign the receipt and then settle the account at the end of the month.'

'Jacobs clearly had bad credit. That being the case, I don't think he did any end-of-the-month account settling.'

'There's no excuse for how he kept his books.'

'You see, Grace. You're more talented than you know. You've got business sense.'

'I never thought about it before.'

'Well, start thinking about it,' he grinned. 'Your future will be whatever you make of it.'

After they'd finished going through the first cabinet, Jack leaned back and scowled. 'There's nothing here but letters from Jacobs' bank threatening foreclosure on his home and nastygrams from the state of Florida for failure to pay alimony and child support. So far he sounds like a prince. What have you got?'

'I've found the statement letter from his credit card company. He owed more than $150,000 and had exceeded his credit limit.'

Jack let out a long whistle. 'Looks like he was ten minutes away from bankruptcy. Why don't you go and see if you can talk Mercy into making us a pot of coffee while I try to put this shit away?'

Jack picked up stacks of paper and files and eased himself off the floor. As he began to shove the mess back into the cabinet drawer, he saw what he'd been looking for: a black leather-bound book.

Grace set a chipped mug of coffee on the desk and looked enquiringly at him.

'What did you find?'

'It's Jacobs' logbook. His real accounting system. Take a look at these entries.'

Grace rested a hand on Jack's shoulder. 'Why, those dates match two of Daniel's visits to Sand Dollars.'

'Yeah. And what's more, the destination is shown as Marathon Key. And there were two passengers.'

'Which means you were right; Daniel didn't travel alone.'

Jack thumbed through the logbook. There were a lot of empty gaps were Jacobs had either forgotten or been too lazy to fill it in.

'Look at this.' He held up a newspaper cutting.

'Oh, my God!' Grace paled. 'That's Daniel! And the guy standing next to him holding the fish is Parous.'

'Do you recognize the third man?'

She took the cutting from him and carried it to the window. 'I'm not sure. His face is turned away from the camera, but he looks like the man from the graveyard. I wonder which newspaper it's from.'

'Let's see if Mercy knows.'

Grace handed Jack the clipping and followed him through to the front office.

Mercy sat at the reception desk nervously fidgeting with the telephone cord.

'You could ask at the local paper. There's an office in town.'

'What about this guy,' Jack asked, 'the one turned sideways to the camera? Do you recognize him?'

Mercy shook her head. 'I'm sorry, Mr West. As I told you, I haven't worked here very long.'

'Never mind, Mercy. Thanks for trying.'

They both shook her hand and left.

The office of the local newspaper was situated up a narrow flight of stairs above a clothes store and staffed by one reporter and a receptionist. Jack strode up to the desk and showed his ID to the young woman with short, curly blonde hair.

'I'm trying to identify the man in this picture and I wondered if it was taken by your staff photographer and published by your newspaper.'

She frowned at the cutting. 'It's not one of ours.'

Jack chuckled in surprise. 'That was a pretty quick assessment. How can you be sure?'

'The name of the photographer is missing.' She pulled a copy of the current issue off the rack and pointed at a picture on the front page. 'See? The photographer's name appears under every photo, even if the picture's sent in by a reader.'

'Any idea when this picture might have been taken?'

'I'd guess during the annual Tarpon Tournament in July, but it's difficult to know for sure.'

Jack thanked her and he and Grace walked back to the car.

'Now what?' she asked.

'We go back to the house, grab a bite to eat, and see there's any news about Kennedy and Mike.'

CHAPTER TWENTY-NINE

'You want to make a start on lunch, while I call the hospital to see how Mike is?' Jack slipped the key into the lock and stepped aside to allow Grace to enter first, and closed the door behind them.

Grace dropped her purse on the table. 'Cat?' She called out from the hallway. 'We're back. Cat?' She turned to Jack. 'Surely, she can't still be in bed, can she?' She started to call out again when Jack put his hand on her arm.

'Leave her be, Grace. She's not worth your concern.'

Grace opened her mouth to defend her sister, but realized Jack was right. He was merely pointing out the truth. She let out a muted sigh.

'It hurts. After all I did for her; it hurts to know she cares only for herself.'

There was nothing Jack could say that would make Grace feel better, so he simply took her hand. He led her down the hall, through the family room at the back of the house and pushed open the door to the office.

'What the hell—'

Catherine stood in front of the open safe. She started to turn away, but wasn't fast enough. Jack's hand closed around her wrist and yanked her back.

'Looking for something?' he asked.

Catherine's lip trembled as she rubbed her wrist. 'It was like this when I came in, I swear.'

Jack shook his head. 'Bullshit! I checked the safe this morning and it was locked tight.'

Catherine's lips drew tightly across her teeth. 'It was open, Jack. You can't blame me for your own ineptitude. It was open and I was curious. Ask my loving sister. She'll tell you my curiosity is how I earned my nickname.'

'That much is true,' said Grace.

Jack pointed a finger at her. 'I couldn't care less if your curiosity got you the name of Snoopy. You're lying, just like you lied about your passport getting stolen.'

'You're crazy.' Catherine turned to her sister. 'You believe me, don't you, Gracie?'

Grace looked at her sister. Catherine's brittle, calculating stare bore into her. 'I'd like to hear your explanation before I decide.'

Catherine shrugged. 'Okay, so I'm lying after all. But I was curious. I thought it would be fun to see if I could open it. I spun the dial, it clicked a few times, and then just opened.'

Jack gave a slow handclap. 'Very good. Only I'm not buying. Was this what you were looking for?' He pulled Elliott's notebook out of his back pocket. He watched the play of emotions on Catherine's face.

'You don't honestly believe I'd steal from my own sister, do you?'

'I don't believe anything you say. Let's put the issue of the safe to one side for the moment. Care to explain how you came by an Irish passport?' He pulled a sheaf of papers out of his pocket and handed them to Grace. 'Diego faxed this to me yesterday. Recognize the woman in the photograph?'

Grace studied the photocopy of the passport. 'Catherine?'

'Okay,' she shouted. 'So I lied. Again. But it's no business of yours what passport I carry.'

'Forgery will earn you a prison sentence. So will murder and theft. You know what bothers me about your story? Grace left messages for you on both your home and cell phones, yet you ignored them. Weren't you the slightest bit interested to know what she wanted? Or did you know Elliott was dead and figured hiding out in Europe until things died down was your best bet?'

Catherine shifted uneasily from one foot to the other.

'I've told you—'

'You can tell me as many times as you want, lady, but it's still a raft of bullshit. I say we take a look in your purse to make sure.' He jerked her towards the door.

'Are you going to stand there and let him treat me like this?' Catherine cried out to Grace.

Grace folded her arms across her chest. 'You brought this on yourself, Cat. Just answer Jack's questions. And let's see what's in your purse.'

'All right. All right. I didn't lose my phone, but the bit about the conference was true.'

'Go on,' said Jack.

'I was supposed to meet Daniel at Heathrow. When Grace started leaving messages I thought she'd found out.'

'Found out that you and Daniel were having an affair?'

Catherine snickered. 'Aren't you the clever one, Jack? What gave me away?'

Grace paled. She'd wondered about it, but never imagined Catherine would say it, and with such complete disregard for her feelings.

'What gave you away?' asked Jack. 'Damned near everything. Your constant lies. Your appearance out of nowhere. Your inability to respond to your sister when she called you in shock and pain. Most of all, your lack of surprise when Grace told you about the Miami bank account, and the fact you knew where the safe was.'

Grace tilted her head back, furious with her sister, but most of all with herself for not seeing what had been happening right under her nose.

'The blue cocktail dress! I knew it was familiar — you wore it last Christmas. And the perfume I smelled on the fabric - it's the one you're wearing now. I knew cats on heat would take on any male, but your own sister's husband? How could you?'

Catherine shrugged. 'Just another reason they call me Cat,' she smiled.

'You heartless bitch!'

'Oh, come on, darling sister. It was easy. Who do you think got you tickets for Wimbledon? Me! And all those conferences Daniel told you he was attending? In reality, he was actually spending time with me here at Sand Dollars. He had a nickname for you. He called you his little nun!' She turned to Jack. 'What does that tell you about what she's like in bed?'

'You... vulgar... whore.' Grace's hand shot out and cracked across Catherine's face.

Stunned, Catherine lifted her hand to her reddened cheek. 'My God... Grace! You've never struck me before.'

'Whose idea was the scam — yours or Elliott's?' Jack asked.

'Why, Daniel's of course,' said Catherine, hand still to her cheek. 'He did it all, you know. Every bit of it was his fault.'

'I don't believe you,' screamed Grace, eyes puffy with tears, shaking her fists in front of Catherine's face. 'Daniel wasn't like that.'

'How do you know, Gracie? You never knew the man. Daniel liked money, but he had no ambition. I introduced him to Salazar, who was looking for an accountant, someone who was prepared to bend the rules and not ask too many questions.'

Jack crossed his arms. 'How'd you meet this Salazar?'

'At a nightclub. I was with a group of other pharmaceutical reps. He said his wife was dying and he'd heard about this new drug my employers had developed, but his doctor wouldn't prescribe it. I felt sorry for him, so I got some for him.'

'Which he copied in his factory along with the other drugs you supplied to him, and no doubt helped sell.'

Catherine ignored Jack 'Daniel transferred Salazar's money around Europe and the U.S. He started skimming some off for himself, just small amounts at first, but then he got greedy. He bought this house and we were going to live here.'

'But there was just the small matter of his wife.'

'She was an inconvenience. He never loved you, Grace. Not for a single minute. In fact, he made me get stuff to poison you with. Yes, that's right. He wanted you to die, darling Gracie. I begged him to divorce you. But no, he wanted you dead. That's how he felt about you, sweetie. I defended you. You're my sister and I wouldn't let him kill you.'

'Shut up, Catherine! I don't believe a word you've said.'

'I don't believe you either,' said Jack. 'You've been in non-stop lying mode since you got here.'

'Believe what you like. I talked him into making arrangements for both of us — in case anything happened to him before we had chance to put his plans into action. He eventually listened to me, he left you pretty well off, I must say.'

'You told him to make arrangements?' said Jack. 'Now why would you do something like that unless you planned his death?'

'Oh, shove it, West. I loved him. I loved my sister more. I had no idea he'd go and die on all of us… and he wasn't supposed to leave her my house!'

Jack grimaced. 'Keep going. You're digging yourself a pretty efficient hole. What happened to him? How did he die?'

'I'm telling you the truth, Jack. I honestly don't know. When he didn't meet me at the airport, I went to work as normal, expecting him to call me later in the day. When he didn't—'

'You packed your bags and ran.'

'The rep who was supposed to attend the conference called in sick. I was asked to go in his place.'

Grace stared at her sister in disgust. 'What will happen to her now?'

Jack's eyes narrowed. 'That'll be up to the judge to decide, but she's looking at a lengthy prison sentence.'

Catherine shoved Grace hard, knocking her sideways into Jack and dashed down the hall. Within seconds she was out of the house and heading for the sand dunes.

CHAPTER THIRTY

'Grace! Wait' shouted Jack, but it was too late. Grace sped after her sister through the garden. He cursed and took off after her, but tripped over the roots of the Banyan tree by the side of the gate and crashed to his knees. He climbed to his feet and caught sight of Grace as she disappeared through the Sea Grape towards the picnic tables on the beach.

A late afternoon rainstorm had drifted in from the gulf, sending sun worshipers and tourists scurrying indoors. Water trickled down Jack's neck and by the time he reached the picnic tables his shirt was plastered to his back. He ignored the discomfort and the waves crashing on the beach, and concentrated on following Grace and her sister.

A lone black BMW sat in the corner of the parking lot adjacent to the state park. Its single occupant clearly visible through the rain splattered windshield. Jack was so furious with Grace that he didn't notice the door open.

'That's far enough, Agent West.' A short, stocky man climbed out, and pointed a heavy revolver at the centre of Jack's chest. 'Drop your weapon. I don't wish to kill you. At least not yet.'

Jack took his gun out of the holder and placed it on the ground in front of him, then slowly raised his arms. 'What do you want, Salazar?'

'I see you know who I am,' He pocketed Jack's gun and patted him down.

'Yeah, Catherine told me what you do for a living.'

'Then you know I've come for my money and the disks.'

'Can't help you, man. Besides, I have to meet someone.' His eyes focused on the grey swelling sea.

Salazar came closer. 'You mean the lovely Mrs Elliott and her equally beautiful sister? I'm afraid that's not a possibility. They met one of my associates along the way while they were out for what appears to be an afternoon run.'

Jack's eyes flickered. 'Where are they?'

'They're safe. Come, I will show you.'

Salazar dug the barrel of his gun into Jack's ribs. 'If you don't let me show you, Agent West, I'm likely to put a large hole right here.'

'I wouldn't want that,' said Jack flatly. 'I just bought this shirt. I wouldn't be able to take it back to Nordstom's.'

'You're every bit as droll as I was led to believe. Let's go see your lady friends, shall we?'

They walked slowly towards the tall white, hexagonal structure of the range light.

Salazar swung the door open, and shoved Jack inside. Weak strands of light from a mottled window thirty feet above his head cast yellowed shadows over the floor.

Grace and Catherine were hunched together on the bottom step of the narrow spiral staircase leading to the lantern room and gallery at the top of the hundred and five foot tower. A thin, wiry man stood guard over them.

Salazar nodded to Catherine. 'Start climbing. You go next, Vasquez.'

Grace was about to scream when Vasquez bent down and shoved her into the corner. She let go a hissing sound as her head connected with the steel wall.

'Bastard!' shouted Jack. 'When I get free, you better—'

'I better what, Agent West? Don't you see how powerless you are?'

Salazar reached over to Catherine and yanked her to her feet. He looked in her in the eye for a long moment. She lifted her head defiantly and, with a smirk, spit into Salazar's left eye. He lost his balance, wiping his eye with his free hand. Then clucking softly in disapproval, he slapped her hard and slammed her against the wall. A low tortured sob escaped her lips and she rubbed her head.

'Let go of my sister,' howled Grace, still dizzy. A trickle of blood flowed down her forehead. 'Let her go, damn you!'

'Of course,' said Salazar. He released his grip on Catherine. She sagged for a moment then Vasquez encircled her neck with his left arm, and forced her up the stairs.

'Now you, Mrs Elliott.'

She looked at Jack, eyes filled with darkness and terror.

'Do as he says, Grace. You're worth more alive than dead to him,' said Jack.

'Take Agent West's advice, Mrs Elliott. If you do not — I'll kill him. With pleasure.'

Grace started to climb, each unsteady step clanging on the metal staircase. 'It's me you want. Let them go.'

'Very touching. But I'm afraid it's too late.'

Catherine stumbled and lurched, and fell head first onto the tread above. Blood trickled from the corner of her mouth onto her T-shirt. Vasquez grabbed a handful of hair and yanked her to her feet. She screamed—the sound reverberating off the steel tower.

'Make him stop!' shrieked Grace. 'Make him stop hurting her.'

'Ah, sisterly love. What a pity Catherine doesn't feel the same way about you, Mrs Elliott.'

'That's enough, Salazar,' Jack growled. 'Call off your gorilla. There's no point hurting them. They don't know anything.' Salazar gouged him in the back with his revolver. Jack groaned in pain. 'And among other sins, you killed Kennedy. Didn't you? Why?'

Salazar shrugged. 'He got greedy. It's quite all right for me to be greedy, Agent West, but not those I hire. So it was a case of bang-bang, bye-bye. Yes. I think that sums it up quite nicely.'

Jack's muscles tensed. Above him, one of the women whimpered loudly. There was another clanging sound. Grace? He had to stay focused. 'What about Anderson?'

'Let's say he won't be coming to your aid anytime soon. He met Vasquez.'

Another muffled cry. Jack couldn't tell if it was Grace or Catherine. He looked into Salazar's empty eyes and searched for a crack in the armour.

'You've got a pretty slick operation, Salazar. It's just too bad you picked the wrong man to launder your money. When did you realize Elliott was skimming cash from your accounts?'

Salazar sighed and shook his head. 'Two months ago. When I asked him about the losses, he blamed the fluctuations in currency exchange rates. At first I believed him, but the sums involved were too large and the losses too regular.'

'So you had him killed.'

Salazar's tongue darted over his lips. 'A large dose of barbiturates slipped into a lunchtime curry ensured that he fell asleep behind the wheel.'

'Let me guess. That lawyer, Parous set up the dummy corporations and bank accounts, and told you about Elliott buying Sand Dollars. And Jacobs flew the counterfeit drugs into the U.S., right?'

Salazar frowned. 'Not even your DEA pays much attention to a seaplane flying between the Barrier islands and mainland.'

Once inside the small lantern room at the top of the tower, Jack studied Salazar. He was breathless and sweaty, but the gun in his hand was rock steady. He mopped his brow with a handkerchief.

'What's the matter, old boy, miss a few aerobics classes?'

'Laugh all you like, Agent West. These are your last few moments on this earth.'

'So tell me, what's in the computer files? Come on, Salazar. You've got the gun and you're going to kill me anyway, so what's the harm? Besides, confession's good for the soul, or so they say.'

Salazar gave a grunt of a laugh. 'I'd heard you had a sense of humour even in dire situations. My sources were not wrong. Very well, records showing the movement of funds from one offshore account to another.'

Salazar levelled his gun at Catherine's pale and bloody face. 'So now my story is done. Give me the disks, Mrs Elliott, or your darling sister dies.'

'Give them to him, Grace,' Catherine whispered hoarsely. 'You can't let him do this to me!'

'I can't,' said Grace, drawing a shaky breath. 'I don't have them.'

'What do you mean?' wailed Catherine. 'Save me, God damn you! He's got a gun in my face!'

'I really don't have them,' Grace stuttered. 'They… they must have been destroyed when Daniel's car caught fire.'

'You're lying!' Salazar yelled, enraged. The gun shook in his hand. Catherine whimpered.

'She's telling the truth,' Jack snarled.

Salazar lowered the gun. 'I believe you. Very well. The disks are an acceptable loss, the cost of doing business here in America. So Vasquez here will keep you and

Catherine company, Agent West, while Mrs Elliott and I go to her bank and arrange to transfer the money to my account.'

Cold sweat trickled down Jack's bruised ribs. He considered the options and didn't like any of them. His thoughts were a flurry. Then it hit him.

'Salazar, you know Elliott went by another name? He also called himself Lionel Lattide?'

The little man spun round and glared at Catherine. 'It was you!'

'What do you mean?' whimpered Catherine.

'You talked Daniel into stealing from me! That's why you asked me to get those fake passports.'

Catherine was suddenly still. Her tears halted. Her trembling lips formed a broad sneer.

'That's right, you creepy, disgusting little gnome. Without me, you're nothing,' Catherine spat. 'Who got you the formulas and samples of the drugs? Me! And what was my share? A measly ten per cent while you raked in millions. Daniel only took from you what was rightfully mine!'

Catherine turned and kneed Vasquez in the balls. He moaned and clutched his groin, dropping his gun and sank to his knees.

Jack lashed out with his right foot, and kicked Salazar's gun out of his hand, then landed an upper cut to his jaw. Salazar spat blood and foam, and stumbled back into the steel wall, then slid slowly down to the floor, unconscious.

Grace grabbed Vasquez's gun from the floor. Her eyes locked with his. Still kneeling in pain, he looked at the barrel and raised one hand, then another.

'Don't you dare move,' she said 'On second thought, please do move so I can blow out what little brains you have!'

Jack's hand's wrapped round hers. 'Easy, Grace.' He took the gun from her, but kept the barrel aimed at Vasquez. 'Get my cell phone. It's in my back pocket. Call the first number you see on speed dial. They'll be here in a heartbeat.'

CHAPTER THIRTY-ONE

Miami
Seventy-two hours later.

Jack knocked on the door of the coronary care unit. 'I hope they'll allow us in,' he said to Grace, who cradled Emilia in her arms.

'Chrissie said it was okay provided we only stayed for a few minutes.'

Jack smiled, and kissed her cheek, then his daughter's, and wondered how he'd gotten so lucky. 'She looks so content.'

'Babies are sensitive, Jack. They know when the person holding them cares.'

'Do you? Do you care?'

Grace looked up at him. Her tear-bright eyes brimmed with happiness. 'How could I not love her, when I love her father so much?'

Jack opened the door. Mike Zupanik sat propped up in bed, a heart monitor strapped to his chest, a drip connected to his arm.

'My God,' said Mike. 'You look like hell.'

Jack grinned. 'Thanks, old man. You look pretty good, considering what you've been through.'

'Nah, could have been worse, although my days with the Bureau are over.'

'I bet Chrissie's pleased.'

'She's been after me to retire for a long time. Guess I just had to nearly die to see the sense of it.'

'And you have.'

Mike snorted. 'I'm a Bureau guy, Jack. What do we know? Nothing. We never figure shit out until we've had it kicked out of us. Which I sort of did, didn't I?'

'Yep, you did.'

Jack pulled out a chair for Grace and stood by her side.

Mike smiled at Grace and the baby. 'Good to see you, Mrs Elliott.'

'I don't think of myself as 'Mrs Elliott' anymore, Mike. I guess you could say I've had the shit kicked out of me too.'

'She's a tough woman, Jack. I like her. I always liked her, but there's something different about her now.'

Grace smiled and looked down at the sleeping baby. 'I had a reality check, you might say. I found out what's really important in life too.'

'So,' Jack said, a little uneasily. 'Is Chrissie going to keep you under lock and key for a while?'

'For a while. But then we're going to take a cruise – I don't know where yet. It doesn't matter. I'm breathing and I've got a woman who loves me, God knows why…'

'I think I know why, 'said Grace, looking first at Mike, then over at Jack.

'Well,' said Mike. 'So how does it feel to crack one of the largest counterfeit prescription drug operations on record?'

'I wish I could say it was because of my brilliance and intuition. Truth is, I was lucky.'

Mike smiled grimly. 'You're a damned good agent, Jack, even if you do bend the rules.'

'Does that mean you've cut my transfer orders?'

Mike laughed. 'Hell, no. They won't let me near a computer yet.'

'I spoke to Anderson's doctor,' said Jack. 'The bullet missed the bone and passed right through his leg. He'll out of hospital in a few days, but he won't be back in action for a while.'

'I'm glad to know he's okay. He's a good man.'

'And it turns out Salazar's been on Interpol's radar for some time, mainly for racketeering. Trafficking fake prescription drugs is a new game for him.'

'What do we know about him apart from the fact he had a Swiss Bank account?' asked Mike

'He's Eurasian. Chinese mother, Portuguese father. My guess is that the narcotics are manufactured in China. Before the vessel reaches the U.S., the drugs get off loaded onto a smaller ship and taken to Salazar's home on Marathon Key and distributed from there.'

'Sounds plausible. Have you notified the FDA?'

'Yeah, and the DEA. And the Swiss authorities have seized the contents of his bank account.'

'The lab extracted DNA off the cigarettes you found in the study.' Mike turned to Grace. 'I'm sorry, but your sister's is a perfect match. I understand you found Elliott's ATM card in her luggage. Don't blame yourself. Catherine's an adult. She made her choices.'

A momentary look of sadness crossed Grace's face. 'She made her choices. That's true, she did. None of them included me.'

'She wanted everything in life and she decided a life of crime was the solution,' said Mike. 'It's not your fault.'

'It feels that way sometimes. A lot.'

Jack squeezed Grace's hand. 'It'll take time, baby. You'll forgive yourself. You did everything you could. Even if you'd have done more, it wouldn't have been enough.'

Mike scratched at his IV drip. 'These nurses. They can't even put on a Band-Aid without messing it all up.'

'The results of the second autopsy on Elliott came through,' said Jack.

'And?'

'His real name is Niall Deloitte. He's the son of Christiano Deloitte, a Mafia boss in New York back in the '50s. When his father was murdered, Niall's mother, who was Irish, sent her son to live with relatives in Dublin.'

'So, why the change of name?'

'I guess she thought she was saving her son from a life of crime.'

'Pity it didn't work out that way,' said Mike. 'By the way, Jack. Did Diego tell you the news?'

'What?'

'Hector Suárez spilled his guts. Turns out his older brother, Estefan, is serving time for drug running and murder.'

'I know. So?'

'Estefan got engaged just before he got busted. Two guesses about his fiancée.'

'Come on, you know I'm not good at this. I give up.'

'Rosa Nunuz.'

Jack swallowed. 'No shit.'

'None whatsoever. And she got arrested this morning for attempted murder of an FBI agent. You, Jack.'

Grace grasped his arm.

'She must have been pretty pissed at you,' Mike said. 'She hired Hector to follow you and kill you.'

Jack shook his head. 'I always knew she used me. At first I thought it was for green cards, but now I can see she wanted revenge.'

'You weren't the first to get suckered by a pretty face, son. She'll be doing some serious time. And when she gets out there isn't a judge alive who'll grant her custody of Emilia.'

At the sound of her name Emilia's eyes fluttered open and she gurgled softly. Grace gently rocked her back and forth.

'Well, Mike, I think it's time we left you to rest.'

'One more thing before you go, Jack.'

'When I retire, I'm recommending that you take my place as Special Agent in Charge of the Miami office.'

'Uh, Mike, well, I—'

'Save your mumbling and humility. You've worked for it. You deserve it. Of course it'll be up to the Director, but I'm betting he'll say yes.'

Jack looked at Grace. 'I don't know what to say, Mike.'

'So don't say anything. That's my recommendation. And I'm finished talking about it.'

'Okay… well, look, Grace and I have a few things to discuss, so we'll be on our way.'

'You two kids get outa here then. Just make sure you invite me and Chrissie to the wedding.'

Jack pulled Grace to her feet and wrapped an arm around her and Emilia. A smile tipped the corners of his mouth as they left the room.

'Well, that's not exactly what I had in mind for a proposal, but you know what they say: 'Out of the mouths of curmudgeons'…

Grace took a breath. 'Are you asking what I think you're saying?'

'Yes to both. What do you say to a Christmas wedding?'

Grace stood on tiptoe and brushed her lips against his. 'I think it sounds perfect.'

'Well, then we'd better get going. Think Emilia's too young to be a flower girl?'

The End

Printed in Great Britain
by Amazon